Rainbow Hands

Rabina Khan

authors OnLine

Visit us online at www.authorsonline.co.uk

About the author

For the past thirteen years, Rabina Khan has lived in Tower Hamlets in the East End of London. She has worked on a variety of community initiatives to help develop understanding between people, to access opportunities in education, housing, health and employment. At present she is working with the Environment Trust and her love of reading has prompted her to write her story.

Rabina is married with two children and her strong desire is to see them grow up in a harmonious, multi-racial society, without fear of prejudice. She wrote her novel to show how people of different backgrounds can come together to challenge racism and bridge gaps between themselves.

Acknowledgements

I would like to thank the following people for their help, support and encouragement:

Wendy, my editor, for reading, guiding, and reassurance
Mehera for the idea of the cover and my many phone calls
Joynal for all the endless lists
Abdul for the front cover
Ruksana and Rohima for suggesting the title
Tahera for help with looking for errors
Anisa, Shakila and Nadia for their ideas for a title
Zakia for asking me every night when the story would be finished and
Nablila for letting me know when to stop typing!

Review of Rainbow Hands

This beautifully told story must make us all sit up and think. It delves into racial tensions without falling into the well-known trap of complete bias.

This author has managed to portray the many issues and cleverly let us see both sides of the same coin.

She has allowed us into two families, one Bangladeshi and one from the East End. We see prejudices from them both.

We start with Mrs Peters, a wonderful elderly lady and truly loyal East Ender, finding a Bangladeshi family moving into the flat next door. She reflects over her life, the good old days when her beloved husband was alive, and recalls their struggle to bring up their children. Every memory evokes images for us all and fills us with nostalgia.

We then learn the true values of the Ali family from Bangladesh and how hard they had to work for any kind of recognition. Each family seems resigned to keep themselves to themselves, but they hadn't reckoned on Ayesha.

This little eight-year-old eats into everyone's hearts and her desire to plant a sunflower, something so simple, draws the families together. She is a delightful, inquisitive child, yet even she cannot penetrate the heart of stone that reigns in Graham, Mrs Peters' youngest child, although now a man.

He hates anyone with different colour skin to himself. His mother tries in vain to get him to change his ways and then she is tragically attacked.

This is an ideal situation for Graham to blame the Ali's son. A couple of prejudiced policemen are called to the scene but they had not reckoned on Detective Sergeant Brown, a pride to any force, as he sets about getting to the bottom of this horrendous attack.

The research is deep and meaningful and steeped in recent historical events. It will make you angry, it will make you smile, it will make you sad, but it will certainly make you want to keep on reading.

– Wendy Lake Writer and Novelist

CHAPTER ONE

Mrs Peters was having her afternoon tea as she watched the new family moving into the flat next to her own. She heard the sounds of furniture, boxes and suitcases being dragged past her window. During the whole of last week people had been in and out, decorating, cleaning and generally preparing the home. Although Mrs Peters did not understand the family's language, the sound of laughter seemed to tell her that they were happy to be together. Why shouldn't she understand? Mrs Peters was also proud of her close-knit family.

With that thought she looked at the selection of photos on her wall unit and smiled warmly knowing that she was loved. There was her wedding photo with her beloved husband Arthur, who had sadly passed away a few years ago after his long struggle with cancer. Then there were photographs of her four children - David, Susan, Vivien and Graham, together with their respective children, all except Vivien, who unhappily could not conceive, and sadness filled her knowing her daughter could never experience the joy of giving birth. Mrs Peters was proud of her children; they hadn't done too badly in their lives, in fact they had made it very well in the world. That was apart from Graham, he had always been troublesome and generally the black sheep. However, he was sorting himself out now and getting on with the rest of the family.

Mrs Peters turned back to the window and looked at her new neighbours; she had a feeling they were probably Bangladeshi. She saw a woman in a sari, a young girl of seven or perhaps eight and a teenage girl climbing out of a mini van. The woman's face was young but the eyes were old. A bald man carried the little girl towards Mrs Peters flat. He suddenly stopped at the door and looked at the window, but she quickly moved away.

His sudden movements had taken her aback. She hadn't counted on him looking at her window, after all she wasn't spying on them... well, she wasn't really. Having lived in her building for fifty years, she felt she had a right to know who was coming and going from the neighbouring flats, in particular the one next door. It had belonged to a close friend and she had passed away leaving her with a sort of responsibility towards the place. Somehow she couldn't understand how all these people were going to fit into the tiny, three bedroomed flat. There seemed so many of them. Then she smiled and realised that she had lived in a tiny one bedroomed flat when her children were young. Overcrowded situations were certainly not a thing of the past. Families just had to cope with what they had and make what they could of their lives. It was as simple as that.

****

Mr Ali had noticed Mrs Peters watching him and his sons working on their new home. He had seen her through the kitchen window and sensed she had never had Bangladeshi neighbours before. He knew she probably had her

1

prejudices about them and smiled as he carried Ayesha around the flat, thinking the old woman was probably planning what kind of complaint she could make about his children to take to the local housing office and the police. Knowing white elderly people from previous experiences, it was probably going to be noise pollution. If she was really unpleasant, she might probably say that his wife's cooking smells were affecting her asthma and causing breathing difficulties.

Eager to show his wife and children around the flat that was now their very own, he stopped thinking of Mrs Peters. He and his sons had worked on the decorations, finding the three bedrooms were actually very big after all the wall units were taken out and the clutter of old furniture removed. They had then cleaned the flat thoroughly. There had been three layers of carpet to cut away, five layers of wallpaper to strip, the kitchen and bathroom had been so wet that underneath the lino there was almost a pool of water. However, they had worked together and plastered and painted in vibrant, modern colours to create a sense of freshness and space, all knowing that Mrs Ali would keep it neat and tidy, especially now it was their own.

"What do you think?" Mr Ali asked his wife in Bengali.

"I think it's lovely. I think you and my sons have worked so hard. I thank Allah for his blessings," replied Mrs Ali almost humbly. He smiled and knew that the years of living in a tiny one bedroomed flat with four children made this flat, which he had purchased, a pure haven. The Ali family had originally lived in a bed-sit and were moved, on an emergency basis, to a one bedroomed flat due to a massive water pipe burst. The council had told them it was a temporary situation and they would then be moved as quickly as possible to a larger property. The temporary situation lasted for ten years and they waited for their transfer with hope that turned to despair.

Mr Ali had then met a mortgage broker a year ago, through a friend, who promised him he could buy a property which would fall at the monthly cost of paying rent to the council. The broker had advised him to buy a property in East London where Mr Ali already lived as he believed, in the future, the price of residential properties would increase dramatically. He had at first found it very difficult to believe or comprehend that the dreary looking flats of the East End could become valuable in a few years time and had spoken to his younger son Hamza who was studying for an Economics degree. Hamza agreed with the broker. Mr Ali had given up his tenancy to the council and was rewarded, under one of the council's housing policies, with a small amount of money which he used as a down payment towards his mortgage.

He had decided that he would no longer stand and watch his family suffer the humiliation of being in an overcrowded situation, especially with growing children. There was no privacy, everyone had to be careful not to disturb one another, and the bathroom was everyone's sanctuary. The family not only suffered overcrowding but, along with it, severe condensation, damp and cockroaches. Ayesha had developed asthma as a result of the damp; Mrs Ali always seemed to feel cold, while the other children had often had colds and coughs. It had been terribly disturbing for Mr and Mrs Ali to realise that their housing situation was having such an effect on themselves and their children. However they were people who had simple and humble values rooted from their religion, Islam and their culture had helped them to make the best of their situation.

All they really wanted was for their children to be good, educated, hardworking and honest people. Perhaps this is what made them both tell their children,

"If you go to school everyday and learn your lessons, then you won't need to be just a factory or restaurant worker…"

The lecture always began with this and it went on about not getting involved in drugs, vandalism, crime, gang fights, having 'good' friends, not forgetting one's religion and culture, not getting too westernised. And so the lecture went on, with Mrs Ali interrupting here and there. However it always ended with Mr Ali saying,

"I want you to have a better life than I could give you in this hole and that will be enough for me, and make white people know that you can be more than what they expect of us."

Of all the things Mr Ali said to his children, the last remark stayed with them, from the eldest to the youngest, as a source of energy to succeed in every possible way. They all in their own way wanted to become more than a 'Paki' or a 'black bastard'.

However this particular remark had an intense impact on Yusuf Ali, the eldest child. In the early years of Yusuf's childhood when he had first arrived in Britain as a seven-year-old, with a younger brother, he had faced the grim reality of the 'Paki' context. Yusuf had arrived in Britain with his mother and younger sibling on a bleak, cold, winters day. He remembered how cold he had felt and how terribly homesick he was for his village and for his grandparents. Everything seemed cold and alien to him - this country of riches of which he had heard so much. When Yusuf and his mother and younger sibling had got their entry clearance, people had joked in their village that he was now a 'Londoni' and how he would have a secure future. Even at that young age he could sense the envy behind the jokes.

People back home in Bangladesh believed that Britain, or London as they said, was a place where immigrants were welcomed and then became rich. One just had to get into the country whether legally or illegally. People felt like this because of the extreme poverty, the hardships and cruel labour of indecent work their bodies endured to earn the rice to feed so many mouths. London was the 'American Dream' for the desperate in Bangladesh. Yusuf and his family ended up living in bed and breakfast accommodation, after spending a few days with relatives. The hotel was filthy, full of mice and cockroaches and it had been terrible adapting to his new environment. The hotel had racist tenants hurling verbal abuse and, on occasions, empty beer

3

cans at Yusuf and his family. His mother often cried and was afraid to leave her room in case she met the other white families which seemed to infuriate them even more, as they believed Yusuf's mother thought she was above them. They did not understand that she lived in fear of them.

English was a foreign language and the whole way of life, with its modern technology, was a stark contrast to the way of life in rural areas in developing countries. Yusuf had been astonished to find how easy it was to access a phone, TV, fridge and iron and his mother had to learn how to use a cooker. It was a new way of life for him and he knew that to fit in he would have to learn the English language fast. Yusuf and his family lived in bed and breakfast for a year. During that time he attended a school close by and he watched TV as soon as he got home and tried to use it as language support to read his schoolbooks. Within six months Yusuf understood the language and spoke it fairly well. Within another six months he spoke and understood a high standard of English, even better than children whose first language was English. He could by then read the Peter and Jane serial books better than his white counterparts.

Yusuf attended St Matthew's Church of England Primary School and that is where he first heard the Lord's Prayer. He and five other children were the only non-white pupils who attended the school. Yusuf found they were friendly towards him but their misconceptions of his colour, which they had picked up from their parents and misinformed teachers, meant on occasions petty disagreements led to racist remarks being made.

As he stood looking at the flat he had helped decorate, Yusuf found himself remembering an incident from his childhood. He was nine years old and the class was studying how people lived around the world, in particular the teacher focused her attention on how people lived in mud huts in India. She asked Yusuf how he had felt living in such a hut.

"I don't come from India and I have never lived in a mud hut," he had replied.

Miss Jennings had been embarrassed and had realised how assuming she had been. She had forgotten Yusuf came from Bangladesh. Later that day a boy in the class named John spoke to him.

"You're a liar, you do come from India and you did live in dirty mud huts. That's why your skin is so brown".

"Where did you get that from?" asked Yusuf.

"My dad said all Pakis come from India 'cause they didn't have proper housing back home and want our jobs and our houses." John answered proudly thinking his dad knew everything. Especially as his dad was the only man down at his local pub who could drink eight pints of beer in a go, regardless of the consequences afterwards.

"Well you're wrong, John. I'm not a Paki and I'm telling you again I don't come from India and didn't live in a mud hut. We didn't come over to take your jobs or homes. We end up getting the leftovers from what's offered to

4

you lot," Yusuf rebuked. He was getting terribly angry with John for being such a pig and felt deeply hurt people could assume such things about him and his people.

John refused to give up his argument and taunted Yusuf.

"Paki in a mud hut, that's what you are Yusuf, and you got cleaned up when you got over here."

Yusuf walked away and joined in the ball game but John carried on taunting him. Yusuf was getting very hot and the playground was getting very quiet apart from John's taunts. The other children were staring at him and though none of them were joining in with John, none of them were siding with him. His anger had been building up as John started to rhyme his words.

"Paki in a mud hut, Mother is a slut. Sister is a tart, Father is fart. Brother is…."

John never got to finish the rhyme as Yusuf's fist found his face. There was a great deal of scuffling and clambering and the other children started screaming.

"Fight, fight, fight, fight…."

He remembered the caretaker and Miss Jennings breaking it up and the discipline both he and John received from the school headmistress for fighting. She was angry over the fight but not the actual roots of why it happened. He remembered his father being asked to come to the school and being warned that if Yusuf caused another such incident he would have to leave. John's parents had received a friendly home visit. But most of all, Yusuf remembered the ugly smirk on the caretaker's face when he had grabbed him away from John for his grasp had been a little too strong on a young child.

Yusuf smiled now, and looked at the 'mud hut' he was now going to live in. He had so much in his life, so many things to achieve and was determined not to be a failure. It was strange how children's lives turn out when they grow up. John had left school after his GCSEs, to become a painter and decorator, whilst Yusuf had worked hard and overcome the various social, cultural and racial barriers hindering him from achieving his goals. He was now studying for his medical degree and had just started training to be a doctor.

Yusuf wanted his parents and his brothers and sisters to live comfortably and not in overbearing circumstances; he wanted them to have a chance to feel secure and peaceful. His parents were humble and generous people who had tried very hard to ensure their children lived in a safe, clean one bed-roomed environment. Yusuf felt angry with the council for the suffering and hardships he and his family had endured for the past decade, without any support or sympathy from their local housing office. It was as though they had turned their backs on them and hoped they would disappear amongst all the statistics in the overcrowded housing figures.

Hamza Ali was looking at the largest bedroom, trying to decide which side to put his new computer. He had saved up his own money from working part time at his local supermarket. His dad had insisted that both Yusuf and Hamza work part time and study, as Mr Ali wanted them to understand the hard ways of studying and appreciate the privileges they had. Like free education, complete with free textbooks, writing books and so many resources which he often reminded his children were not free in Bangladesh. He believed by encouraging his sons to be focused on education and working at the same time would help them to become more responsible and mature and it would also help Hamza spend less time with his friends.

Mr and Mrs Ali worried desperately about Hamza getting involved in local Bangladeshi gang fights. The gang fights had turned almost to gang warfare between rival gangs with the use of machetes, knives and chainsaws. It had touched most Bangladeshi families with young sons and the tragedies that unfolded from gang warfare were partly ignored by the local police and were almost seen by them as something normal amongst Asian youths. Drugs were a major problem in the area and its consequence was the increased crime amongst the Bangladeshi community. Many families found it hard to help their children to become more in control of their lives.

However, recently, determined parents, wanting something better for their children than a life of drugs and violence, campaigned for support networks to deal with the problem. Suddenly the police and the council were facing very embarrassing and serious allegations. They suddenly had a very loud wake up call ringing in their ears. Community groups, voluntary organisations and the local authority services came together to take the concerns of families on board and to tackle the underlying problems. Hamza's father joined a local parents' group to find out how he could ensure his children were able to lead lives without being influenced by drugs and gang fights or be victims of racial harassment.

Hamza was a very intelligent nineteen-year-old doing the first year of an Economics degree. Had he studied with more determination, his A level results would have being of a standard topping grammar schools exam results. However his GCSE and A level days had being very unstable with him spending more and more time outside with other young men 'wanting a good time'. His parents and Yusuf knew how easily Hamza could be influenced by peer pressure and they all made an effort to ensure Hamza went away to relatives living outside London during school holidays so that he could not access his so called friends. He was even sent on holiday to Bangladesh where the atmosphere seemed to help him become more settled.

Hamza knew what his goals were in life and he knew exactly how he was going to achieve them. He wanted to be rich and he wanted to buy a proper house for his parents. He had a talent for numbers and he was going to use it to work for the stock exchange. Hamza had tried to persuade Yusuf to go into the finance and trading world. But Yusuf was such a martyr; he wanted to do good for people in need.

Bloody hell, when we were in need, did anyone give a shit, Hamza had thought. No one had cared when he and his siblings had being in the flat with no hot water and heating for three weeks in the winter. They had all been very young then and Mr Ali had gone away to Bangladesh for a couple of weeks visiting his sick mother leaving Mrs Ali looking after them on her own. She had tried very hard to explain to the housing officers how cold she and her children were. Without an interpreter Mrs Ali had not managed to convey the seriousness of her situation and finally Mrs Ali had taken ten year old Yusuf with her to the housing office.

Yusuf had explained the situation clearly but the sour faced Housing Officer had questioned him in detail about why he was not in school and asked if his father was claiming Income Support whilst being abroad. Yusuf had assured them that he would not be there if the Housing Officer had a Bengali interpreter, and that his father did not claim Income Support. The officer had found the child's confident response rather unexpected as she had thought he was as timid as his mother. She was very wrong; Yusuf was angry at her total incompetence. Hamza, remembered that after his brother's visit, a worker came round to their home and fixed the heating and water supply. They had at last felt warm enough to stop living like Eskimos.

Hamza was staring at the garden adjacent to the flat. Due to it being on the ground floor, residents were able to get a piece of garden space for themselves that was separated from the rest of the communal grounds. A great place to play football, thought Hamza cynically, as he remembered playing ball near to the block of flats where he had lived before. One day, he and his friends had been playing ball and the white caretaker had caught them, as ball playing on the grounds was prohibited. The caretaker had taken the ball and screamed at them for ignoring the warning sign, but Hamza and his friends had quietly listened to him ranting and raving. He had eventually said to the caretaker,

"We're really sorry. It won't happen again. Just give the ball back to us."

"You ain't getting the ball back. Don't you get it; football's a white man's sport. Go and play cricket, that's what you Indians are good at. Be like that Imran Khan."

"Fuck You!" Hamza had replied. "We'll play what we like"

"Don't you talk to me like that boy 'cause I work for the council, I don't need to take lip from you. I'm stating a fact. Football is a white man's game." The caretaker had countered and walked closer to Hamza.

"Football is for everyone and anyone who enjoys it. It's even for the tooth fairy if she gets a kick out of it. So you can take your facts and shove it up your arse."

"You fucking Paki prick! You won't be talking like that after I've finished with you." And with that the big burly caretaker had punched Hamza in the stomach. His friends had grabbed the caretaker but he seemed to be made of steel as he shoved and pushed them aside. By now the sound of police sirens could be heard in the distance; Hamza and his friends knew they were in trouble.

His parents were horrified when a policeman turned up with Hamza sporting a black eye. The policeman gave a warning to Mr and Mrs Ali about controlling Hamza's temper towards defenceless council staff carrying out their duties. Mr Ali had enquired as to how his son had managed to end up with a black eye if he was the aggressor.

"Because, mate, the caretaker had to take defensive action against your son," the policeman answered angrily then left saying they would receive a crime report from the police. His parents, after they had heard Hamza's version of the event, had howled at him for playing football in the first place, and for replying back to the caretaker's racist comments.

"What am I supposed to do,' he had angrily replied, "be patient and understanding like you two are with the housing officers when they say there are more desperate people than us?"

"Well, if you want the police to give you a criminal record which they would love to do, then go ahead and show them what kind of a man you are," Mr Ali had shouted back to his son.

It had then dawned on Hamza just how truly frightened his parents were of the white authoritative figure and how they wished to live their lives without causing trouble to the rulers of their host country. The imperialistic and colonialist figures of the past had left such a mark of fear and insecurity on those they had ruled.

****

Shazia Ali stared at the bedroom; she had asked her brothers to paint it in lilac. She had then stencilled Arabic style designs as a boarder in a darker shade of lilac and she could not believe that she and Ayesha were finally able to have a room to share without a third person. Shazia remembered how her parents had divided the large sitting room in the one bedroomed flat into two separate sections using heavy curtains. They had done the same in the large bedroom to ensure one section was a sitting area. How embarrassing it had been when visitors had called, especially for Shazia, as her friends often came round. They didn't seem to care; they were too much in awe of Yusuf.

Shazia had felt ashamed. Living like that meant everyone had to tiptoe around each other to ensure some kind of privacy existed for all. Shazia smiled warmly; she was going to create an ethnic look about her room, and Ayesha wouldn't really care as long as Shazia let her play with some of her make up. Shazia was what the west would call 'a typical teenage girl', interested in clothes, music, make up, looking good and having a laugh. However, the image did not include such things as covering ones' head, ensuring prayers were completed, not going out with boys or out to clubs, learning how to cook and entertain guests with the right food and hospitality.

She accepted these things as part of her life for she was really a Bangladeshi at heart. She was into her Hindi films, Bengali pop music, the Bollywood heart throbs, the songs, the clothes, she loved going to weddings and being part of the preparation of a wedding, finding out whose 'Babi' (sister-in-law) was the nicest, which girl had run away with a boy. Well gossip was part of every community be it the Bangladeshi, cockney East Enders or the middle class elite. Gossip existed in Shazia's eyes because a good bitch about someone or something united people. It overcame their differences as they found something common they agreed or disagreed upon.

Shazia had a bunk bed in her room just like in her brothers' room. Bunk beds were a common sight in council flats, like graffiti, vandalism, dog shit, litter and syringes. These seemed characteristic of poor council estates, especially in inner city areas. Families wanted to live decently with what they had and it was their dignity and pride to be able to say, 'this is my home'. However, that did not always happen. Conflict arises amongst people in poor communities when the grass seems greener on the neighbour's lawn. It was often this which led to the "they and us" syndrome between ethnic communities and their white counterparts.

Shazia went to a 'girls only' school attended mainly by Bangladeshis. There were other girls from Somali, Chinese, Vietnamese and white communities but they were the minority. Most Bangladeshi parents hoped their daughters would attend Evergreen Girls School so they could be in a sheltered environment where religion and culture ruled. The school was almost viewed as a middle class grammar school by many parents and it was a fight to get their daughters into it. Shazia had been able to get into the school because her parents had appealed to an educational panel but in the interim she had had to attend an 'all girls' Roman Catholic school.

It had been the unhappiest episode of her school days. She had been the indigenous minority in a mainly white majority and the girls did not want to know her. The teachers almost found her a problem as they felt they had to teach her gently in case she did not understand their English although it was very obvious that she spoke fluent English. The teachers smiled at Shazia too much, trying to disguise their misguided preconceptions of her and she in turn, dutifully smiled back at them, looking like the forlorn immigrant whose first language was not English. Shazia had found the complete atmosphere a joke. All she had wanted was to be treated the same as the other girls.

Her headscarf had been the centre of attention for many of the white pupils at St Anne's Roman Catholic School. They had made jokes out loud about it in class.

"Has someone got a cold in the class, especially if they need to cover their ears?"

Or "Is it to cover the nits up?"

Shazia was not intimidated by the racist taunts for after all she had grown up with crude racist jokes from neighbours, youth, people in authority, elderly people, bus drivers, even in story books for children. Shazia knew how to react to them and respond to them in an even cruder manner. Responses to the 'cold' joke about her headscarf got retorts such as

"It's not a cold I've got. I'm just avoiding catching AIDS from slags like you."

She had long ago decided that a white girl could never really be a friend to her for she would be expected to compromise her values to meet their understanding and acceptance. Once though, when she was young, Shazia had become friendly with the white girl who lived next door. She and Louise played together on the balcony in their block. Louise's parents were not exactly friendly, but they allowed her to play with Shazia. She never went into their house as her mother had warned her to stay in front of their flat where she could keep an eye on her. One day whilst playing ball, Shazia missed the ball and it rolled into Louise's hallway. Without thinking Shazia ran in and retrieved it. Moments later Louise had been called in.

From outside the kitchen window, Shazia could hear Mrs Brady telling Louise off.

"Louise, I told you to play with the Paki outside, what was she doing inside the flat?"

"Mum, Shazia was only getting the ball. And so what if she came in."

"Don't so what me, Louise. These people don't wash properly, they're filthy and they need to know that this is white people's country. They don't belong here."

"Mum, Shazia ain't dirty. I've seen her mum washing five times a day 'cause they have to be clean when they pray," said Louise defensively.

"You what Louise? You've been in their home, ain't you? Your dad and me have told you, white kids don't go to Paki people's homes. It ain't being British. That's it you're not playing outside again." Louise was moaning and almost begging her mum to let her play with Shazia. She was going to miss Shazia, Mrs Ali's treats and baby Ayesha and she felt suddenly very lonely. It was not fair; Shazia was the same as herself, she thought.

Shazia had heard everything and she felt hurt; she was not going to cry over some white woman's racist comments. She did not smell, her family did not smell and her home did not smell. Shazia thought about how much her mother stressed the importance of cleanliness, not just for hygiene reasons, but also for religion. Angels and the goodness of God would not enter an unclean home. From that day Shazia never played with Louise or any other white child in school. She stuck to her own as it was not worth the hassle to be friendly with white people.

Shazia stared again at her room and knew exactly how to hang her new curtains. She had bought a plain lilac sari to drape over the curtain rail, to give the room a mystical atmosphere. She thought how the West now complimented their clothes, interior designs, furniture and food with so much from Asian and Eastern culture. Yet the West still felt superior as if people from the other side are savages, thought Shazia, remembering the word 'savages' from the novel 'The Heart of Darkness'. White people tan themselves to become dark like us but yet they find us repulsive. They are full of contradictions and hypocrisy thought Shazia angrily.

****

Ayesha Ali was busy running around in the garden amongst the weeds and grass. She was seven years old and she could not believe the number of rooms in the flat and the fact it also had a garden. She was a good-natured and friendly little girl and there was something about her cheeky and engaging smile that made people look twice at her. Ayesha laughed a lot; she had an unspoilt character even though she was the youngest of the Ali children. She was the surviving one of twins born to Mrs Ali. Her twin brother had died a few hours after birth. They had been born prematurely, at a gestation of thirty weeks. Mrs Ali had started labour early and she had dilated too far for anything to be done by medical staff.

The tragedy helped the family to love and protect Ayesha even more. Death can change the way people feel about each other, their attitudes and behaviour, and for the Ali family, they learnt that they needed to watch over each other and the importance of family unity.

Ayesha went to a primary school which was mainly attended by Bangladeshi children. The number of white children could easily be counted, as there were only five. The other seven were Somali and three were Chinese children. Ayesha played with any child who wished to play with her. She did not see the colour first, she just saw another child. Ayesha had heard her mother being called Paki. She had seen her mother being spat upon by white men and women and she understood that these white people were just silly. They did not really mean it in her eyes; they had got out of the wrong side of the bed.

Ayesha played with Jade and Simon at school sometimes, especially if there was a game of rounders. She enjoyed playing with them as they always had a laugh together. Even Jade's mum had a laugh with Ayesha because she made a point of talking to Jade's mum. It had been a shock for Jade's mum when Ayesha had first spoken to her.

The other mainly Bangladeshi parents did not speak to Jade's mum. Mrs Smith had reluctantly enrolled Jade in Blue Berry Primary School as there had been no vacancies at other schools. Ayesha had seen Mrs Smith waiting for Jade outside the classroom.

"Are you Jade's Mummy?" she asked with a smile as she walked out of the class.

Mrs Smith had looked down and seen a smiling, cheeky-looking little Asian girl with big black eyes. She hadn't known how to respond, yet managed to splutter, "Yes I am"

"Oh, well she's gone to the loo, she'll be back soon."

"Oh, okay then," Mrs Smith had said, not encouraging Ayesha to carry on the conversation. But the little girl had not been deterred for she didn't need encouragement.

"I play with Jade. She's my friend. Sometimes we play house games and rounders. Jade and me always hit the ball," chatted on Ayesha smiling as she talked and Mrs Smith really didn't know what to say to this child. She didn't even know Asian children played rounders. Of course they do, they're children as well she finally chided herself.

"Really, that's nice. Do you beat the boys?" Mrs Smith found herself asking.

"Course we do. Remember girls are better than boys, my dad always tells me that," laughed Ayesha. Mrs Smith started laughing too.

"Yeah, girls are better than boys. Your dad's right."

But Mrs Smith did find it strange that an Asian man could really say that because she had heard that they preferred to have sons to daughters. Well, she could be wrong. By then Jade had come back from the toilet and Mrs Ali was gesturing to Ayesha to hurry up. Mrs Ali was already worried about what Ayesha had been chatting about. She knew if an Asian person failed to understand something or communicated the wrong message it could sometimes easily trigger off nasty comments from a white person.

From that day Mrs Smith and Ayesha always had a chat, even Mrs Ali sometimes joined in. It was strange how children could easily make friends with strangers whilst adults stood afar.

Ayesha had seen Mrs Peters from her kitchen window. Shazia had tried to frighten her as they went past by saying that Mrs Peters was an old witch. A witch who liked little children for her spells but she had told Shazia off for telling lies, especially as her big sister knew nothing about Mrs Peters. All she cared about was what sari she would wear on her wedding day and Shazia did not really know how to be friendly, decided Ayesha.

Ayesha had smiled at Mrs Peters through the window and she thought that the smile had been faintly returned. It was only when her asthma affected her that she felt down and weak and even then the asthma had to be really bad to get her down. Ayesha got on well with the rest of her siblings. Obviously now and then she caused a bit of trouble for Shazia and Hamza, but only when she couldn't find anything to do. However she loved Yusuf. In Ayesha's eyes he had a heart of gold. He was generous, kind, patient and a very helpful person and he was terribly honest; she thought there couldn't possibly be a girl worthy of her brother.

Ayesha looked around the garden and wondered if her parents would let her have a little patch of her own to grow flowers. She wanted to plant a sunflower if she was allowed but knew that her mum was already planning to have some of the garden tiled and the rest of it was going to be adorned with coriander, spinach, tomatoes and other vegetables, wherever they could be fitted in. Mrs Ali was the typical Bangladeshi gardener, harvesting the popular food from Bangladeshi culture, but her youngest daughter was getting more and more determined to plant a sunflower.

The sunflower would be a new beginning for the family, thought Ayesha, something that would shine in the garden and make the family think of her. She would tell her parents it would be like a gift for them to remember her and her brother who had died. Ayesha knew about her twin brother and sometimes she felt guilty that she was alive and he was dead. But her mother told her it was Allah's will for him to die and for her to live and it was not her fault.

****

Mrs Ali was inspecting the kitchen. The boys had tiled the majority of the wall with creamy peach tiles and the rest had been painted in lemon. The kitchen was big enough to contain six chairs and a matching rectangular table as her sons had fixed new cabinets without overcrowding the kitchen. One thing Mrs Ali had learnt, living in a council property, was to maximise the storage facilities without minimising the space. Rokiya Ali was a slender petite woman of thirty seven years; she was fair skinned and looked much younger than her years. She had been the youngest daughter of a poor farmer in Bangladesh living close to Mr Ali's family village.

Rokiya Ali came from a family of eight children and by the time she had reached puberty, she had only three remaining siblings still surviving. The rest had died of various illnesses such as TB, pneumonia and typhoid as her parents had not been able to pay for medical care for their children and so they had died. It was part of life in developing countries, to bury their young at an early age or even straight after birth. Parents almost expected one or more of their children to die due to illnesses. Young deaths were more common in these countries than the West and the people accepted them far more readily.

Rokiya's marriage had being arranged by her mother-in-law when she turned sixteen. Mrs Ali senior thought that her future daughter-in-law would make a perfect match for her son. Mr Ali senior thought otherwise. He thought Rokiya was not a match for his son, after all, his son was a 'Londoni' and he was much wealthier than Rokiya's family. The only thing Rokiya's father had was his name and background, as at one time her family had been very well known in the district. However her grandfather had dwindled away his wealth and poverty had slowly crept in. Their quality of life fell and Rokiya never saw the way her parents had once lived but only heard about it.

Mrs Ali senior had somehow managed to persuade the family to agree to the marriage between her son and Rokiya. Rokiya was asked once about the marriage but she knew this was her ticket to something better and so the marriage took place with Mr Ali junior arriving one week before the wedding. He was secretly pleased with his mother's choice of bride and only Mr Ali senior remained aloof throughout the wedding and afterwards because he still believed his son could have found a better wife.

Rokiya knew that her future father-in-law was not too happy with her marriage to his son. She knew she had to work on him to win the family over. She was a clever young woman and her poverty had brought the best out of her. She was a talented cook, craftswoman, her needlework was beautiful and her weaving of mats was talked about by many, but most of all Rokiya had learnt to live within her means. These talents had enabled her to pay for some of her education fees as well as something towards her marriage. Rokiya had resolved to win the lion of the Ali family over. Making her husband happy would be simple as she already knew that he was pleased when he had met her on the marriage arrangement day. Rokiya knew how to win her father-in-law over too.

After Rokiya's marriage, she took care of the cooking and the various delicacies necessary in a large Bangladeshi household. With the help of the two women servants, she ensured the farm workers were well fed, did not steal from the kitchen, kept no favourites and encouraged them to pray. Rokiya knew Bangladeshi servants were the greatest news distributors. The servants talked about the new "Bhui" (daughter-in-law) in admiration and it did not take long for her father-in-law to hear about her behaviour. He had tasted her food and found it delicious, he had seen Rokiya's hand made bedspreads and the beautiful bed nets. Most of all, Mr Ali had noticed his workers becoming more prayerful, more committed to their work and less quarrelsome. Workers became like that when they had seen good in the kitchen where they ate their food.

Mr Ali remarked about this to several people and finally admitted in public,

"My wife made a fine choice for my son. The daughter-in-law has brought luck. Even the fields look greener." Rokiya Ali had won the lion over. For a Bangladeshi woman to gain respect like that from an older generation showed how intellectual a woman of her time could be but Rokiya never forgot her humble beginnings. She was fond of her in-laws as they had treated her well for she had given so much. They were good people and, for Rokiya Ali, her mother-in-law was a woman who had inspired the best in the moulding of her relationship with the rest of the extended family.

Rokiya Ali was relieved that her new kitchen was bigger than the previous one. She was a very tidy and clean person and it reflected in the appearance of her home as nothing was ever out of place. Mrs Ali had hammered tidiness and cleanliness into her children's heads, apart from Hamza, whose head was made of stone in Mrs Ali's opinion. Mrs Ali would not give up though; she would at least chisel it in, for the sake of a future daughter-in-law.

Mrs Ali remembered arriving in England after the sorrowful goodbyes to both her own and her husband's families. How terribly homesick she had felt, so lonely and isolated. She had felt frightened, insecure in her new environment and she had a right to feel that way. There had been no warm welcomes from the white tenants living in the bed and breakfast

14

accommodation where the family had first lived. Mrs Ali and her children had been verbally abused, spat on, had beer cans thrown at them, their door had Paki written on it and dead animals had been put through the letterbox. Mrs Ali had led a very frightened and helpless existence during the first few months of her arrival, but like so many other hardships in her life, she learnt to deal with it and live with the reality of racial prejudice. It was something that came with living in a host country when strangers from one race saw another as an intruder and felt superior to them. It was the humiliation of others that made the 'bully' feel secure and proud. It was also this aspect which made the frightened stronger.

Once, Mrs Ali was shopping in her local supermarket with Ayesha and Shazia. Ayesha had been a baby in her pushchair and Shazia about eight. Whilst waiting patiently in the queue, a white woman pushed past Mrs Ali and jumped in front of her, claiming she had been first. She had ignored her and carried on waiting for her turn but it had not gone unnoticed by the black cashier. The white woman had seen Mrs Ali's indifference and put her trolley near to Ayesha's pushchair. The trolley was full of pork, chops, sausages, alcohol and other items and Mrs Ali got the white woman's jibe instantly. She had moved Ayesha's pushchair to the side and placed her trolley right next to the white woman's trolley.

"Fucking bitch. You fucking taking the piss?" the white woman had snarled at Mrs Ali. Although petite in size, she had looked at the white woman as though she was filth and then looked away. All this time, the black cashier was watching the white woman's actions and when she went to unload her shopping, the cashier stopped her.

"I'm afraid Madam, the lady behind you was first. You jumped the queue. Our manager wishes to ensure all customers are treated equally and with respect. I must serve the customer behind you before I can serve you." The white woman looked as though the cashier had smacked her in the face.

"You got a fucking cheek. I ain't buying anything. You're like the Paki, that's why you ain't serving me. You fucking nigger..."

She did not get to finish her racist rhetoric; the cashier had sounded the alarm and two security guards had escorted the white woman outside. She continued with her racist taunts. The store manager called the police and insisted that Mrs Ali pay half of everything priced on her shopping. The manager had been a white man who had evidently drilled equal opportunities into his staff.

Mrs Ali remembered that day because it always made her feel hopeful when she felt the racist taunts in the street had hurt her a little too much. Hope sometimes lay in the actions, words and looks of strangers when one felt defeated in the face of prejudice and ignorance. It made Mrs Ali realise hope was better than hate. If she had taken hate into her everyday life, she knew her children would not have had such a strong sense of their religious and cultural identity. Hate would not have taught them about honesty, respect, tolerance, and to aspire to do better in a society that held so many odds against them. Mrs Ali was a humble but strong woman and it was this that shone in her children.

The Ali family stood and admired their new home, each with memories of the road they had travelled to find it. Life's experiences had taught them so much, they had grown from strength to strength and had dreams and expectations to live, all bonded together through their need for each other. Each with a desire for a new beginning, a new sense of hope for a prosperous future, for the Self was only human.

CHAPTER TWO

Mrs Beryl Peters was in her sitting room wondering what the family next door were doing. The smell of cooking wafted through her garden door making her feel suddenly very hungry. She went into her kitchen to make a ham sandwich and another cup of tea, but the sandwich didn't exactly look appetising, nor did it smell delicious. The strange odour from next door seemed really intoxicating. Mrs Peters hadn't had a cooked dinner for nearly two weeks. What was the point? There was no one else to share a cooked meal with, apart from Tabby, her cat. Tabby was her companion till death; for someone who was lonely, a pet helped to fill that empty human vacuum in their life.

Her children usually came to visit her every week but for the last two weeks, none of the four had visited, due to various engagements. All of them 'phoned daily, but it was not the same as when they called. She loved to cook for her children as she was still a very mobile woman for her seventy-two years, and she loved to be independent. She had a little bit of arthritis but that still didn't stop her from doing her own shopping, cleaning and cooking. Independence was just as important for older people as for younger people; it upheld their dignity and esteem.

Mrs Peters remembered the last stages of Arthur's fight against bowel cancer. Having lost control of his bowel movements, he had been forced to wear incontinence pads and then have a catheter fitted. He had become too weak to carry out his personal tasks and she had, with the help of a district nurse and social services care worker, looked after Arthur's personal care. Her eyes started to sting as she remembered just how much pain Arthur had been in before he died, but the most painful part for someone like Arthur, who after years of being a strong and independent man, the breadwinner of the family, was to come to terms with becoming dependent on others for everyday living tasks. Having to be fed had probably been the most humiliating experience of his life.

Mrs Peters remembered her husband's words.

"Beryl, don't ever leave me. I can't face this on my own. I'm sorry you have to clean my dirt. I wish I had it in me to do it myself. I can't, and it kills me when you and the nurse have to clean me. I'm sixty nine years old and I feel like a baby."

Arthur died in her arms; only Vivien was there at the time. All of her children should have been there but he had died suddenly and quickly with the words of love whispered in her ear.

Mrs Peters had made sure Arthur received a good and respectful send off for funerals in the East End, although sad events, needed much preparation - just like a christening or wedding. Arthur had been laid in state in his sitting room, family members paid their respect, and the reception was held at his local pub with lots of food and drink. Family and friends attended, although looking sad, and had ended up singing good old East End songs. Mrs Peters had hired a horse and carriage, just like in the old days. On his coffin was a wreath shaped into an anchor because Arthur had worked as a docker till the docks had closed down. The East Enders loved to ensure there were enough flowers and wreaths for the deceased.

She missed her husband deeply and she hadn't imagined a life without him. When she had married, she had taken her marriage vows very seriously having grown up with the understanding that through thick and thin, a couple stuck together just like her parents and her grandparents. Marriage was a lifetime commitment. Mrs Peters had come from a generation where she had known families whose children went hungry and a Sunday roast was a rare and heavenly meal.

The East End was her home and she had never strayed away from her birthplace. The furthest she had moved was from Poplar to Stepney. When Mrs Peters thought of the East End she had once known, it was with warmth, where everyone knew each other. Within a couple of streets, you had your own neighbourhood with your local bobby, your local corner shop, and the rag and bone man came round, together with various traders selling their wares.

Beryl Peters had been an only child, born in 1928, to a couple who owned an Eel and Pie shop, now known as Pie and Mash shop. They had been seen as quite a well off family by the local community in comparison to the poverty of so many others living closely, especially as there were less mouths to feed in the family. However, Beryl's parents were very kind and generous hearted people who always helped others in times of trouble and the local neighbourhood had respected Mr and Mrs Jones.

Beryl and her parents had lived over the shop. Beryl's room had been very small - almost a tiny cloakroom; her parents' room wasn't that much bigger and there had been a small sitting room, a kitchen and the toilet was outside. There had been rows and rows of houses, all wedged together, to house as many families as possible. Mrs Peters remembered how families had lived in such appalling and overcrowded conditions; she had known of children sleeping four to a bed.

Sanitation had been so difficult during those times with toilets outside and tin baths in the kitchen in front of the fire. People were much less private in those days but it made up for the fact that they felt bonded together to support one another. There seemed to be more security in friendship and there was a real sense of community. Mrs Peters remembered how neighbours were not strangers, but friends - part of the family - for it was them you turned to in times of crisis. She smiled and remembered when women borrowed a few biscuits or a cup of sugar from each other if their man was out of work. In those days broken biscuits were a bit cheaper to buy, and mothers used to buy them for their children as a treat after tea, leaving the unbroken biscuits for fathers and guests.

It was these acts of generosity, sometimes very simple, which made the shared interest of ones' community go from strength to strength. The sound of children running and shouting with each other as they raced past her kitchen window interrupted Mrs Peters' thoughts. She heard the clash of the security doors bang as the children ran up the stairs of her block and remembered when she was growing up children lived more outside than inside.

She also remembered the cramped living conditions and the lack of television, which meant that children and even mums were out in the streets till late at night. The men were often down at the pub enjoying each other's company after a hard days work. Children never really got up to too much mischief because the local bobby knew where everyone lived. Such a way of life meant you always had people around and never felt alone; everyone kept an eye on all the children in the street and was wary of any strangers. This meant that people knew each other's business and gossiping was a great entertainment.

Mrs Peters thought people being so 'close' would be very overwhelming for the young generation of today as people led such private lives and there was less unity amongst friends, families, neighbours and the community as a whole. No wonder, she thought, there were so many single parents, teenagers going off the rails, runaways, and children being beaten by parents; there were so many social problems. Families and people needed the support network the community had provided years ago when she had been growing up and after her marriage. It was a support network institutions like Social Services and the Police could never really replace.

Mrs Peters remembered when her mother had found a child going though the dustbins at the back of the shop. The child had looked terribly underfed, dirty and had been searching for scraps of food. Mrs Peter's mother had found out that the child's mother was ill and the father was desperately seeking work. The family were new to the street and there were six young children all very hungry. Immediately Mrs Jones had rallied the community on their street together to look out for the family and Beryl remembered with warmth how generous people had been, despite their own poverty and hardships. Some had provided food, some clothes, others had done the housework, scrubbed the rooms clean, washed the clothes, bathed the children and the doctor had waived his fee when he came to visit the mother. The men had helped the father to get three days work in the docks, at least for a couple of months, as he sought more permanent work. This was what community spirit was and what the present so called neighbourhood watch or scheme should be about.

She also remembered with pride how the family had felt no longer alone but part of their new community. There was a time when poor people were rich in generosity, loyalty, friendship and security, but these values no longer seemed to exist. Maybe these values had enabled her to meet her Arthur. Beryl Jones and Arthur Peters had grown up almost on the same street and had played together as children. It was when she was sixteen and he almost nineteen, that their relationship took a different turning when Arthur had asked her for a dance at a wedding.

In those days it was important for a young man to court his lady right and proper with the approval of her parents, especially as the whole neighbourhood would be watching. Wooing was a serious aspect of life, one had to make sure nature did not take over too fast as they did so often these days, thought Mrs Peters wryly. She remembered a distant cousin of hers getting fat when she was growing up, and then suddenly disappearing for the summer. She had come back looking much smaller and very quiet. Relationships were influenced by the views of parents about what was best for their children and courting was not simply a matter between the young couple but of two families sizing each other up before becoming united together.

Arthur worked in the docks and Beryl got a job in a bakery. It had been hard saving money for the wedding and for household items after setting up home together. Her mother had spoken to a landlord about renting a couple of rooms and kitchen, with an outside toilet, for herself and Arthur just before they got married. The place had been in the same neighbourhood they had grown up in, almost a street away from their respective homes. The problem was, although the rent was cheap, the landlord had clearly stated no pets or children. The only sanitation was water from the kitchen sink and Arthur and Beryl often had to visit the public baths in Stepney Green.

However, Mrs Jones always helped out by telling them both to have baths at her place in front of a hot fire. Arthur had been the third in a family of eight children; his mother had looked as though she was in her sixties at their wedding. She had actually been a woman in her mid thirties but had died a few years after his wedding. Her body had being racked by tuberculosis which had been rife in those days, with everyone coughing and turning their cheeks red. The burden of bearing eight children one after the other, the housework, washing, cooking and the severe lack of a well balanced diet, had all contributed to her early death.

There were no washing machines, vacuum cleaners, fridge or freezers, and certainly no gentle cleaning products for women's hands. Women were tougher and stronger years ago, thought Mrs Peters. For women, housework and running a household on a tight budget, was more tiring than for the men going out to work. They had seemed to have lower expectations of their men in those days and were more committed to their families and their loved ones. It was mothers, wives and sisters who made families strong and they were the ones men drew their strength from.

In 1935, when she was seven years old, her dad had taken her to see King George's Jubilee. She had seen King George and Queen Mary driving in an open coach so that all the crowds could see them. Beryl had loved the day and as a child had dreamt of her wedding being similar - of driving in a horse and carriage through her neighbourhood.

In reality, Beryl and Arthur's wedding had taken place in a church and her dress had been a simple white long gown with a veil. Her mother had sewn the dress. The food had been prepared by members of their family and friends. Most of the people in the neighbourhood had attended as weddings were important social gatherings. Even poor families tried to put on a good show and people bought all types of gifts for the newlyweds; some gave money, others bits of cutlery, pictures, flowers, ornaments, they gave what they could and that was much appreciated. It wasn't a matter of who could give the most expensive gift for everyone was in the same boat. It was the generosity of their hearts and the warmth of happiness that made such gatherings special.

Arthur and Beryl's mothers used to say,

"We ain't got no airs and graces. We ain't got much money. But there ain't any shame in being poor. There's shame though feeling sorry for oneself. The poor knows about giving and the rich knows about taking and keeping."

Mrs Peters thought the poor did know about giving for they had given their best in the war. She remembered in 1944, a few weeks after her dance with Arthur, he had been posted to France, like so many others from their neighbourhood. How unfair the world had seemed, how her heart had wept for Arthur, but Beryl had known that it was her duty to send Arthur off with a brave face, like other sweethearts of those days.

Those times were hard during the war. She remembered only too well that down at the Royal Docks, people were unloading the cargo of canned meat from the United States during the days of rationing and food shortages. Chicken and meat had been so scarce and most families had more fish to eat than meat and poultry. Beryl recalled that herring was often given to the men for tea after a hard day at work. There had been many fish dishes at her wedding, including jellied eels; sausages and chicken sandwiches had been such a treat. Nowadays, young people only ate fish if it was fish fingers.

Beryl smiled thinking how the East End had celebrated VE Day on 8 May 1945. After nearly six long years of war, bombs landing in many streets, children being sent away to the country, deaths and the news of men killed in action, the celebrations were needed by people everywhere in the country, especially in the East End. It showed how people coped with tragedies, their loss and heartaches. They became stronger and carried on in the celebration of life and the East End had celebrated on the streets with rows and rows of tables and chairs for dinner brought through a community collection. They had high hopes that the end of the war would be a new beginning for jobs, new housing with the clearance of the slums, better health and the end of poverty for families. It was not as easy as people had hoped as the road to prosperity was a difficult and laborious one, filled with bittersweet memories.

After Arthur and Beryl were married, Arthur left his job helping a Rag and Bone trader. He got a job in the Royal Docks and Beryl got a job in a bakery and they saved every penny they could for the future. Arthur came from a family of Dockers and was well paid. He worked from eight in the morning, till seven at night, eleven hours a day and five and half days a week, sometimes Sundays as well. Arthur used to put Vaseline up his nose and cotton wool in his ears to stop the asbestos from going down into his chest, but the affects of asbestos caused many a docker to become fatally ill in later years. His dad had managed to become a stevedore and his younger brothers had become stokers by the age of eighteen.

Arthur and Beryl wanted small things in life; a decent home, enough to eat and give away, a place where children could grow up in peace and honesty. In 1951 Beryl became pregnant with her first child and it was time to look for bigger accommodation. There had been many people in the East End who had moved to estates like Dagenham, while the council's promise of better housing in the 1930s carried on being promises. The council had managed to build a limited number of small houses, still shared by two families with one living upstairs and one downstairs, on streets that had been bombed during the war. The new houses had an indoor toilet but still no bathing facilities.

Beryl and Arthur moved to one of these homes and she had thought how lovely it was to live in a fresh and newly decorated environment. It would be good for the new baby. At the time the National Health Service had been established and that helped so many families, especially expectant mothers and children, thought Beryl after her four experiences. It had been extremely difficult, living in one bedroomed accommodation, with another family living downstairs. At the beginning it had been three to a bed with the baby in the cot and then as the children had got older it was two to a bed. Mrs Peters had lived like that with her family for nearly ten years, with her mother helping out as much as possible. Families, especially mothers, were there for their daughters, supporting them as best they could, whether it was watching the children one afternoon or with housework. Social services could not have done a better job than mothers and friends.

In 1962, the Peters' housing situation was finally noted and they were offered the three bedroomed flat that she still occupied. The family had thought how wonderful the flat was. Arthur continued to work in the docks and Beryl looked after the children. The Peters family made friends with their neighbours and gradually became part of the community on their estate. It wasn't quite like when Beryl was growing up, but it was cosy and everyone knew each other, yet there were changes from the old community Beryl had known but things change with the times and Beryl was happy with what she had. One's childhood always looked rosy in adulthood. By the mid 1960s Beryl had noticed changes that were getting increasingly evident. Bengali speaking workers, mostly men, came with the intention of earning money and many worked on the docks and Beryl remembered the first time Arthur talked about a man called 'Abdul'.

"Abdul, the new bloke, he wants to learn everything. Although his English isn't that good, he seems to pick up everything as he sees it. Got no family, all back home in Bangladesh. I said to him, come down the pub but all he had was a coke. He said he don't drink. Something about being a Muslim 'cause he ain't a Jew."

Mrs Peters remembered almost bitterly now, the gradual arrival of those Bangladeshi workers' families in the 1960s. It was the arrival of wives and children that identified a community as previous residents moved out to take advantage of better opportunities elsewhere. The new residents took old trades and introduced new ones. Suddenly there had been shops springing up selling strange vegetables, wares and providing clothes for the new community that had emerged. The old corner shops had long been sold to the new residents as people moved on to other places, travelling up the social ladder.

Geographical mobility, sociologists would have called it, but white residents did not see it in that context. They saw their jobs, trades and homes been taken over by foreigners, at least it looked that way to Mrs Peters. Gradually, with the increasing influx of immigrants moving in to the East End, social and community problems started to develop. The housing shortage, although not acute at the time, the lack of social and community facilities for the young, and the lack of innovative education and training opportunities, started to show as underlying problems for many families and the conflicts began between the diverse communities in the East End. In reality immigrant families, especially the women, found it difficult to settle in due to the lack of language, communication, and cultural and religious problems.

By then it was 1968 but the white community did not understand the problems and Enoch Powell's politically well-timed 'Rivers of blood' speech went down jubilantly with many white people. As far as many white people were concerned, the Bangladeshi families were in the same boat as them and had to cope with their lot. Why should Bangladeshi families be spoon-fed and white families expected to get on with it on their own? Mrs Peters had sent all her children to Church of England schools to ensure they got a decent education and did not mix with the wrong crowd. She thought this was the only way white children could get access to better opportunities for jobs in the future, but in actual fact her children could have enjoyed being in the company of children from other cultures, if they had been given the opportunity.

Mrs Peters remembered when David, as a young child had come home and said,

"We've got a Bangladeshi kid in our school now. He don't know how to speak English. Even the teachers don't know what to do with him."

At the time she and her good neighbour, Vera, God rest her soul, were having a cup of tea in the kitchen.

"Don't know why they didn't learn English before they came over, Beryl. It might have saved a lot of time and effort for them and us. Mind you, I got nothing against them." Vera had said

Beryl had somehow found herself agreeing, Vera was absolutely right she'd thought. Why didn't these newcomers learn English when they came over? Vera had been a good friend since 1953 when they had organised the street party, to celebrate the Coronation of Queen Elizabeth. It had been a big party and people had really got together for the celebration. Later the two friends, along with others, had done a similar event during the wedding of Prince Charles and the late Diana for they had wanted to keep the community spirit of the good old days alive within their children's generation. For them it was part of their cultural heritage and they were proud of it.

There's nothing like that now thought Mrs Peters, it's so empty and lonely. Many of her old friends had passed away and she felt so incredibly lonely and isolated and often found herself looking through old family photographs and reading newspaper cuttings. There were so many memories in the passages of her life and her heart ached for something of the old to come back and fill the deep loneliness she now felt.

David was her eldest son, an electrician who lived in Essex. David had three grown up children with families of their own and they all lived near to each other, just as Beryl and Arthur had lived near their parents. He had tried hard to persuade his mother to live with him in Essex but she had insisted in living where she had been born. Beryl's second child and older daughter, Susan, also lived in Essex and, she too had tried to persuade Mrs Peters to move there, especially after Mr Peters' death. But to no avail. Mrs Peters loved her East End roots and she was going to live there until her death. Susan and her husband owned a furniture shop and her two grown up children had moved out and lived with their partners.

Vivien, Mrs Peters' third and younger daughter, led a solitary and private life although she worked in the city close to where she lived. She had never married and lived on her own. Vivien often visited her mother and on every visit Mrs Peters urged her to find herself a husband. Mrs Peters worried about Vivien's lonely life, but she seemed unaffected by it, for as a child she had got on with people and was never one to complain. Vivien was by far the most ambitious of the Peters' children and she had travelled a great deal - well she could afford it with the amount of money she earned, smiled Mrs Peters proudly. David and Susan as children had been the homely type, putting family and kinship first. They had been 'average' kind of children and they had never had non-white friends, although there were many black and Asian children living on other estates. As children and then as teenagers, David and Susan hadn't liked or hated the Bangladeshi community.

They had seen many changes in the East End, especially with white children learning foreign languages, learning their ways and dressing like them. Susan and David had seen the festivals integrating communities in the area but for them there were no traditional East End festivals or celebrations held anymore. It was all about mixing with each other, like an exotic cocktail. They had found the Bangladeshis dirty and filthy, well they had looked greasy, the older women were always chewing some sort of leaf with nuts and making their mouths red, the kids had lice, they always smelt of curry and they wore funny clothes. As far as David and Susan were concerned, if the

Bangladeshis were living in England then they had to live like the English, like decent British white people.

David and Susan had moved out of the East End, to a white populated area, to ensure their children did not forget their British roots and learnt their English language properly. In reality, to an outsider, David and Susan were trying to become more middle class by leaving their working class roots behind and by trying to nurture their children to behave in a more middle class fashion. How strange for them to believe that moving away from an area of diverse ethnic cultures would not influence their children. David's daughters enjoyed wearing clothes influenced by Indian-subcontinent fashion and designs. For various social occasions, they had worn clothes from shops that sold ethnic clothing and fashion accessories. His daughters used henna on their hands and feet and wore ethnic jewellery. As for David's son, he was having an affair with an Indian woman at his office and cheating on his wife.

Susan's son worked for a Japanese bank and her daughter dressed in a Gothic manner. For David and Susan, moving away to another area to ensure their children grew up as 'fresh English roses' had not in actual fact happened for their children had still been touched by other cultures and traditions. How could they possibly not be? The mass media and the changing face of Britain touched the lives of all children and people from all races with varied responses. It was change from the old to the new that people found hard to deal with. It didn't matter which community, race, creed or culture one came from, change was an aspect of life which could either be painful or joyful, but had to be accepted or acknowledged eventually by individuals.

Vivien Peters thought that was the difference between the left and right wing parties - one party wanted change from the old to the new in leaps and bounds and the other - a slow passive change, or may be none at all. Vivien Peters understood about change. She was by far more accepting of change than members of the community she had grown up with for she hadn't wanted to be a hairdresser or on a Youth Training Scheme placement. She had wanted to make money and so had managed to get herself an admin place in a large foreign bank and gradually worked her way to the top. She had a knack for understanding about stocks and shares and with the right investments had accumulated a small fortune. She had 'made it' as the East Enders would say but, as far as Vivien was concerned, she had made it because she had an open mind.

She was more tolerant towards other individuals, different from the small world of the East End. Vivien had travelled to many countries, witnessed many walks of life and had seen how different people lived with what they had, and yet they all had something in common. From the Indian farmers to the white cockney painters and decorators of the East End, the will to live and work for the survival of the family was evident in the way they helped each other.

On many occasions Vivien found David and Susan overbearing. With their narrow views and 'stuck up ways' they always tried to make out that the Cockney East End was lost because of the newcomers. David and Susan thought that the good old days had been without crime or muggings, there had been good jobs, decent homes and great schools. She remembered growing up with old people being mugged, burglaries taking place, schools not being refurbished, David and Susan on unemployment benefit while waiting for apprenticeship places, Graham getting into trouble with the law. The past had not been a rosy picture of peace and prosperity, there had always been problems whoever had come and gone in the East End. The problems had just looked worse because there had been someone else of a different colour to blame apart from the local council.

Graham Peters lived very near his mum and he also visited her often. He lived in a bed-sit, but Graham believed that his life could have been a lot better if there had been less 'Pakis' around. As a child, Graham had kept to mainly white friends for he deeply believed that the Pakis got priority in everything and he never really believed in making friends with any Bangladeshi children. Why should he? They lived another way of life and it had been them that had made him lose the chance to work in a top-notch bank. He had once gone for an interview, after leaving school, but the bank had given the job to a Bangladeshi young man. He had apparently completed all the interview tasks correctly, but Graham believed otherwise. The 'Paki' had been given the job because of the new age of equal opportunities and equal opportunities were about giving more chances to the newcomers, the people who wanted handouts.

In the past Graham had lived with his wife and two young children in his mother's flat. They had had to wait until the council found them suitable accommodation. It had been unfair living off his mum as he had been unemployed at the time, but then he had worked a bit on the side while he was on benefit because he couldn't make ends meet. Now and then, many poor families dodged the benefit system, like the rich now and then evaded the taxman; the poor were under pressure to ensure they lived just above the poverty line. Or may be the pressure of Graham's ex-wife, ever demanding needs for herself and the children, was what led him to cheat the benefit system and his mother had known about his little secret. Well, her son had to survive and he would have survived even better if he had never married Sharon.

Mrs Peters had never really approved of Sharon; she had been bad news from the day Graham had a fight over her in the pub where they had met. She was a spoilt, lazy, greedy and manipulative woman in Mrs Peters' opinion. He had been married to Sharon for twenty stormy years, but last year she had finally kicked him out of their flat. His children, now in their late teens, still lived with their mother because they had nowhere else to live. His wife claimed that Graham had beaten and abused her for the last ten years and she would not put up with his violence anymore, but Mrs Peters did not believe a word of her daughter-in-law's claims.

Graham's life had gone down hill when he'd lost his job at the construction company where he'd worked for most of his life. He'd always been a 'problem child' as his teachers had called him, but Mrs Peters thought he hadn't had the same opportunities his siblings had enjoyed. She tended to forget that David had found him an apprenticeship with the electricity board where he worked when Graham had left school with no qualifications, but Graham had messed up. He hadn't turned up on time to work; he had got drunk while on duty and finally he had a fight with another apprentice. Vivien had later found him a placement in another bank, but again he messed up due to his own selfish attitude.

Mrs Peters had spoilt Graham. He was the youngest and he'd been the only one left at home and she had felt useless after the others had left. She had made such a fuss of Graham and always sympathised with him when anything went wrong. Finally one day Arthur had come home from work and found Graham sleeping the afternoon away, a couple of empty beer cans laying nearby.

"You're ruining the boy's life," Arthur had said angrily to Beryl. "He's got to face up to his responsibilities and he has to take the blame for some of the trouble that he causes for us and other people. For Christ's sake I'm still at work and what makes him any different from me. Graham is not a child anymore and he needs to mend his ways or I'll kick him out of the house. You hear me, woman?"

She had heard all right, the whole neighbourhood had probably heard Arthur that day. Beryl Peters had been frightened of Arthur's temper, which prompted Graham to go down the job centre. The job seekers' officers had finally found Graham the construction job and he had stayed there for twenty years until his redundancy. He had found great mates to have a laugh with as they were all heavy drinkers like him and developed beer bellies over the years. Vivien found Graham to be pathetic and ignorant whenever she met him at her mother's flat for in reality he was a middle-aged man who thought he was still the rebellious teenager of long ago.

Graham and his mates lived near to each other and met down at their local pub as much as possible. Their conversation consisted of which birds had big boobs and a hard arse, what they had for last night's dinner and who was the man in the house. But most of all they had fierce discussions about the local Pakis, Bangladeshis, black bastards and niggers, because Graham and his little group saw themselves as patriots to the British flag. They were for Queen and country and he thought the Queen represented them as the British whites. After the tragic death of Diana, Graham had displayed no sign of sympathy.

"The Royal family are probably feeling bloody relieved that Di's dead," he'd said to his mates. "The slag was going out with that black bastard and to top up with that he was rich and famous. Diana bought shame to the Royals and to us whites 'cause she let a black man touch her."

27

Graham was racist and his prejudices had become worse over the years as he encountered one failure after another. In his opinion, if there were less niggers, Pakis and chinks there'd be less failures for white people to go through, white people couldn't even get a decent job without being overlooked to give hand outs to the newcomers. The National Health Service would be in a better condition if there were less black or Asian babies being delivered as they always seemed to be reproducing. If there were less people needed to teach English, there would be more money for schools and his children could have done better. If there were less coloureds with big families to re-house, then he would be in bigger accommodation. The British society was a total mess with so many coloured faces and it shouldn't be like that. Graham often told his mates, "There ain't no black in the Union Jack."

Mrs Peters shook her head; her ham sandwich was untouched and dusk was drawing close. The family next door had made her think so much today, she had never had Bangladeshi people living next door to her. She got up and drew her curtains and as she did so, she looked out of her sitting room window and saw the children still playing in the communal gardens. It was twilight and the summer breeze was a little cold now but she saw the white children playing on one side and the Bangladeshi children playing on the other side. It was always like that, never different, they never played with each other. They only met in the middle to hurl abusive names at each other. Mrs Peters did not feel any different seeing these children segregated in their play. Each to their own, she thought, best that way for they would never understand each other since they spoke different languages so they couldn't really enjoy playing with each other. It never really occurred to her that the language of play and laughter could be universal for children for if they were given the opportunity children were more accepting towards people, places and differences than adults. Their play could have been the celebration of their differences and similarities; they just needed the chance to play together.

Mrs Peters sat back down on her settee and switched on the television (her other companion, along with Tabby) and started to eat her dry sandwich. How different the East End was now, so many different faces, names and strange ways. She still found it hard to understand why the London Hospital had translated so many of its signs into Bengali underneath the English. She found it such a cheek that these little things had to be done for the Bangladeshis. No wonder so many young white people felt angry. On top of that, many of the local pubs and small churches had shut down and yet everywhere else, all these temples were springing up with a priest singing at odd hours.

She often felt frightened because she felt like a stranger in the place she had loved so much. Going shopping to her local fish and chip shop, or to the post office, Mrs Peters often felt fear when she saw groups of Bangladeshi boys. She had once been pushed at a bus stop and nearly had her purse stolen by a Bangladeshi boy. Mrs Peters was scared to leave her home after dark and on a number of occasions she had run out of milk but she had not dared to go out because she knew by the time she came home it would be dark. She often forgot bits of her shopping and did without because of going out again. It really was not fair for her to live like a bird trapped in a cage, trying to flutter when its wings had been wounded. It was no wonder that Mrs Peters longed for the days when she had felt safe and secure and most of all not alone.

A short time later, she switched off the television and put the light on in the corridor as she went from room to room shutting the curtains. She caught sight of a photo of Arthur and the dockers he had worked with, something made her choke and she pushed back her tears. The government had shut the docks down years ago; they had killed a whole way of life that had been passed from generations of families to each other. They had taken the livelihood of many families and the dignity of the men. In 1969 the London Docks closed followed by St Katherine's Docks, the East India Docks shut in 1970 and a few years later the West India Docks closed. And finally the Royal Docks were the last to go and her Arthur had being made redundant in 1971. He was forty-six years old at the time, too old for a career change and too young for retirement.

Arthur had found it difficult to accept he was no longer at work and had to claim unemployment benefit. He was angry and frustrated at first, then he gradually became quiet and withdrawn. Beryl started to worry about his behaviour and she had talked to Vera about him.

"I'm really worried about Arthur. He don't go out, he's ever so quiet. The dock closures have hit him hard and he thinks he's useless now."

"Oh, luv. It'll get better. Get him into something else."

"But he's being a docker all his life," cried out Beryl.

"Well that don't matter; my Harry's a dustman. Maybe Arthur might want to join him. Harry could get him in," Vera said comfortingly.

"I don't know if Arthur would," said Beryl.

"Why not?" Vera had said getting a bit touchy. "Arthur used to help a rag and bone man."

"All right Vera, I'll have a chat with Arthur at tea time."

So Beryl talked to Arthur, but it had being difficult to get him to agree to join Harry but finally he relented and said he would try it for a week. Arthur stayed a week and then worked as a dustman until he was sixty. He and Harry were always in a team together but one day Harry had a stroke, leaving him paralysed on his right side. Arthur and Beryl made it their duty to help Vera, giving her company and help to keep his spirit alive and to help him to face his life with strength and dignity.

Closing the docks had cost the whole area socially and financially but the government at that time would never understand how important the docklands had been to the Cockney East Enders. It had been the end of an era, but still the East End spirit rose above its loss and carried on. The tide change, however dramatic or gradual, did not bring the benefits promised by the conservative government for the East Enders. In their eyes, the rich got richer at the expense of the poor and the poor got poorer. There were two types of people who had screwed the East Enders - the 'Yuppies' and the 'Pakis', as Graham put it. How unfair the distribution of wealth was; many people in power had screwed the East Enders and lined their pockets. Closing the docks had been about making profits, not about welfare or traditions.

Like many East Enders Mrs Peters saw the stark differences of the rich and the poor. It was so shamelessly flaunted in front of them but they failed to see the Bangladeshis were in the same boat as themselves. Poverty and deprivation often made people blind to the truth. The beautiful, modern apartments built in the docklands were only affordable if you were earning a fortune, the jobs were only for those who had a city look and spoke with a 'posh' accent. Even the nightlife was different and so the line between the bourgeoisie and the proletariat was defined.

Generations of East End families had given their labour and their health to make a financial success of the riverside economy and it was this that had contributed to the development of the City. The City's financial power rooted back to the East End and East Enders had a right to be angry and resentful for they felt they had been cheated. The policy makers, the rich investors and new modernisation also contributed to the unrest and conflicts arose from social and financial burdens on families and it led to prejudice and racism both verbal and physical. Life had just remained as hard as it had been years ago but the only difference was that it was tougher now for people to cope with their hardships because the grass looked greener on the other side all the time. The community was fragmented now and to walk amongst strangers in one's birthplace was the hardest thing to accept.

Mrs Peters went to run her bath and as the water ran from the taps she remembered the same sounds of the river water at the docks when workers worked together loading and unloading the cargo from ships that had travelled from ports all over the world. Many a time she had gone to meet Arthur with the kids after work and it had been a lovely outing for them. It seemed nothing much of an outing, but it had been exciting for Beryl and her children. They hadn't much money for holidays and expensive outings, yet joy was found in the smallest of things.

The phone suddenly rang and Mrs Peters went back into the sitting room and picked up the receiver.

"Hello," she answered.

"Hello mum." It was Vivien.

"Hello luv. How are you?" asked Mrs Peters fondly.

"I'm all right. How have you been?" Vivien answered.

"Not bad. Got some new neighbours who moved in today. Bangladeshi, they are."

"Have you met them then?"

"No, they've only just moved in. They might not be able to speak English."

"That doesn't matter Mum, it's nice if you go and say hello. It doesn't matter whether their Bangladeshi or cockney. It's being neighbourly, you taught us that," Vivien gently reminded her mother.

"I suppose so but it ain't the same at it used to be," argued Mrs Peters with a touch of bitterness.

"No, mum it ain't, but we cockneys have got a good heart," Vivien said with her most cockney accent. Over the years working in the city had changed her accent developing it into more pronounced English. Working with high-powered financial professionals one had to prove that one had the power of speech, an important factor in negotiating deals and exchanging contracts.

"Yes you're right Vivien. We have got good hearts. Anyway when are you coming down?" asked Mrs Peters cheerfully.

"Probably this weekend," Vivien answered.

"Well, stay the night because I could do with the company. Vera's gone and all and I feel a bit lonely, I'll cook you some nice supper." There was a tone of desperation in Mrs Peters' voice and Vivien caught it and felt her mother's loneliness. She refused to move to Essex near David and Susan and she would not move in with her for Beryl loved her East End.

Vivien had been thinking of buying a flat near her mother so she could keep an eye on her. She could afford to buy a flat with cash if she sold her present accommodation. She hadn't said anything yet; she didn't want to get her hopes up.

"All right mum, I'll stay over," said Vivien making her mother very happy. Mother and daughter said their goodbyes and once again Mrs Peters was alone in her home with only Tabby for company.

CHAPTER THREE

It was nearly three weeks since the Ali family had moved into their new flat. They had settled in very well and met a few of the other Bangladeshi residents. In the block where they lived, there were fifty-five flats of which twenty-five belonged to white families, twenty to Bangladeshi residents, five to Chinese and five to Somali residents. It was strange how the majority of white residents were housed in the east wing and the majority of Bangladeshi families were housed in the west wing.

The Ali family lived in one of the seven flats that divided the east from the west side and these flats directly faced the street. They were the only Bangladeshi family in that row. The rest were all white, but not all East Enders. Mrs Peters flat was on their right and the flat on the left was rented by three young men who worked in the city. The Ali family had met the three young men in passing and had introduced themselves and found they were friendly people from counties outside of London.

However, they had not met Mrs Peters in circumstances which would have prompted them to speak and felt rather daunted by the prospect. The times they had seen her, she had not exactly had a friendly look on her face and neither did she give an impression that she wanted an introduction. They didn't even know her name and they lived right next door to her and this disturbed Ayesha very much. She really wanted to talk to Mrs Peters and be friends with her.

One afternoon Ayesha sat in her bedroom with Shazia who was preparing for her exams. She was finding it difficult to concentrate with Ayesha's chatter.

"Afa, I just want the old woman next door to know that we are a nice family and we don't mean any harm to her. She might be frightened of us, I just want to say hello."

"Ayesha you're just a busy body because all you really want to know about the old woman is her life history, especially as she's white. White old women are bad news; they'll say you tried to give them a stroke if you ask too many questions," Shazia snapped at Ayesha.

"Shut up, Afa, you're being nasty 'cause you aren't as brave as me. I'm just a nice person and you aren't..," said Ayesha angrily.

"Get out and stay out. The whole day you've being going on about how to be buddies with the old cow next door!" snapped Shazia.

"I'm going, there's a funny smell in the room." Ayesha stormed out and slammed the door shut behind her.

It was Saturday and Ayesha was bored. She was not allowed out on her own in the communal gardens and she had nothing to do. Ayesha had no one to play with and that was very serious for her, she didn't really know the other Bangladeshi children very well yet and was very concerned how she was going to spend her holidays without playmates. She went into the garden and sat down on the plastic chair in the shade.

Ayesha had an idea; she would start to plan how to plant her sunflower by clearing a patch in the garden where the sun shone the most and so set to work. She found the washing up gloves in the kitchen and a large metal spoon to dig with, and a carrier bag to put the rubbish in and went back into the garden and started to dig. The sunflower is going to grow so high and tower above the garden fence and people will see it and think it was Ayesha who had planted such a beautiful plant, she thought to herself as she carried on digging. She was going to paint some stones and make a border around the sunflower to separate it from the rest of the garden.

She wondered if Shazia would help her plant the sunflower, it was hard work digging. Her sister was preparing for her exams and she felt guilty for disturbing her. Ayesha suddenly felt as though someone was watching her. Straight away she turned around and found the old woman next door having a little peep at what she was doing. She automatically smiled at her but the old woman quickly went back to putting her washing out on the line.

"Hello, how are you?" Obviously Ayesha had failed to recognise the old woman's reaction to her being caught peeping and there was no response. Again she said loudly but sweetly:

"I said hello, how are you?"

Mrs Peters stopped for a second and said "Hello" without turning around and carried on with her task.

"How are you?" asked Ayesha again.

"I'm fine," replied Mrs Peters stiffly. She was in a very uncomfortable position as she really didn't want to get friendly with this pestering Bangladeshi child.

"My name's Ayesha. What's your name?" Ayesha asked, completely ignoring the obvious unfriendly response.

"Beryl Peters but Mrs Peters to you. You're a bit nosy," Mrs Peters added haughtily, hoping Ayesha would be put off from making any further conversation with her.

"Mrs Peters, I'm not trying to be nosy, I'm trying to be nice and friendly. My sister, Shazia, said the same thing about me but I think its nice being nice to your neighbour," said Ayesha sweetly. Mrs Peters turned around for the child had voiced Vivien's words, something she had taught her daughter and she suddenly felt a little ashamed.

"Yes sometimes being nice and asking questions can look as though you're being nosy, but it doesn't matter," she said, as a sign of being sorry without actually saying it.

"That means we're friends. Oh, Mrs Peters, your garden is so pretty," Ayesha said admiringly.

Mrs Peters felt very pleased with Ayesha for noting her garden.

"Oh, thank you," she replied.

"Mrs Peters, it reminds me of Mary, Mary Quite Contrary's Garden but even prettier than that," Ayesha theatrically commented with her hands clasped and her eyes wide open and Mrs Peters really could not help but smile.

"My garden looked much prettier when my husband used to look after it. I can't always manage to do it on my own."

"Where is he?" asked Ayesha. She had really had to know.

"He's dead, gone to the Lord's garden," she replied with a frown.

Ayesha looked at her with sympathy as though she felt her pain.

"You'll find him one day because every one finds the people they love," she said reassuringly.

Mrs Peters looked at Ayesha properly for the first time. With her big shiny dark eyes and the lovely dark curly hair that hung over her face, she looked so innocent, she kept pushing her hair back behind her ears and for some reason Mrs Peters found this Bangladeshi child looked so sweet. Maybe because Mrs Peters had really looked at her and talked to her and found she was just like another child.

"I hope our garden looks as nice as yours when it's done up. Do you think it will?" Ayesha asked. She had noticed Mrs Peters had looked a little sombre, for she was a very alert little girl, insightful to people's feelings, emotions and reactions.

"I'm sure it will." Mrs Peters gathered her pegs to go back inside. Ayesha was not going to let her go in for it was such a sunny day and Mrs Peters really should enjoy the sun and have a chat with her. Ayesha loved having a chat with who ever could spare her some free time.

"Mrs Peters," called Ayesha, "I want to tell you a secret."

Mrs Peters stopped in her tracks and turned back to Ayesha; whatever was the little girl going to tell her. It must be something very important, maybe about her family because she had heard strange stories about Bangladeshi families, like child brides.

"What secret?" she asked in a hushed voice.

"Come over here and let me tell you quietly. I don't want anyone to hear," Ayesha said solemnly and her elderly neighbour lent over near to Ayesha's side of the fence and bent down to her.

"I want to plant a sunflower but my mum and dad don't know yet and the sunflower's going to remind everyone of me and someone else," whispered Ayesha.

Mrs Peters chuckled to herself as she had thought Ayesha was going to tell her something dreadful like her parents had arranged for her to get married.

"Well, the secret's safe with me," she whispered back.

"Why don't you get a chair and I'll tell you all about my sunflower," Ayesha said in a quiet voice.

Mrs Peters thought, why not, it's not like I've left company inside to entertain. Anyway let's see what the child's got to say. The child just would not take the hint that she was not too keen on making friends, but then she didn't have to be friends with her.

"Okay then," she decided and got one of her garden chairs and sat near to her neighbour's side of the fence while Ayesha went back to dig her little patch in the garden.

"Do you know much about sunflowers?" asked Ayesha.

"No, not really, but Arthur, my husband, knew lots about flowers and David knows a lot like him too. I suppose he'd know about sunflowers."

"Who's David?" asked Ayesha.

"My eldest son," replied Mrs Peters.

"How many children have you got then?"

"I've got four but they're all grown up and got families of their own. Some of their children have got families of their own," said Mrs Peters proudly.

"You must be really old then, Mrs Peters," Ayesha said in her innocent way.

Mrs Peters smiled. "Yes I am, I'm seventy two years old."

"Well, I'm eight," Ayesha competed, feeling very grown up.

"Yes, you'll nearly be my age soon," teased Mrs Peters, for she was enjoying herself.

"Do you think I ask too many questions?" asked Ayesha as she stopped her digging for a breather.

"Yes, I do. I haven't asked you any, if you haven't noticed."

"Well, you can ask me as many questions as you like and I'll ask you as many as I like. We'll be same then," Ayesha said. She smiled confidently inside knowing Mrs Peters couldn't possibly beat her at question time.

"Who was the other someone you're planting the sunflower for?" asked Mrs Peters.

"My brother," Ayesha said sadly and Mrs Peters noticed her face.

"Why do you look so glum if it's for your brother?" she asked.

"Because he's with Mr Peters," said Ayesha staring at her. Suddenly Mrs Peters felt a wave of emotion for this child and she wanted to hold her. How odd to feel like this, for a stranger of another race.

"What happened?" asked Mrs Peters. She needed to know, to understand the tragedy. She felt really bad probing into the little girl's sadness but she was desperate to know, to feel.

"My brother and me were twins but he died after he was born and I lived. We were both premature," said Ayesha with something akin to guilt in her eyes and this did not go amiss on her listener.

"It's not your fault luv, your brother died because it was meant to be and I'm sure he doesn't blame you," said Mrs Peters comfortingly. "I'm sure he'd be happy with the sunflower. Got any other brothers or sisters?"

Ayesha told her about her family and who did what in the house, who she liked the best, her fights with Shazia and Mrs Peters told her about her family too. They told each other what programmes they watched on television, what they liked to eat, what clothes they liked, who was their favourite pop star and they both realised they had so much in common. From enjoying fish and chips, watching East Enders, listening to Cliff Richard's songs and reading. Ayesha and Mrs Peters loved singing We're all Going on a Summer Holiday, especially as Ayesha had practiced it in school.

****

From afar it looked peaceful to see an old white woman chatting to a little Bangladeshi girl as though they had known each other for many years. Mr and Mrs Ali had been watching Ayesha and Mrs Peters from their sitting room window for their youngest child had somehow managed to break the ice with the old woman and may be she might not be as bad as they had assumed. Perhaps in a little while I'll go out with Rokiya and introduce ourselves, it might show we aren't as bad to talk to as she might think, thought Mr Ali.

****

In the garden, Mrs Peters and Ayesha were talking about the weather and how it was so unpredictable. The old white woman was finding it so enjoyable to talk to someone, a child rather than Tabby, the television, the telephone, or her own thoughts, it was so lovely to have company. The little girl spoke such good English, even better than me, thought Mrs Peters as she had believed that Ayesha might speak with an accent, but she was very wrong.

Ayesha's parents came out and Mrs Peters saw them from the corner of her eye, but she pretended she hadn't noticed them. She carried on talking to Ayesha while Mr and Mrs Ali stood looking at their garden, trying to discuss it quietly in Bengali. They were aware the old woman was ignoring them and they felt uncomfortable. Perhaps it had been wrong for them to come outside to introduce themselves, but it was a contradictory sight with Mrs Peters talking to Ayesha and yet not attempting to acknowledge her parents.

It was Ayesha who broke the ice.

"Mrs Peters, that's my mum and dad standing over there looking a bit silly," she said. What a way to introduce her parents to me, thought Mrs Peters but secretly she had a giggle about it and it showed on her face. Ayesha noticed and laughed with her.

"Well, you best call them over," Mrs Peters said.

Ayesha called to her parents in Bengali, to come over and be introduced.

"We were going to come round and introduce ourselves but we didn't get round to it," said Mr Ali apologetically.

"Well, your daughter's gone and done it for you and I hear you're going to do your garden up?" Mrs Peters replied.

"Yes we want to do a patio and on the sides we want to grow vegetables. My wife wants to, I wanted flowers but she wants potatoes."

"Well, your wife rules otherwise you won't get any tea," chuckled Mrs Peters.

"My sons and me will do the garden. Builders cost too much money and my pocket is empty," said Mr Ali.

"My sons, good boys. They hard work do," Mrs Ali said in her broken English trying to express herself.

Mrs Peters smiled at Ayesha's mother trying to join in the conversation. She couldn't speak English, but she had tried to join in using the words she knew. She had made an attempt to learn the English language and that was what counted.

"Yes, my sons and daughters are hard working too," she said instead.

"We buy our flat with our own money," volunteered Mr Ali, an expression of his hard work.

"The flat belonged to my best friend, Vera, but she died and her children sold it. I didn't want them to sell it but I suppose they had to, seeing as none of them were going to live in it. They've all moved out of the area."

"Yes children grow up and change and they become different from us and move on. It's hard to make them understand to live like how we lived," said Mr Ali wistfully thinking of his sons and elder daughter.

"How old are your sons?" asked Mrs Peters.

"My big son nearly finished medicine degree, my second son in first year of degree in Economics and my daughter do A-levels at girl's school. Ayesha still baby," said Mrs Ali proudly.

Mrs Peters couldn't hide her surprise at how well Mr and Mrs Ali's children were doing as she had expected them to be in work since the age of school. She hadn't counted on them studying at university, but the family certainly were trying to bring up their children to be as educated as they could. They were probably loaded and the father worked and claimed benefit to help his family.

"What do you do then?" Mrs Peters asked Mr Ali.

"I work as a mini cab driver. When I first came to this country I worked in the docks. It was good work and people were nice," said Mr Ali remembering the early years when he first came to Britain. He had always worked hard and sent money back home to his parents, like many other Bangladeshi men who had come to Britain. Bangladeshi families living in Britain had one foot in Britain and the other back home in Bangladesh. That was the cycle of the financial burden on so many Bangladeshi families. One never forgot the deprivation left behind.

"My Arthur worked for the docks, but then they closed down and he became a dustman. He was a good docker and he came from a family of Dockers. It was sad to see the docks close," said Mrs Peters.

"It was wrong for government to do that," Mr Ali said and he continued, "they hurt many families and many men lose jobs they could have had for years. It was unfair. The people living here suffered but the new people who have the docks now have been the winners."

Mrs Peters looked at the bald Bangladeshi man and realised he understood about the unfairness of the dock closures; he seemed to have been affected too. She had thought only the white East Enders felt sad and angry at the dock closures, but perhaps she was wrong, perhaps life was not as green on the other side as she had thought.

"Mrs Peters, my sons and father help clean your garden when they do my garden," offered Mrs Ali as a statement, rather than a question.

Mrs Peters was a little taken aback by Mrs Ali's generosity and did not really know how to respond. Fearing they had offended the old white woman, Mrs Ali looked hastily at her husband, who added,

"That is if you want us to. If you don't mind."

"Okay, that's very kind of you. My children don't always get the time and you know they have been a bit busy." Secretly, Graham had had the time and she had asked him, but he had just come round and gone to sleep on the settee, had his tea and gone down the pub. He had said he would do the garden but he just hadn't had the time.

"If you need anything, like getting any milk, any help, please just come and ask. We will all help," said Mr Ali.

"Why that's good of you," said Mrs Peters. This is what neighbours did for each other. Perhaps they had learnt this from the East End, or perhaps this is the way they treated each other in their custom.

"If you need anything, I might be able to help. I know I'm old but I can still get round." Mrs Peters generously offered.

"Thank you," said Mr Ali. Frankly he couldn't really see what an old woman like Mrs Peters could possibly do for them or perhaps she could.

"Your mum's all right with her English, I suppose she gets by. Did you teach her?" Mrs Peters asked Ayesha.

"No, I haven't got the time. When my brothers were a bit older she went to a language class and learnt a few words. My dad said she had to learn a little because she couldn't speak to the health visitor and in case there was an emergency at home when he was at work," replied Ayesha.

"Well your dad used his common sense because I see a lot of Bangladeshi ladies down the post office, taking their kids to do the translating when they should be in school. It's a pity they can't learn a bit of English since they're living in Britain," said Mrs Peters.

"Sometimes Bangladeshi women are afraid to join English classes because they're not confident and too scared," Mr Ali defended gently. He knew many white people found it hard to accept why Bangladeshi women and even men did not always speak English or fluent English.

The sitting room opened and Shazia came out of the flat. She observed the scene before her with her parents and Ayesha talking to the old woman from next door and knew Ayesha had had something to do with creating this, but it was time for her to get involved. I wonder what the old woman thinks of mum's English language skills, thought Shazia. She walked over to them and spoke to Mrs Peters.

"Hello, how are you?"

"I'm fine and what's your name?" said Mrs Peters as she inspected Shazia,

38

up and down. The young girl was extremely pretty and she almost did not realise how pretty she was. Her face was clear of make up which she was pleased to see as many girls she saw had faces plastered thick with it. In her day, women used a little to enhance themselves, not to scare people. Shazia had long, shiny, straight, black hair that reached down to her waist and thank God there was no hair spray.

"My name's Shazia."

"You got a pretty face, you know. Bet you get a lot of lads chasing after you."

Shazia could feel herself blushing very deeply for this was not the kind of thing people said to a nice Bangladeshi girl in front of her parents, especially her father. She made a muttering sound and was about to go in, but Mrs Peters, unaware of the embarrassment she had caused, called out,

"Don't go in, come and have a chat with us. Your sister told me about the fights you both have with each other."

"Oh, did she really? I suppose she made out she was such a victim," said Shazia suddenly deciding it might be a good idea to stay. She was going to set the record straight about a few things the new neighbour might have been misled about by her dear sister. She smiled at her sister with a loving look.

"I'm sure Ayesha would love me to stay," she said.

Ayesha smiled lovingly back and Mrs Peters noticed the little exchange of words between the two sisters and burst into laughter.

"It's good to see a little squabble amongst sisters. Ishaa hasn't said anything bad about you Sharon," said Mrs Peters.

Ayesha and Shazia looked at Mrs Peters for they did really hate it when people didn't say their names properly. They looked at the white old woman and corrected her politely.

"It's Ayesha and Shazia."

Mrs Peters noted the way the two sisters corrected her straight away, and knew she would get a bit annoyed if someone didn't pronounce her name properly and their parents did pronounce her name properly. Mrs Peters judged herself to be fair.

"Sorry luvies, I didn't quite get your names properly the first time. It's what, Ayesha and Shaz, Shazia ain't it?" She pronounced the names slowly. "Anyway, what do you do Shazia?" asked Mrs Peters.

"I'm studying A levels; I want to become a teacher. I want to teach English to secondary school pupils," said Shazia.

"Do you read a lot of books?" asked Mrs Peters.

"Yea, I read thriller books like Wilbur Smith ones but when I was a bit younger I read all of Virginia Andrews and Catherine Cookson books."

"Yea, I enjoy reading the Virginia Andrews and Catherine Cookson books but I'm like you a bit now I read the thriller books," said Mrs Peters. She spent a lot of time going to and from the library for she had so much spare time and in the last few years she had read many books.

"I read other books by black and Asian writers now like Alice Walker, Toni Morrison and Anita Desai."

"What, do they write in their language?" asked Mrs Peters politely.

"No, they write in English like many other writers and many of them write about things they have experienced or know of like slavery, colonialism and racism," said Shazia looking straight into Mrs Peters' eyes. In the background Mr and Mrs Ali were muttering in Bengali for Shazia to change the subject. They were worried in case Mrs Peters got the wrong end of the stick but their daughter pretended she hadn't heard.

Mrs Peters really didn't know what to say to the young Bangladeshi woman in front of her.

"Everyone has problems but we just have to be a bit nicer to each other," she said.

"That's right Mrs Peters, like me and you are going to be best neighbours. I can't make you my best friend because I've already got a best friend but I haven't got a best neighbour. Is that all right?" asked Ayesha.

"'Course we can be," said Mrs Peters cheerfully and smiled at Shazia, who smiled back thinking may be this old woman might not be that bad after all.

Mr and Mrs Ali said they were going indoors and told Shazia not to be too long because she had to do her prayers.

"What's your mum and dad going to do indoors now?" Mrs Peters asked Shazia.

"They have to do their prayers. We're Muslims so we pray five times a day," she answered.

"Is that why sometimes we hear a man singing at different times of the day?" asked Mrs Peters seriously.

"He isn't singing, he calls people to prayer," said Ayesha and by now she was tired of digging and she looked dirty with soil on her face and clothes.

"The man is called the muezzin. Christians are called to prayer by church bells and we are called by the voice of another person," explained Shazia very logically. Some people really did not know other peoples religions very well and when they did, the knowledge was only the negative aspects portrayed by the media and the distorted truths they heard about.

"I understand, each religion has its different call to prayer. You explained it very nicely," Mrs Peters said. Shazia smiled for at least she listened to her properly rather than half listening and coming to ignorant conclusions, maybe she wasn't that prejudiced. One only knew a white person properly when they met their children, as their children's attitude might show what they really thought of Bangladeshis. Parents usually had a major influence on the thoughts of their children.

"I have to go in now but if you need anything, just give me a shout. It was nice meeting you," she added as she started to turn round to go indoors.

"All right luv, I might need a bit of help now and then. I might want to go to

40

the library with you," smiled Mrs Peters.

"Mrs Peters, I'll get my brothers to meet you soon. They're just as nice as me," Ayesha said.

"And who said you were nice?" Mrs Peters said pertly.

"You didn't say it, but if I wasn't nice, you wouldn't talk to me," said Ayesha logically. The child was exactly right for she had perceived the obvious… Mrs Peters' efforts to ignore her at the beginning of the afternoon.

"Mrs Peters, because you thought I was nice, you met my mum and dad and talked to them," continued Ayesha.

How true the child's words were thought Mrs Peters. At the beginning of the afternoon she'd had no intention of making friends with her new Bangladeshi neighbours but it had been Ayesha's innocent persistence of wanting to be her friend, of trying to make her talk to her, that she had let her guard down about Bangladeshi people. She had relented and conversed with Ayesha and her family and gradually, during the afternoon, Mrs Peters had discovered things about the Ali family she had not thought possible. She had assumed that none of them would be in education and presumed that perhaps they were probably part of a gang, into drugs and other criminal activities. They seemed to be more educated than Graham's children, who had been brought up in the same area. Mrs Peters discovered that like her, the Ali family had their own ways and beliefs, which they observed, just like she did as a Christian. This afternoon, spent for the first time in her life in the company of a family of colour, race, religion and background so different from her own, had left her confused and made her question her attitude and secretly, her prejudices.

"Mrs Peters are you angry with me?" asked Ayesha concerned at the old woman's silence. Mrs Peters looked at the little girl and thought, how could I be angry with a child who wants to be my good neighbour, something I taught my children. How can I be angry with a little child who wants to be a friend rather than a stranger? When she had watched the white and Bangladeshi children in their play, she had thought it best they did not play with each other. Maybe she was wrong, maybe they could play together just as she had found a way of talking to her little Bangladeshi neighbour.

"Mrs Peters, I'm going in now to have a wash but could you do me a favour?" asked Ayesha earnestly.

"What luv?" replied Mrs Peters - she could not help but call Ayesha 'luv' just like when she talked to her children and grandchildren. She had wanted to keep her distance but she couldn't help but respond to Ayesha in that way. There was something about the East Enders which responded so well to the genuine smile and offer of friendship from a stranger. It was called having a big heart, the generosity and good will of people.

"Could you find out from your son about growing sunflowers?" instructed Ayesha.

41

"Yes of course I can," said Mrs Peters eagerly, for she loved doing something for others, it made her feel wanted and needed and it gave her something to do.

"All right, bye now. I'll be going to my cousins' house tomorrow but Monday morning look out of the window and I'll wave to you on my way to school," said Ayesha.

"All right, see you then. My daughter's coming to see me tomorrow but next time, you might be able to meet her," Mrs Peters said. It was Vivien who was coming round and she wanted to show Vivien that she could be friendly to strangers from other countries. As if reading her mind Ayesha teased.

"Do you want to show me off? Because, I'm going to show you off to my friends and cousins."

Mrs Peters laughed loudly, for Ayesha was a little charmer.

"Flattery will get you everywhere," she said.

"Bye then." And as if by her natural instinct, Ayesha squeezed Mrs Peters' hand, almost cementing their new found friendship and Mrs Peters found herself squeezing Ayesha's hand back.

Ayesha went in, Mrs Peters put her garden chair back and went in reflecting her strange afternoon, because she had met members of the family she had been watching over the past few weeks, moving in and settling down in their new home. She had never really known any of the Bangladeshi families who had settled down in the East End as they had always been unwanted strangers, watched by white East Enders, keeping their distance about knowing them. Perhaps, by knowing them, it would close the distance and it would be harder to see one's black or Asian neighbours as unwanted strangers. The question was, for Mrs Peters, how close does one become to their Bangladeshi neighbours.

****

Ayesha found her family in the sitting room. While her dad and brothers were watching the football, her mum was on the phone to someone and Shazia was reading the local newspaper. They all looked at her and she knew she looked filthy from the dirt and soil outside.

"What's this then, Ayesha? Are you the new gardener?" asked Yusuf laughingly.

"I hope not. The garden will look a wreck if Ayesha has anything to do with it...," said Hamza sarcastically.

"Shh, Hamza Bhai. You're so mean. Anyway I'm going to be given some gardening advice from Mrs Peters' son," said Ayesha proudly.

"Who's Mrs Peters and who's her son?" asked Hamza and Yusuf together.

"It's Ayesha's new friend. She hasn't got any of her own age, so she made friends with the old woman from next door," Shazia answered.

"At least I can make friends. You scare people off with that slavery and black talk," retorted Ayesha.

"Shazia, you didn't give your heavy talk to the old woman, she might have a heart condition," chided Yusuf.

"No, I didn't, we just told each other what we enjoyed reading and I was a little bit more explicit than her," said Shazia.

"Will you all be quiet," said Mr Ali in Bengali. "I'm trying to watch the game. Ayesha did a very good thing by making friends with the old woman from next door. We live in a row of flats where we are the only Bangladeshi family and I told Mrs Peters when we do our garden, we'll tidy up her garden too."

"Oh God!" groaned Hamza.

"Hamza, it's best we do it to keep her friendly with us and we don't want any trouble around this area. I've got next Saturday off so you'll have to be free Hamza, I made concessions the last time," said Yusuf.

"It's all your fault. As far as I can see, we're not being friendly with her, we're licking up to her and it seems we're the slaves."

By then Ayesha had already disappeared into the bathroom. Mrs Ali had finished her conversation on the phone and spoke to her sons and Shazia in Bengali.

"The old white woman lives on her own. We need to ask her if she needs help now and then. I never understand why children never keep their parents with them. They should look after them in their old age. Anyway Mrs Peters didn't really want to speak to us, it was Ayesha who changed her mind with her never ending chatter. All of you make sure you're polite and helpful to her."

Mr and Mrs Ali mainly spoke in Bengali to their children at home and they liked their children to leave the English language outside. It was incredibly important for them that their children spoke Bengali - it was a way of keeping their cultural identity alive in them. After all, Bangladesh had fought for their right to speak their language which had led to civil war when it had been part of Pakistan. Bangladesh had been born in 1971 but so many had died for their freedom as many atrocities had been committed against women, children and innocent people by the Pakistani army. History should never be forgotten or repeated.

Mr and Mrs Ali viewed Mrs Peters as the white long standing East End pensioner, who knew the Bangladeshi community through stereotypes, shaped by a number of factors such as the general community gossip and fuelled by various television dramas, documentaries and other reports. They all seemed to focus on negative aspects of the Asian community. The couple felt that their elderly white neighbour was the kind of person who didn't really like Bangladeshi people - the kind who felt they had taken the white jobs, spoilt the schools and generally changed the East End's good old days.

However this did not mean Mr and Mrs Ali were not going to be friendly with Mrs Peters for they were the typical passive 'bending over backwards to avoid arguments or confrontations' Bangladeshi parents. Their children understood this very well. Although they did not always agree with their parents, something about their upbringing of respecting elders made them stay quiet. Hamza and Yusuf carried on watching the football with their dad but they got the warning message from their parents.

Hamza was thinking the old woman was probably a bundle of trouble and Yusuf was thinking how could an old woman live on her own. Their parents were wondering if they were going to have a peaceful relationship with their new neighbour or would it be the start of a series of complaints; too much noise, funny smell, strange songs and the list would go on covering a variety of aspects and issues. It was Ayesha who thought her neighbour was going to be a friend. In her innocent eyes she did not see the colour first as she saw the person first, unlike her siblings and her parents. For Ayesha it only seemed natural to talk to people and be kind to them because there was no point being unfriendly, one needed friendship far more than aggression.

****

Mrs Peters sat in her home drinking tea and thought how the enchanting little girl was such enjoyable company and, through her, she had found her new neighbours not to be as she had imagined. In fact, she actually did not know what to make of them. They had offered to do her garden but she would see if they lived up to their offer, some people said one thing and did another. As for the woman, she had tried to be friendly with her broken English, probably out of politeness, and their teenage daughter with her righteous talk had seemed off putting at first, but she was probably going through that adolescent period of her life. But all in all, she had been pleasantly surprised. Mrs Peters had yet to meet the boys and decide what she thought of them. Her mother had once said, you never really know your neighbours until you've walked in their lives and they had walked in yours.

However, it was Ayesha whom Mrs Peters had gradually developed a fondness for during the course of the afternoon. She had felt Ayesha's sadness at the loss of her brother and it brought home to her that Ayesha and her family had suffered just like any white East End family. In essence it was this she was finding it hard to comprehend and understand for all families, regardless of their background, had various experiences of sadness and joy in their lives and she had a feeling Ayesha would show these experiences in her childlike manner.

****

The following Monday morning, just before nine, Mrs Peters found herself looking out of her kitchen window watching out for Ayesha and, true to her word, Ayesha walked past on the way to school with her older sister. She pointedly looked at Mrs Peters' window and saw her standing there and they waved to each other. She and Shazia walked along down to the road to cross over and as she turned around and saw Mrs Peters still at the window, she waved again and to the old woman's surprise blew her a kiss.

Mrs Peters blew a kiss back to Ayesha whilst laughing to herself for the child was so cheeky and perhaps her attitude had rubbed on to Shazia who had also waved to her. She watched the two sisters walk off together hand in hand and saw they were still close even if they had their little squabbles. The little scene between Shazia, Ayesha and Mrs Peters had been watched by some of the other white and Bangladeshi residents. One white resident wondered why Mrs Peters was getting cosy with her Paki neighbours? The Bangladeshi resident wondered if the new Bangladeshi family thought they were so high and mighty getting cosy with the old white woman who had never spoken to any Bangladeshi person or child in the block. The relationship between the Ali family and Mrs Peters was being watched by both sets of residents and to them it was really a little alien to see such friendliness.

Mrs Peters went back into her sitting room to finish her cleaning and suddenly remembered Ayesha's little request. She went to the phone and rang David but he wasn't at home so she instinctively phoned him on his mobile. He answered very concerned.

"Mum, is that you? What's the matter? Are you all right?"

"Yes, I'm fine and there's nothing the matter," reassured Mrs Peters.

"It's just you never ring me on my mobile. I thought it was some sort of emergency." It was true Mrs Peters never phoned him on the mobile.

"No, luv, there's no emergency. I just wanted you to tell me about planting a sunflower," said Mrs Peters. David started laughing.

"Is it for your garden?"

"No, it's for my new neighbours' little girl's garden. She asked me about planting a sunflower and I said you knew a lot about such things," said Mrs Peters.

"Mum, I've got a baby sunflower at home in a pot which I haven't planted in my garden. If you want me to, I'll plant it in the little girl's garden this weekend, perhaps next Sunday."

"Oh, lovely. She's going to be so happy," exclaimed Mrs Peters but she did not tell David her new neighbours were Bangladeshi.

"All right, mum. Hang up now 'cause your bill's going up ringing me on the mobile so early in the morning. That little girl's one lucky kid to have you as a neighbour," said David. His mum had a big heart.

"Bye luv." And with that Mrs Peters hung up. Ayesha would be so happy about it and she planned on telling her when she got back from school. She was subconsciously becoming fonder of little Ayesha, although she believed she was keeping a distance between herself and the little girl but such distances closed in with the understanding that time often brings.

That afternoon Mrs Peters was waiting near her front door, watching the children go home from school. She was looking out for Ayesha. In the distance she caught sight of a young man holding Ayesha's hand walking towards her and they crossed the road and came nearer, Ayesha let go of the

45

young man's hand and ran towards her.

"Hello, Mrs Peters. How are you today?" said an excited Ayesha.

"I'm all right luv. I got some good news about your sunflower, though," said Mrs Peters.

"What is it?" Ayesha asked excitedly.

"I phoned my son, David and he's got a baby sunflower for you and he's going to plant it in your patch next Sunday. That is if your mum and dad are all right."

"That means I have to tell them about my secret sunflower," groaned Ayesha.

"What secret sunflower?" asked Hamza as he approached them. Mrs Peters looked at Hamza, he was a tall young man, a bit on the thin side, but a rough kind of good-looking lad.

"Well they don't have to know what it's for," said Mrs Peters comfortingly.

"What secret about sunflowers," repeated Hamza ignoring Mrs Peters and his little sister saw how he had behaved and was very annoyed with him.

"Well, I'm not going to tell you with your rude behaviour. Say hello to my friend," demanded Ayesha. Hamza looked embarrassed at the way he had behaved, especially as it had been pointed out by his younger sister and he looked at Mrs Peters apologetically. He spoke without actually meeting her eyes.

"Hello Mrs Peters."

"So, you know my name, young man," she said sharply.

"My sister told me the other day. My name's Hamza," he offered hesitantly.

"Well, nice to meet you. Ayesha's going to plant a sunflower and she'll inform her mum and dad in good time so you don't need to inform them any earlier," warned Mrs Peters smiling. Hamza smiled meekly at her, he had got the message. Ayesha's new friend was watching over her and she didn't want any trouble from any troubling siblings. He had an idea to impress her.

"Why don't you come round this week for a cup of tea, Mrs Peters? You can see the decoration that I did in the flat," Hamza said proudly.

"No, Bhai, you, Abba and Boro Bhai did the decoration together," corrected Ayesha immediately. Her brother scowled at her.

"Who's Boro Bhai and Abba and why do you call Hamza Bhai?" asked Mrs Peters pronouncing Hamza's name in two syllables - Ham-Za.

"I call my brothers Boro Bhai and Sutu Bhai which means big brother and little brother. Abba means dad in our language and Afa means big sister. We don't call our elders by their names because it is not polite and it shows our respect," explained Ayesha, and Hamza nodded in agreement.

Strange, thought Mrs Peters but the she recalled as a child calling many of her neighbours Uncle this and Aunt that. They hadn't really been her uncles and aunts or any relative but it had been more polite and family like than Mr this and Mrs that. She understood Ayesha, it was their way of living and she made sense of it by drawing a parallel to experiences in her life.

All right, luv, I'll come round one day this week," said Mrs Peters. "You both run along and get something to eat and I'll speak to you soon."

Hamza smiled politely thinking didn't this woman realise he was almost twenty, a man, but then his grandmother back home in Bangladesh still thought he was a child too.

****

Later that evening, Mrs Peters was again trying to decide what she should eat for her tea. Suddenly there was a knock at the door and she wondered who it could be at this time; her children usually let her know when they were coming round and many of her friends who used to visit had passed away. She went to the door, put the safety chain on, opened it and peeped through the gap and to her surprise, saw Shazia and Ayesha standing at the door. Mrs Peters opened the door and curiously asked them what the matter was.

"Nothing's the matter," said Ayesha smiling.

"My mum sent some chicken with rice round for you, it's here in a container," said Shazia handing the container to her.

"Oh, I see," said Mrs Peters. She really didn't see at all for she was taken aback by Mrs Ali's kind thought.

"My mum cooked the chicken very mild for you. You do like curry?" asked Ayesha anxiously.

"Oh yes I treat myself now and then to a curry and Chinese food," said Mrs Peters as though she was a woman of the world.

"That's good 'cause you'll enjoy my mum's cooking. I love it," said Ayesha looking almost relieved.

"Well that was real nice of your mum to send me some supper, I'm sure it's going to be delicious," said Mrs Peters.

"Well it was really Hamza who gave her the idea because he was talking about our grandmother back home and he just thought of you afterwards," said Shazia.

Mrs Peters felt touched by the way the family had thought of her, as though they had known her for years. It was so unexpected for her because she had no expectations of a Bangladeshi family to do such a neighbourly thing and it showed Hamza wasn't as hard hearted as he had made out to her during the day.

"Listen luv, it's getting a bit windy and dark. Go home now 'cause you got school in the morning. I'll see you later this week and give your mum my love," added Mrs Peters. She felt some kind of bond towards the family; she hardly knew them, but they were beginning to become less strange and more familiar. It brought memories of the neighbourly feelings of years ago when a neighbour was not a stranger but a friend.

CHAPTER FOUR

It was Saturday morning and Mr Ali was up at seven watching the sun gradually ascending to its mighty and fiery grace through his bedroom window. Today was going to be very warm and a day full of hard work, thought Mr Ali, for himself and his sons. He looked over at his sleeping wife and smiled warmly. The garden was going to be done today - his wife would not let him or their sons rest until they had finished and in spite of her petite stature, she had great determination and will. Characteristics which ran through their children, rooted from the passionate side of a person. Mr Ali smiled again at his wife, his mother had chosen well for him; he loved his wife deeply, but he rarely told her. Perhaps for him it was his insecurity for her to see such emotion in him.

All his life Mr Ali had worked hard. He had arrived in Britain and worked continuously from the second week. He found his independence to be one of the most important aspects of his life and had felt empathy for Mrs Peters when she had talked about the closure of the docks for he had worked there on his initial arrival. He had seen the white Dockers working hard and going home to their families and there was something about the way they had worked which reminded of him of the farmers in their rice fields back home in Bangladesh.

Perhaps it was something to do with each man's basic instinct of survival both for himself and his family. A man's pride and dignity to ensure he provided for his family and Mr Ali had seen this vital aspect of life amongst the white East Enders, just like men from his own community. He had seen the white women bringing up their children, just like in his own community and it was the same simple principle in the cycle of life but just a different way of living out that principle. The sad thing was, both communities failed to recognise the similarities they shared.

Mr Ali went to the kitchen and made his own breakfast and as he did so, he remembered when he had first arrived in Britain there had never been the luxury of finding a home cooked dinner. He had shared rented accommodation with a number of other Bangladeshi men like himself who had come to Britain to seek their fortune and those days had been very hard and lonely times. There had been no family with him, which was so important for Bangladeshi men to fill the gap of living in a host country. Yes, there had been other men from his native land living with him but like him they worked long and varied hours and rarely had time for social gatherings.

The system was that men in the accommodation he shared with worked different hours and so they missed the time to see each other. When a few men were at home they were either too tired or hungry to talk. The food they ate was of poor quality. The problem was that it was difficult to cook food similar to that of back home. They lacked the culinary skills and on many occasions, the right ingredients. The poor, unhealthy diet consisted of too much oil in the meat and chicken, not enough vegetables other than potatoes, not enough fibre and the lack of fish dishes that many of the men missed and craved for. Years later, many of these men suffered coronary heart disease, diabetes and developed high blood pressure. The earlier years of eating the wrong food and the lack of a well balanced diet had a major effect on their health in later years. Years which they had hoped to enjoy in tranquillity with the arrival of their families.

Mr Ali called his sons to wake up and get ready for the long day ahead. Yusuf did not need much waking, but Hamza needed a push. The boys woke up and ate breakfast cooked by their father and by then it was eight. He and his sons started to work in the garden, with Hamza moaning and groaning about how he had not had enough sleep. By ten the rest of the Ali family were up and Mrs Ali had already started her cooking. Cooking a variety of dishes, especially fish, was an almost compulsory aspect of Bangladeshi life and Shazia helped her mother with the cooking at the weekends. It was more of a demand from her mother than a choice for Shazia as she wanted to ensure both her daughters learnt the art of cooking and other household tasks. It was what shaped a future wife and mother and although her parents wanted to educate their daughters, they viewed the basics of family and household duties to be an equally important part of that education.

Shazia had made a snack for her brothers and father along with drinks and she took it out to them in the garden. Hamza was the first to grab the food and he ate as though he had not eaten in days.

"Hamza Bhai, you stink terribly," said Shazia. He didn't actually smell that bad, she just liked to wind him up.

"Well what do you think I'm doing out here, sunbathing? Of course I'm going to stink with the amount of hard work I'm doing," said Hamza looking at his sister as though she was stupid.

"You're always feeling sorry for yourself whenever you've got to do any hard work, whether it's washing your socks or doing a bit of gardening," she in turn retorted.

"All right you two," their father called out, "now which one of you two are going to do our neighbours' garden?" He smiled at Hamza and Yusuf.

"I don't mind," Yusuf said.

"No, Bhai, Hamza gets on with Mrs Peters very well. He should do it," said Shazia smiling at Hamza.

"Do you want to do it?" asked Yusuf.

Hamza scowled, Shazia smiled sweetly at him and Yusuf waited for an answer. Unexpectedly Hamza said, "All right I'll do it."

"Are you sure Mrs Peters isn't going to bite you?" asked Shazia.

By then Hamza had already gone into the flat to wash his hands to go next door, for he was determined to show Shazia he could do a good job for Mrs Peters. Or was it because he secretly felt sorry for her as he knocked on her door?

"Morning, Hamza," Mrs Peter said, opening her door. She still pronounced his name in two syllables, but Hamza didn't care. His mother pronounced many English words in a variety of different ways, like television as 'tellybision'.

"Good morning, Mrs Peters," greeted Hamza, "Um, er. My dad sent me round to tidy your garden for you."

The old woman smiled, her neighbours had lived up to their word and she had much respect for people who kept their word. Secretly she hadn't expected them to but she had been proven wrong now, then again she hadn't expected the tea Mrs Ali had sent round the other day.

"All right luv, you don't mind do you?" she said as if she was testing him.

"No Mrs Peters, I wouldn't come round if I did mind. My dad told us last week that when we did our garden, either myself or my brother would tidy your garden too," said Hamza firmly, for the old woman could be a bit testing at times, probably because she can't understand Bangladeshis can help others.

"Well come in and I'll show you what I need done," smiled Mrs Peters, this time much more warmly.

Hamza walked into her flat and waited in the sitting room while she went to get the garden door keys. The sitting room sort of reflected the owner of the flat and the furniture wasn't old looking; it was what elderly people of Mrs Peters' age tended to choose. The settee was a floral print; the wall unit was an oak wood effect with a matching tea table, an assortment of family photos were displayed on the wall unit. There was a large crucifix on one side of the room and a bunch of fresh flowers was set on the tea table. A variety of animal ornaments, made from china, decorated the rest of the wall unit along with different ornaments from abroad, maybe gifts given to her from someone who travelled in her family, and an old fashioned tea set displayed in one section of the wall unit.

It displayed the character of a person - loving towards her family, perhaps a love for animals, religious in some ways, someone who treasured ornaments and gifts given to her. It was a clean room, especially for someone elderly like Mrs Peters living on her own. It was a simple and almost humble home, as if the owner hadn't expected much out of life, just a family and love.

Mrs Peters had already opened the garden door and beckoned Hamza to follow her into the garden. The garden was very unkempt although one caught a glimpse of what it could be like if it was tidied up. Where the hell were her children, he thought almost angrily, they should have at least tidied this up for her let alone look after her. He resented the western ideology of children leaving the nest for their parents to enjoy their lives in their retirement age. What happened when the parents became elderly or one of them died? How did they cope on their own? In Bangladesh sons and daughters-in-law looked after the elderly parents in their homes as there was no welfare state and residential homes to take on the responsibility.

"Well Hamza, if you can start with trimming the hedge and giving the lawn a mow it would be very helpful." Mrs Peters said. She also wanted him to tidy the flowers as well, pick up the rubbish and the rogue weeds and generally tidy the garden but she did not say this as she thought what he was going to do would be enough for him and it would be unfair to take advantage of his generosity. She caught sight of Mr Ali working with his older son in their garden, both engrossed in their work and not aware Mrs Peters and Hamza were standing in her garden.

"Hello Mr Ali, thank you very much for sending Hamza round to do my garden, you certainly kept your word. How are you anyway?" Mrs Peters called out.

"Hello Mrs Peters. It's okay about Hamza, he wanted to help out. This is my eldest son, Yusuf," he called back looking over from where he was kneeling cementing the tiles down on the garden earth.

"Hello, Mrs Peters, nice to meet you," said Yusuf taking a pause from his work.

"Nice to meet you, young man. What do you do other than helping your old man out?" Mrs Peters asked.

"I'm studying medicine. I'd like to be a doctor and I work part time as well," Yusuf replied.

"My, you've got clever kids, Mr Ali, they'll make you proud," she said genuinely impressed.

"I pray they be good people. Make no trouble for people. Live their life without fighting, lying and stealing. Their mother always she pray for them," Mr Ali said earnestly.

"That's right, luv. That's what it's all about, living decent lives and I've always wanted enough to live on and enough to give away," agreed Mrs Peters softly.

"Shall I get started then, Mrs Peters?" interrupted Hamza.

"'Course you can lad. Come on I'll show you the garden tools, they're kept in the shed. I'll speak to you later then Mr Ali," said Mrs Peters.

Hamza got started on his work and his father and brother went back to theirs and Mrs Peters went inside to fix lunch. He worked steadily on the hedge putting as much effort into the job in hand as possible as he planned to do more than what his elderly neighbour had asked of him. He had noticed the flowers needed tidying up, the weeds needed to be pulled out and he would sweep up the rubbish and leave everything tidy for her. Mrs Peters had gone straight to her fridge freezer to find what she could cook for herself and Hamza. She wanted him to have lunch with her to show her gratitude, it was the least she could do for his trouble. She looked through the boxes and packages in the freezer and could not decide what to take out because she didn't know what he enjoyed eating. Well, she thought, he's working so hard, he probably needs a bit of meat in him because he'll be hungry from the work and so Mrs Peters got out some pork sausages, chips and peas. She also had apple pie, which she would serve with custard, and had some coke in the fridge or would he want a cold beer. She smiled as she got to work on preparing lunch for Hamza and herself, it was so nice making dinner to share with someone else.

By half past twelve, Mrs Peters had prepared a tray for Hamza and it consisted of a large plate of chips, three pork sausages, peas and a small jug of beef gravy and a can of cold beer for him. She proudly took it out and found he had finished the hedge and was halfway through mowing the lawn. He had thoughtfully spent time in putting the rubbish into black bags and taken them out to the main rubbish bin. She was impressed with Hamza's work for it was very tidy.

"Hamza, luv. I got some lunch ready for you. Come on, wash up and tuck in and I'll join you as well," said Mrs Peters. She was talking to him as though he was her grandchild, quite unaware that she was doing it as she was learning to treat him as she would her own.

"Oh, thanks Mrs Peters," said Hamza smiling. He was getting a bit hungry and walked forward to the tray to have a look at the food. Oh shit, thought Hamza, I should have told her what I eat or rather what I don't eat and if I tell her she might feel pissed off with me. As if reading his face Mrs Peters asked,

"What's the matter, don't you eat chips and sausages? You're not on a diet are you?"

"No, no everything's been put on the tray so thoughtfully. Um it's just, er, look um I'm not hungry right now," stammered Hamza. He felt really stuck because he was afraid she would not understand if he told her the truth.

"Now, I think you're telling me a lot of cobblers. Just tell me what the matter is, I won't bite your head off," she said encouragingly putting the tray down on the garden table. She wanted to know why he didn't want to eat the food because she certainly didn't believe he wasn't hungry. Wasn't her food good enough for this Asian boy? But then he might have a good reason why he didn't want it.

"You won't mind if I tell you?" asked Hamza hesitantly.

"Try me," said Mrs Peters putting her hands on her hips.

"You're Christian aren't you?" began Hamza.

"Yes, I see myself as a good Christian," she replied proudly.

"Well, we Bangladeshis are mainly Muslims and Christians have different beliefs to us. Jews, Hindus and Buddhists, they all have different beliefs. In our religion, Islam, we are not allowed to eat pork or drink alcohol; in addition we are only allowed to eat meat and poultry if it has been slaughtered according to our Islamic rites. Similar to Jewish people eating kosher meat and we don't drink alcohol because it can poison the body. Do you understand Mrs Peters?" Hamza looked at her as though hoping she would understand.

Mrs Peters looked at him and she sort of did understand for people were often different according to the way they had been brought up by their religion and had different ways and beliefs. Some people observed their religion and others did not, but Hamza and his family observed their religious beliefs. Mrs Peters knew deep down, Hamza had not wanted to tell her because he thought he would offend her. Inside she knew he had not really expected her to understand or even respect his religious beliefs, but Mrs Peters thought she could prove him wrong.

"Hamza I'm trying to understand. I just have to get used to it and this is all new to me. Do you understand?" asked Mrs Peters looking at him squarely. Just as he felt hesitant about telling her of his reasons why he did not want to eat the food, she had a right to feel that discovering new beliefs was strange to her.

Hamza looked at the white woman in front of him. He understood for the first time that, to a stranger, his religion and culture would seem unfamiliar, especially if they had been living side by side in the same community, feeling threatened that their own way of life would be underestimated and taken away from them. Hamza understood this because his grandfather had told him how the British occupation of India had affected the lives of the Bangladeshi people when they had been made into second-class citizens in their birth country.

"Yes, I do understand. I'm glad you understand what I'm trying to tell you," Hamza said.

"All right, luv. You know what I'm going to do? I'm gonna fry you some chips in vegetable oil, fry a piece of cod and boil some fresh peas and I've got coke in the fridge. How about that?" asked Mrs Peters cheerfully.

"Great, I'll look forward to that," said Hamza gratified.

"And I'll have your dinner so it won't go to waste. It's a big dinner to have but I feel very hungry today."

"You need it. You need to put on weight," said Hamza.

"Lad, you know very well I don't need to put on weight," laughed Mrs Peters.

Hamza grinned and Mrs Peters went back inside to make a fresh meal for her Muslim gardener while he went back to work in the garden of his Christian neighbour.

Hamza worked away and felt relieved that the elderly woman had made an effort to understand, rather than taking offence and he felt respect for her, not just because she was an elder but an elder who seemed to have an open mind. She had encouraged him to tell her so she could understand and for him to express himself without feeling she was going to be angry. Mrs Peters started to cook again and felt relieved that it wasn't her cooking that Hamza hadn't wanted to taste, but the actual food was against his religion and she had understood a little, though he had been brave to tell her the real reasons. He had made things clearer, easier for her to comprehend.

Whether Mrs Peters and Hamza realised it, they had both taken a step forward to understanding each other, compromising along the way according to each other's way of life to be able to communicate and find common ground where they could walk together. From a distance a person looks strange, but when you walk alongside them, one often found out different aspects of their life and things looked less strange. She came back with a fresh tray of food and put it on the garden table, then went back in and ate her dinner while Hamza went to wash up in the kitchen and came out to settle down for his lunch.

"Mrs Peters, how did you know that I wanted the chips and cod to be fried in vegetable oil?" Hamza asked as he tucked into his food. He had wondered how she'd known about the chips having to be fried in vegetable and not animal oil.

"Well if you can't eat the meat and chicken sold in the English supermarkets, how can you eat food that's fried in animal oil or lard. It's quite clear to me," said Mrs Peters priding herself on her new outlook on the Bangladeshi community. Hamza smiled to himself; he could tell she felt knowledgeable having learnt something new about her neighbours from another race.

****

"Hamza, Hamza, come and eat your dinner," shouted Shazia from their garden. Her father and Yusuf had long gone in to have their dinner and were now taking a short break before continuing with their work. She walked near Mrs Peters' garden fence and nearly tripped over at the scene before her in the other garden, for there in front of her was Hamza and Mrs Peters eating their lunch. Most of all she noticed Hamza eating a fish dish and Mrs Peters eating the meat dish.

"I'm eating with Mrs Peters. She kindly invited me to lunch at her house," Hamza said to his sister smugly.

"Yes Shazia, your brother's having lunch here with me and has been working very hard. You run along dear and have yours," smiled Mrs Peters at Shazia.

"Yes Shazia run along now and have your lunch before it gets cold or are you going to skip lunch?" smiled Hamza.

"You don't miss meals do you, Shazia? Because you really shouldn't, you're too skinny as it is; your mum needs to fatten you up," Mrs Peters chided.

"My mum's always fighting to feed her and all of us. She thinks the fatter her children, the more beautiful we look. But then that's what a lot of Bangladeshi mothers do, beat their children to eat," Hamza laughed with his sister as though it was such a joke but Mrs Peters didn't quite understand but was enlightened by Shazia.

"Mrs Peters, many Bangladeshi mothers we know almost have a fit if their children don't eat their dinner properly. They see the fatter their children are, the healthier they are which in fact is not really true."

54

Mrs Peters laughed with Shazia and remembered how Susan had got fat in primary school and her worries about whether she would lose the weight or not, yet Mrs Ali was fighting to feed her children to fatten them up.

"Mrs Peters, I'm going to have my lunch now but please don't be surprised if my mum pops along to see how much Hamza's eating. She needs confirmation," said Shazia.

"Don't worry luv, I'll make sure he gets another plateful," she replied.

"Oh, no way. I'm not having any more seconds, I'll have my pudding now," declared Hamza getting a bit frightened.

Just as Shazia had predicted, her mother came out smiling to have a peep at Hamza and Mrs Peters who smiled at each other and waited for Mrs Ali's words.

"Hello, Mrs Peters. My son being good boy. He eating your dinner with you. He fussy with dinner. But he good worker in garden, huh," said Mrs Ali quickly noticing a large empty plate and a pudding bowl, which Hamza was devouring.

"He's fine luv, he's been working real hard and I thought I'd feed him a good dinner. He needs to be fat," added Mrs Peters for good measure.

Mrs Ali beamed at Mrs Peters, pleased that she wanted to fatten her son up because he ate so little but then all her children ate less than she wanted, she decided.

"You eat food I send?"

"Yes and it was lovely, you're a good cook like myself," said Mrs Peters. Hamza almost choked on his food because his neighbour and mum would certainly get along since they admired their own cooking. His mum was extremely proud of her cooking talents and she became concerned when someone commented negatively about her food.

"Mrs Peters, anytime you need help or you scared, you call me. My sons, my daughters and Mr Ali, we help you," Mrs Ali said. She had been thinking about Mrs Peters living alone and she had found herself remembering her mother and mother-in-law, she found it hard to accept Mrs Peters living on her own. She truly wanted to watch over the elderly woman for it was something culturally inbred in her, to take care of the elderly and to have genuine respect for them.

"Mrs Peters, sugar, tea, bread, come my home. I give when you have none. Understand?" Mrs Ali said earnestly.

"Understood luv. Thanks luv for the offer. I might take up the offer 'cause now and then I get short for a bit of milk and when it gets a bit dark I don't like going out to get it," said Mrs Peters warmly. She was feeling somehow close to Mrs Ali, the first stage of a trusting relationship, especially as she appreciated Mrs Ali's efforts to practice her English by conversing with her. It was really positive to see foreigners learning the language of the country they lived in.

"Your garden's taking shape and it's going to look neat and tidy by the time the men have finished working on it," said Mrs Peters.

"Thank you. Good news for me," said Mrs Ali as she looked at the garden because the concrete slabs had been put down and the cementing was nearly finished. Yusuf and his father had made such an effort of clearing all the weeds and various plants to leave part of the garden free for Mrs Ali to plant her vegetables. She looked at the garden and remembered how, as a little girl, her grandmother had taught her to grow various vegetables and the valuable gardening lessons had being a source of income before she got married. The garden brought back so many memories of the hardships Mrs Ali had endured as a young girl and the heartache poverty caused could only be explained by those who had endured such times and had risen above it. Mrs Ali looked at the garden almost lovingly as though each vegetable she would plant would nurture and ease the sadness of the years of uncertainty she had known as a child and then poignantly as a young girl on the verge of marriage.

Mrs Peters had watched Mrs Ali look at the garden as though she were remembering something sad and touching from years ago, the marks of memories.

"What's the matter, luv?" she asked gently. Mrs Ali looked at the old woman and thought, how do I explain to her about losing so many brothers and sisters as children; about eating dhal and potato for endless months at a time? How do I explain to her that my father was unable to give furniture with me at the time of my marriage? How do I explain the worries of a Bangladeshi mother on whether or not her daughter would be able to find a suitable husband for herself? As if reading her mind Mrs Peters said,

"Go on try me. Tell me what you're thinking of?"

Mrs Ali looked at Hamza and told him in Bengali to explain how poor she had been and the hardships she had faced as a child.

"Mrs Peters, my mother came from a very poor family back home before she married my father. I had many uncles and aunts who died in childhood because my grandparents could not afford to pay for the doctor's fee. My mum understands about growing vegetables because as a young girl she grew them as a source of food for her father's house, she learnt many forms of needlecraft and sold them to earn money. This garden means a lot to her, poor people are proud, they don't always like taking handouts and my mother always wanted to stand on her own two feet in her own way," Hamza explained proudly. He also knew how much his mother had been looked down upon initially when she had married his father by his paternal grandfather and members of his father's family.

"I suppose your dad's side was a lot better off," said Mrs Peters thoughtfully.

"Yes, they certainly were."

"Did your mum have a tough time after she got married because they thought she wasn't good enough?" Mrs Peters said knowingly and Mrs Ali smiled, she had understood Mrs Peters' words completely.

"I poor, Mr Ali rich. My father-in-law, very angry with mother-in-law. But I work very hard and make everyone happy. Anger go, they feel happy now. Very hard for me. I clever woman," Mrs Ali said cheekily.

"Good on you gal. That's what we women are – clever. Men are full of big talk 'cause I know what it feels like to be poor and working hard to make ends meet. I ain't lost as many people I loved as you did though and that's tough for you to accept." Mrs Peters really felt sympathetic to Mrs Ali's past. She understood about poverty but to lose so many siblings and then later a child was something that she had not experienced and would never want to experience. Mrs Ali was a tough woman, like an East End woman. She understood about the prejudices people often perceived of the poor working class. Hamza's mother went back in leaving her son and neighbour in each other's company.

"How come so many of your aunts and uncles died?" asked Mrs Peters.

"Lots of children die in Bangladesh; it's something that happens all the time. Bangladesh is a very poor country and people suffer terribly to survive. Diseases which have been eradicated years ago are still rife in Bangladesh; there are even cases where healthy people in Bangladesh sell their organs for money to feed their families, or even one of their children to feed the rest of the family," said Hamza.

Mrs Peters listened and felt suddenly torn between the poverty she saw in the East End and the poverty Hamza described back in Bangladesh, for she did not know who to sympathise with more - her East End or people back in Bangladesh. Who was she to judge which was worse? Why did Hamza have to tell her such details? She suddenly felt frustrated about the situation and almost snapped at Hamza.

"Hamza, just like people are having a hard time back home, there are a lot of families here who are having a tough time."

Hamza was startled at her reaction and bit back politely.

"I think perhaps there is a difference in the living standards between families back in Bangladesh and over here. You don't actually see children suffering extreme malnutrition walking the streets unless they have been neglected by their parents."

"Hamza, everyone has to get on with what gets dished out to them just like your mother because she didn't feel sorry for herself."

"That's right, she didn't feel sorry for herself and she was lucky and there are lots of people like her back in Bangladesh. But sometimes things go wrong and farmers work in the hot sun planting their rice, nature takes its course and brings floods and washes away all the seeds and the hard work. Children go without food and in the winter there is no money for firewood and people die in the cold. There are different sides to a story because nothing is black and white." Hamza had managed to remain calm but had still got his point across but he was terribly worried he had offended the old white woman.

Mrs Peters looked at him and said stiffly,

"Well if you've finished your lunch, Hamza, I'll go back inside."

"Mrs Peters I'll finish off the garden and the lunch was lovely," Hamza said gently as though apologising for any offence he had caused her. The old white woman felt the apology in his tone and walked inside. She sat down in her sitting room and reflected on what Hamza had said because she knew people were poorer in other countries but what could British white people do about it? They could not solve all the world's problems as, in the midst of solving world problems, the problems at home often got forgotten. There was something about making her East End cause more important to Hamza than listening to what he had said. It was Mrs Peters' loyalty to her East End roots that made her not forget there were needs just as important where she lived as there were abroad. However, she knew she should not have snapped at Hamza, who was just telling her the reality of living in a poor, developing country for she had been the one who had wanted to know about Mrs Ali's sad memories. Sometimes ignorance was better than knowing and reflecting and ignorance made the world look black and white - knowledge brought shades of grey into the picture.

****

It was nearly evening time and Mrs Peters looked out into her garden. She hadn't looked out since her heated conversation with Hamza. She went outside and found him tidying the last remains of the rubbish. The garden looked beautifully tidy. He had made a great effort in trimming the hedge and tidying the flowerbeds, he had swept and watered the garden and it looked as though it would not need work for a good many months. Mrs Peters felt a little ashamed at her earlier snappy remarks because Hamza could have left the garden in a fit of temper as many of his age group would have done, but he had shown maturity for accepting her behaviour and trying to make amends for his behaviour as well. Hamza saw Mrs Peters approaching and was uncertain what to say to her, but he didn't need to, she said it for him.

"Thanks a lot, luv, sorry about my snappy remarks a bit earlier on," she looked at him searchingly.

"It's all right Mrs Peters. Look Mrs Peters there are poor people everywhere and people should make sure that they don't do things to make it harder for them to live and cause greater sufferings," said Hamza.

"That's right, darling. Where we can, we should help each other, no matter what our differences are," she added thoughtfully. Hamza was right, there were people suffering everywhere in the world.

"Go, on home luv. You've being working really hard, you must be real tired. I haven't seen Ayesha all day, has she gone out?" asked Mrs Peters.

"Yes, my cousin was supposed to pick her up today. She'll be back soon."

"Would you tell her to pop round to see me, Hamza?" Mrs Peters requested.

"Yea, 'course I can. Well I'll be going now. See you soon," said Hamza and with that he made his way out.

Mrs Peters saw Mr Ali and Yusuf at work together and she remembered when Arthur and their boys used to go to play ball in Victoria Park. Vicky Park was not the same anymore - there were used syringes, condoms, dog mess and litter lying around because people didn't look after the park as they used to in the old days. They had so much other entertainment in their lives, why bother taking the time to look after an old park. She called out to Mr Ali.

"Could I have a word with you for a moment."

He looked up and saw Mrs Peters and walked over to her wondering if Hamza had done anything wrong.

"Mr Ali, first of all thank you for lending me your son for the day. He's done a very good job in my garden, a proper gardener, he is."

"That's no problem. I'm happy to help," Mr Ali said, almost relieved.

"But I've got a favour to ask you."

"Oh, what?" Mr Ali said, dreading what it might be.

"Ayesha might have told you she wants to plant a sunflower. Well my son David's going to come round tomorrow with a baby sunflower to plant for her in a corner in your garden. Is that all right?" asked Mrs Peters.

"Yes, yes, fine. Very good. Ayesha did say something about planting a sunflower," said Mr Ali. "Now please excuse me, I go back to work."

Yusuf had being listening and called out to Mrs Peters.

"Mrs Peters, is there a particular reason why Ayesha wants to plant a sunflower?"

"Oh, no, she just wanted to plant it," she said slowly.

"Maybe it's for school," Mr Ali said.

"No, no. She just wanted to plant a sunflower," laughed Mrs Peters.

Yusuf knew his little sister well for him to enquire why she wanted to plant a sunflower, thought Mrs Peters. She looked at the Ali family garden.

"You've done a lovely job, Yusuf, for your mum."

"Thanks and my mum's been on my back to get this done non stop."

"Do you two want a drink?" asked Mrs Peters.

"No, we had a drink just a while ago," Yusuf said.

"So, you want to be a doctor, I hope you listen to your patients properly. My GP doesn't even have the time to listen to me properly and it's like I'm in and before you know it, I'm out again. He really doesn't have the time to see his patients properly," moaned Mrs Peters.

"Well I hope I'm a doctor who listens well and takes the time to talk to my patients sensitively."

"I think you will. You've got a good mum and dad," Mrs Peters encouraged.

"Yes, you're right, my parents are decent people, that's how kids become decent as well," Yusuf said. "But then sometimes some kids lose it along the way even if their parents are decent," he added thinking of good Bangladeshi families who had one child addicted on drugs in spite of their efforts to keep them clean. Mrs Peters smiled in agreement and walked back inside her flat leaving the sun to slowly descend behind the two men.

Later during the early evening hours Ayesha knocked on Mrs Peters' door.

"Hello Ayesha," said Mrs Peters excitedly.

"Hello Mrs Peters," Ayesha said, with Shazia behind her.

"Hello Shazia, come in for a while."

"All right, just for a little while because I've got homework to finish," said Shazia.

Mrs Peters led them into her sitting room and both sisters sat down and took in the sitting room's décor, for it was certainly Mrs Peters, they both concluded, from the flowers to the photos and the floral settee.

"Ayesha, do you want to come round tomorrow in the afternoon? My David will be here to plant your sunflower," said Mrs Peters.

"Oh yeah. I'll come round tomorrow but Shazia's too busy," said Ayesha. She didn't really know whether her older sister was busy or not, she just wanted come round on her own. Ayesha's mum usually liked to ensure she was chaperoned as much as possible as her mother had a strong fear of strangers.

"No, Mrs Peters I'm not, I'll come with Ayesha," said Shazia giving Ayesha daggers.

"Okay, that's settled and I'll expect you both at two tomorrow," said Mrs Peters. Nodding in agreement, the two Ali sisters said their goodbyes and went home looking forward to the next day.

****

On Sunday morning in the Ali family, Mrs Ali was telling her daughters to behave properly when they went to visit Mrs Peters. She had made vegetable somosas for Shazia and Ayesha to take round on their visit and was also worried in case Ayesha babbled on too much and if Shazia said anything to offend her. Mrs Ali also wondered whether Mrs Peter's children knew that she had made friends with her Bangladeshi neighbours. Sometimes white children did not approve of their parents interacting with people of a different colour and Mrs Ali had a feeling Mrs Peter's children would not be as forthcoming as their mother had been, after her initial hostility. Maybe Ayesha could work some of her magic on them.

****

Mrs Peters was baking and cooking a Sunday dinner. David was coming and so was his son, Jamie. Susan and Vivien had suddenly phoned Saturday night to say they would be popping around. At the back of her mind Mrs Peters had a small worry of how David and Susan would react to Ayesha and Shazia. It would not really be their fault if they found it a little strange to find two Bangladeshi neighbours in her home. Mrs Peters had never attempted to make friends with Bangladeshi families or any other Asian families in the past when her children had been growing up. There had never been any reason to, she had never wanted to, perhaps secretly she had seen them as an excuse for a scapegoat for failures in her family and that of her children. But then Ayesha had appeared and made a crossing from the other side, which Mrs Peters had never expected to happen. Now it was a situation where Mrs Peters knew her neighbours and felt a bond with them even if there were differences. It was a turning point in Mrs Peter's life, so late in her life, a time for reflection for perhaps she had mellowed over the years.

Mrs Peters nearly finished cooking when the phone rang and she picked it up.

"Hello, mum," said a muffled voice.

"Hello, is that you Graham?" asked Mrs Peters hesitantly.

"Yeah. How are you?" he said, his voice a little clearer.

"I'm all right. Have you got a cold?" asked his mother.

"Nah, I had a late night, me and the lads," laughed Graham as though something was funny.

"You shouldn't keep drinking all the time. Have you found a job yet?" carried on his mother sharply.

"No, not yet. Will do soon. I was thinking, I'll come round to see you today," said her youngest son cheerfully.

"Oh, um Susan, David, Vivien and Jamie are coming round today..." Mrs Peters said slowly. She really did not want Graham to come too.

"Yeah, I'll come round and cheer everyone up. Or don't you want me to come?" asked Graham suspiciously.

"No, no, of course I do," lied Mrs Peters.

"Right, I'll see you then," Graham replied.

"Yes, I'll see you at lunch," Mrs Peters said. As she put the phone down slowly, many thoughts ran through her mind for she had much to weigh up as Graham had put her on a balancing act.

Mrs Peters was worried about Graham coming round because she knew her son was a deeply prejudiced man, especially against the local Bangladeshi community, although she did not publicly admit it. In the past she had tried to cover up his prejudiced behaviour making various excuses to herself and others. That was one of the reasons Vivien did not see eye to eye with her younger brother and Mrs Peters was worried how Graham would react to Ayesha and Shazia. Her only option was to make an excuse to her neighbours to avoid such a situation.

But then Mrs Peters gradually decided if she were to remain friends with the family next door, sooner or later Graham would know about them. Such a situation would eventually creep up another day in the future and why should she feel torn between Graham's misconceptions and her loyalty to the Ali family. Yes, loyalty was what Mrs Peters felt for them. They were good, hardworking people wanting to live a peaceful life. They had done no wrong to her or her family for in fact, they had been good to her. Mrs Peters mentally resolved that she would not make excuses to Ayesha and Shazia as she would

61

invite who she wanted to her home. Graham would have to accept it and he could keep his opinions to himself and with that resolution she went back to her work.

****

Vivien was the first to arrive and turned up with flowers and shopping for her mum, which she often did.

"Mum, something smells delicious," she exclaimed as she kissed her.

"Thanks, luv," said Mrs Peters. It was nice to feel her child in her arms. It reminded her of when they were so little and helpless.

"Vivien, you look lovely - so tanned and glowing," Mrs Peters added.

"Mum, it's not natural and I'm old now," giggled Vivien.

"Well I don't care, you're lovely anyway. If you're old, what am I?" said Mrs Peters faking shock. "Go on, lay the table while I make a cuppa for both of us."

Vivien laid the table and her mother finished off decorating her fairy cakes and made two cups of tea. Mrs Peters brought the tea into the sitting room and sat down on the settee and waited for her daughter to join her. She would talk to Vivien about her problem and hear what her daughter thought.

"Viv, you know I told you that I had Bangladeshi neighbours," began Mrs Peters.

"Oh, mum, don't tell me you haven't spoken to them because you think they're not good enough" said Vivien.

"No, I did talk to them," snapped Mrs Peters. "In fact over the last couple of weeks we've become quite good friends. Hamza, Mr Ali's son tidied my garden yesterday."

"Really?" Vivien exclaimed in surprise.

"Yes and Mrs Ali sent me round some chicken curry the other day. Ayesha and Shazia are coming round today because David's going to plant a sunflower for little Ayesha," said Mrs Peters looking ahead of her.

Vivien stared at her mother and could not believe what she was hearing. Her mother had never been friendly with black or Asian people and suddenly she was friends with the Bangladeshi family living next door. She remembered the conversation a few weeks ago when her mother had seemed hostile towards the family, but it was marvellous of her mother to take such a different approach in her life by making friends with people from a different background. Vivien had many friends of various backgrounds but she never really introduced them to her family for they had a different outlook and had different ideals. Perhaps if she had, maybe it would have helped them to have a more positive outlook on viewing people of different races, cultures, creeds and so many other different backgrounds.

"Mum, you've never been friends with people from other races because you've always stuck to your old cockney bunch. Why the sudden change? Whatever the reasons, I'm really happy that you've made an effort to be friends with them. It's a nice change from your boring bunch," laughed Vivien. She was really proud of her mum for making the effort, no matter how late in her life. "Oh, by the way, do the others know about your visitors today?" asked Vivien lightly.

"Yes, well I'm a nice East Ender and I wanted to show I was decent just like them. No, the others do not know and I'm just wondering what they'll say when they see Ayesha and Shazia," said Mrs Peters.

"Oh, I think David and Susan will be all right about it once they get used to the idea. I mean look at their children, they're all into this era of ethnic clothing and fashion."

"Yes, I suppose. It's Graham I'm afraid of."

"Oh, Christ, is he coming?" wailed Vivien. She just did not want to see him.

"Yes, he rang me this morning to say he's coming. I tried to sound off but he invited himself round so I started thinking of making excuses to the girls but then I thought I want them to come round since I promised Ayesha about the sunflower."

"Mum, I'm glad you didn't change your mind about inviting your visitors. You invite whom you please. Graham is racist and he will have to learn to keep his views to himself in front of them and me," said Vivien.

"No, luv, he's just got a few things mixed up…" said Mrs Peters.

"No, Mum, you know Graham is racist. Susan and David are mixed up. You always deny his faults and that's why he's spoilt, lazy and aggressive and you also know deep down that maybe Sharon was telling the truth about her beatings from him. Mum you have to accept Graham is no longer a child and most definitely not an angel." Vivien was almost seething as she spoke.

"But, what about today…" began Mrs Peters.

"No buts," interrupted Vivien again. "Your home is yours to invite who ever you wish and do as you please. In your house Graham abides by your rules and your morals."

Mrs Peters looked at Vivien because she was right. Graham would have to live by her rules if he came into her house and that included being polite to her visitors and she would make sure he stuck by those rules.

"Yes, Graham will have to do as I say if he comes to visit me in my home. Vivien, you may have to help me though," said Mrs Peters like a child seeking help from an adult.

Vivien squeezed her mother's hand and smiled.

"Yes, mum I'll stand right by you. I'm so proud of you for being brave enough to do this and taking the step to look beyond the East End."

Both mother and daughter sat waiting for the rest of the guests to arrive.

CHAPTER FIVE

The doorbell rang and Vivien went to open the door. David, Susan and James were there and just behind them was Graham.

"Hello you lot, how are you?" greeted Vivien cheerfully.

"All right, Sis," said David giving her a kiss on the cheek.

"Hello, Aunt Viv," Jamie mumbled.

"All right, Viv," smiled Susan.

"Watch, yea, Viv and I like your fake tan," sniggered Graham thinking he had cracked a joke. Vivien gave him a filthy look in return.

They all gathered in the sitting room and kissed their mother for it felt good to be home with their mum, bringing back many fond memories. Memories which would never be forgotten, engraved into their hearts. Mrs Peters looked at her children and grandson and appreciated that she had had a fulfilled life. Many spent their lives not knowing about the bonds of family. It was a life well spent.

"I cooked you all a Sunday roast. You all need a good meal now and then, but that doesn't mean you don't watch what you eat," said Mrs Peters.

"Yea, I know what you mean, Mum. I've got to watch what I eat 'cause the doctor said I've got a high cholesterol level," David said, touching his big belly.

"Oh, that's rubbish. I eat what I want and just sod the doctor," bellowed Graham.

Vivien looked at him in distaste, he was already getting on her nerves and she didn't know how she was going to tolerate him for the rest of the afternoon.

"Graham, when you've had a heart attack and *if* you live, please tell me how it feels when you come round," said Susan sarcastically. She wished he would grow up and take things more seriously because everything seemed such a joke to him and he certainly wasn't funny.

"Gran, I'm looking forward to dinner, I didn't have breakfast," said a skinny James.

"Jamie, luvie, why didn't you say? Come on everyone, let's get washed and ready for dinner. Viv's laid the table."

Everyone sat down for their dinner, helping themselves to the food on the big table. Graham helped himself to more than everyone else and Vivien could not bear to look at him. She wondered how she had managed to live, at one time in her life, in the same house as her younger brother. They all tucked in and made small talk about different things in their lives, other family members and the good old days of their childhood.

"When's your little girl from next door coming round for her sunflower then?" David suddenly asked his mum.

"Oh, she will," said Mrs Peters smiling at Vivien across the table.

"You got new neighbours, Mum?" Graham asked with a mouthful of roast potato and meat.

"Yes, I've got new neighbours and very helpful ones at that. They're good people."

"That's good for you Mum because it's nice to have helpful neighbours. It fills the gap for you at least after losing Aunt Vera," Susan added and her mother decided at that point to enlighten her children a little, in preparation for the visitors who would call later.

"Yes, that's true and no one can replace Vera. They are different people, but decent and friendly," said Mrs Peters. "They sent me some tea round the other day and one of their sons did my garden yesterday."

"Right on, Mum. That's the kind of good East End neighbours you want, not like some of the Pakis around here," said Graham.

"If you don't mind Graham, I don't want that kind of language at my dinner table," Mrs Peters stated, slowly looking at her son.

"Oh, come on, Mum, you know as well as I do we don't like Pakis in our country," Graham said, a little taken aback by his mother's reaction to his reference to the local Bangladeshi community. He had always talked and aired his racist views in front of her and she had never said anything before. There had even been occasions when his mother had agreed with him because Graham spoke for the family when he spoke against Pakis, niggers and Chinks. He thought he was doing the family a favour by ensuring they knew who they were - British whites and natives of the land.

It was silent at the dinner table as everyone absorbed the sudden tension. Then Jamie broke the silence.

"Gran, can I have my pudding please and a large helping if you don't mind."

"Go on luv, help yourself," said Mrs Peters.

Dinner again resumed, but the incident was on everyone's mind, especially Graham, who did not like being told what to do and what not to do.

Everyone helped clear the dinner table, apart from Graham, after they had finished and the family laughter and chat shared in work was apparent in the Peters' home. They all sat down to an afternoon tea in front of the television after the clearing up when there was a knock at the door.

"That must be the little girl from next door," David said. "I'll get the door 'cause I best get the sunflower from the car, I'd forgotten about it." With that he got up to open the front door as his mother looked at Vivien and she smiled reassuringly.

David opened the door and there were two Asian girls in front of him. One girl was about seven or eight and the other a teenager. He looked at them puzzled and then frowned.

"Yeah, what do you two want?"

"Hello, where's Mrs Peters? She's expecting us," Ayesha smiled. Shazia made an effort to smile, because she knew from the look on David's face, that he had not expected his mother's visitors to be of a different colour. She knew that their visit was going to be difficult and strained.

"Um. Oh, right, well you best come in. I'm gonna just pop out to the car and get the sunflower," stumbled David. He felt uncomfortable and was a little lost for words because apart from swearing at Asian children and teenagers, he hadn't actually spoken to them as one human to another. "You know the way to the sitting room I suppose," he added questioningly, now knowing why his mother had snapped at Graham at dinner.

"Yes we do," said Shazia pertly and walked past him. Shit, thought Shazia holding on to Ayesha's hand, there's a herd of them for us to face, as she heard the chatter in the sitting room, I should have sat at home and done my essay.

There they stood at the doorway of Mrs Peter's sitting room, two girls of colour, like red roses nestled in a bundle of thorns waiting for the first thorn to prick with the wind of change. The Peters family stopped chatting and looked at them and Graham nearly dropped his beer can. Oh, fucking hell, what the fuck has Mum got herself into, she's going senile living on her own, thought Graham. Vivien smiled warmly at Ayesha and Shazia whilst Susan made an awkward attempt of a smile and Jamie gaped at Shazia.

"Hello darlings, come on in. David's just popped out to get the sunflower, come over here," said Mrs Peters indicating for the girls to sit near her. She could feel Graham staring at her, frustrated and shocked at her behaviour.

"Hello, how are you?" Ayesha smiled. She knew that Mrs Peter's children were staring at her, but she didn't care and she was not going to let them make her feel uncomfortable, especially the man who looked as though he was half drunk. So she walked over to Mrs Peters letting go of Shazia's hand and before she sat down she gave her elderly neighbour a hug and the elderly white woman gave her one back. Graham could not believe that his mother was actually hugging a Paki child, this should not be happening in his father's house. Shazia followed and as if she wanted to wind Graham up, she also hugged Mrs Peters.

"Mrs Peters, my mother sent you some vegetable somosas to eat with tea," said Shazia, handing a plastic box to Mrs Peters. Her silver bracelets twinkled in the sunshine as she put out her slender, golden arm to Mrs Peters. Vivien thought the young girl was incredibly beautiful, the natural youth on her face gleaming like an unspoilt innocence. Jamie had also noted Shazia's beauty, just like his Aunt and Susan knew the girl was exceptionally pretty, but she would not acknowledge it. As for Graham, he thought she needed a few lessons from him in bed, to make sure she knew who the master was and where her place was.

"Shazia, Ayesha, these are my daughters Susan and Vivien. This is my youngest son Graham and this is my grandson Jamie, David's son. And all of you, this is Shazia and Ayesha, they are my new next door neighbours."

Mrs Peters introduced them to her children proudly because, she realized, she was proud.

"Hello, I'm glad to meet you," Vivien smiled.

"Me too," agreed Jamie grinning at Shazia, but she ignored him; she knew when a white boy or man was lusting after her.

"All right you two," said Susan half smiling. This was rather uncomfortable for her and she wished her mother had told her beforehand. Not that she had any bad feeling against the Asian kids, but they were different from white children. Graham did not say a word but carried on drinking his beer sullenly.

"How old are you two?" asked Vivien.

"I'm eight and Shazia's seventeen," said Ayesha. "And how old are you?"

Vivien laughed and Shazia said apologetically,

"Ayesha, you don't ask people their age straight away. Sorry, she tends to say whatever's on her mind."

"No, no. I don't mind and it's good to say what's on one's mind anyway. I do. My staff at work get scared of me when I do," Vivien stated.

"Are you studying or working?" asked Jamie to Shazia. Ayesha assumed he was asking her and so she answered.

"I'm studying at primary school," James looked at Ayesha puzzled and then laughed.

Shazia was about to answer when Graham looked at her.

"Or are you married, is the question that we should ask?" he said sarcastically.

Before Mrs Peters could scold her son, Shazia looked at Graham squarely.

"No, I am not married like my old school mate, Tracy, who had a baby at sixteen. I'm doing my A levels and working part time in a local chemist on Saturdays. I do not plan to get married in the near future and neither do my parents plan to marry me off."

Shazia made sure her cream chiffon headscarf was on her head when she replied. Bloody pig, thought Shazia and she looked at Mrs Peters for her reaction. She found her smiling at her as though she were saying, good for you for stating the facts to my ignorant son. Graham was flaring his nostrils but bit back his retort when he saw his mother's face.

"Shazia, I do like your headscarf, it really matches with your clothes," Vivien said, admiring both her clothes and her confidence to speak her mind. Shazia's clothes were a creamy embroidered tunic with matching pants, they looked so delicate on her, making her look almost fragile.

"Do you always wear a headscarf?" asked Susan. She felt suddenly sorry for her little brother Graham; he had asked a question which was only fair seeing as so many of these young Asian girls got married so young. That girl's got such a cheek for talking about white girls the way she did, thought Susan and as for Vivien, licking up to her with flattery. That's why she had asked her question about the headscarves, to see if Shazia would be able to answer without feeling stuck for an answer.

Oh, here we go, the Paki inquisition has begun, thought Shazia. She looked at Susan's bleached blonde hair and her heavy jewellery and planned a well-formed answer.

"Yes I do. I wear a variety of different scarves, many which seemed to be favoured by actresses, models and pop stars. It's part of my religion. Do you find it strange that I wear a headscarf?"

"Well, you see luv, many white women don't wear headscarves, so perhaps I do find it strange?" said Susan smiling very sweetly. By now David was panting in the sitting room with the sunflower pot in hand.

"Well, I don't think it should be strange for you to see women wearing headscarves. At one time, in Britain, in fact just before the war and even after, women did not leave their homes with out wearing a headscarf to the shops, school or any where else. Do you not agree Mrs Peters?"

"Yes, Shazia is right. My mother wore a headscarf and even I wear one when I go out sometimes," agreed Mrs Peters and Shazia continued looking straight on at Susan.

"The headscarf is seen as something prudish, but for us it is our beauty. Yet in the Victorian times in this country, people covered the legs of tables because it reminded them of women's naked legs. I wonder what is prudish these days and what isn't?"

"Well I'm no prude," laughed James at Shazia. What an idiot, thought Shazia and David scowled at his son. He then spoke to his mother.

"What do you want me to do with the sunflower?"

"Well let's have some tea and cakes and the lovely somosas Mrs Ali sent round; then, Ayesha and I will take you to her garden and she can show you where to plant the sunflower. All right?" Mrs Peters replied.

"Fine with me," said Vivien.

"I suppose so," replied Susan, but she felt disloyal to Graham as he did not say anything but stared at the television.

"Great," said James as it gave him more time to take a good look at Shazia.

"Yea, I'm dying for a cuppa and those delicious cakes of yours, Mum," David added, squeezing himself in between Susan and Vivien on the sofa.

"Umm, yum," said Ayesha and Shazia smiled politely in agreement. The East Enders just like the Bangladeshis loved their tea.

Mrs Peters went to make a fresh pot of tea and Susan followed to help her as she didn't know what conversation might creep up that would make her feel torn between her mother and Graham. Vivien decided she would have a long chat with Shazia and Ayesha; it would give her a chance to ignore Graham and wind him up.

"Have you always lived in the East End?" she asked Shazia.

"Yes, I was born here, at the London Hospital. My two older brothers were born back home and came to Britain very young," answered Shazia, as she thought, 'here we go, another family history' because maybe they're wondering who was the original slave master of my family's forefathers. But maybe she's just being friendly, Shazia wondered as an afterthought.

"I love the East End. I love going to Stepping Stone Farm, Victoria Park to see the swans. I love going to London Tower. I've won a Blue Peter badge, which means I can go free to lots of places like the London Eye, Madam Tussauds, London Zoo and other places," Ayesha said all in a rush.

"Those places ain't the East End," bit out Graham, because the kid was getting on his nerves.

"Yes, I know that but they're still nice places to visit," said Ayesha as though she was trying to make a spoilt child understand the obvious.

Vivien wanted to laugh out loud at Ayesha's words for she reminded her of herself.

"That's right darling, they're all lovely places to visit. How did you win a Blue Peter badge?" asked Vivien. She had never met anyone who had won one.

Shazia and Ayesha looked at each other and Shazia encouraged Ayesha with her eyes, to explain how she had won the badge. Vivien noticed they both gave darting looks at Graham for his attitude was not lost on them.

"I drew an educational robot for a robot competition held by Blue Peter," said Ayesha.

"Oh, it must have been a very special robot for you to win a badge," said Jamie. He had once entered a Blue Peter competition but had won nothing.

"It was special," said Shazia. Jamie smiled at her thinking God you're bloody special.

"Why was it so special, Ayesha?" Vivien asked.

Ayesha looked at Graham as if trying to read his face but he seemed busy watching East Enders. She was a little hesitant, but Vivien smiled at her encouragingly and Mrs Peters came in with the tea and Susan followed with the tray of cookies and cakes. Mrs Peters looked at Ayesha and felt her nervousness and gave her wink and that was all she needed to carry on.

"My educational robot for Blue Peter was to help people and children to learn each others' language so that they could talk to each other. I put buttons on the robot so people and children could put words in the robot's mouth and then press the buttons to translate the meanings. I thought it was a good way of learning and becoming friends with each other. I've got a friend called Jade at school and I taught her some of my language," Ayesha said proudly and Shazia added,

"Yes, Ayesha you taught her all the swear words in our language, because you both thought it was so funny." The pride was wiped off Ayesha's face and she felt a little embarrassed.

"That's really original," said Jamie laughing.

"Yes, absolutely and it's a great invention. I wish had a robot like that when I go on my holidays, instead of my having to go through my hand guide book of translations," said Vivien.

She was impressed by Ayesha's wish of wanting people to understand each other, regardless of what language they spoke. Susan and David listened but found it difficult to comment. They had moved their children away from languages foreign to them, spoken in their children's schools, to other schools where English was the dominant language. They had wanted to ensure their children spoke fluent English and were well brought up without any alien influence. Here was a little girl, whose first language was not English, trying to find ways of making people speak to each other in whatever language they spoke, via a robot so they could all be friends. She had an understanding of appreciating all languages and people.

However, Graham was horrified at what Ayesha had said for it was exactly what he disagreed with. He found the child's talk of some kind of friendly integration between white people and coloured people completely distasteful as he was against this kind of social inclusion and fusion, but he was in favour of exclusion. He found it difficult not to comment on the child's innocent wish.

"Listen and listen carefully, little girl, not all people want to speak to each other and be cosy with the person next door, especially if they don't speak English. Your little wish is not a reality in this hard world. You should be glad the British let you in and let you enter a Blue Peter competition. They probably let you win 'cause you're an ethnic minority. Get the picture?"

Graham gritted his teeth as he spoke. He knew his mother was becoming angry with him from the way she was standing with the teapot in mid air. He did not have to wait long before his mother spoke with a steel assertion.

"That's enough, Graham. If you can't behave like a decent human being in the company of guests in my home then you should either be quiet or leave. Have I made myself clear?" How dare Graham speak to an innocent child like that? He sounded as though he wanted to rip her apart for wanting peace and joy with people of all backgrounds. Something that, if everyone could get a chance to explore, could prove to be astounding. There was a silence from the tension created by Graham's outburst and his mother's reaction. Even David and Susan felt embarrassed at Graham's outburst for had he forgotten Ayesha was only a child, not some sort of teenage rebel.

She hadn't actually said anything to aggravate him as such but something had triggered Graham off. But then he seemed to get triggered off at the slightest of things on occasions and as for Vivien, she was totally disgusted by such behaviour. The other two, David and Susan, looked like two lemons sitting there without apologising for what their brother had said. Well, she would not stay silent.

"Mum is right. How dare you talk to Ayesha as though you're one shelf above her? If you can't manage to speak without causing offence, then don't speak at all."

"I don't mind if Graham speaks because he might need some answers in return," said Shazia with a look that sent darts through Graham. Jamie thought she looked terrific when angry.

"Yes, Shazia might want to answer Uncle Graham. Don't you think she should, Gran?" asked Jamie and smiled at Shazia as though he was giving her comfort.

At least the fool's done some good for me, thought Shazia giving him the first smile since she had met him.

"Go on, luv, say your piece and let's get the air cleared here," said Mrs Peters as she stared at her son. What a predicament, but she was going to confront this. For years she had learnt to dislike, almost hate the local Bangladeshi community for any woes she and her family experienced. They had been the scapegoats she had needed in the past, she realised that many white families had used them during times of deprivation and distress. The time had now come, although late in her life, where a child from the other side had somehow reached out and touched a part of her, making her realise that there was good and bad in all communities and that one community could not be all bad and could not be excluded at the expense and wish of another for problems created beyond their doing.

"Well, firstly you're right, not all people want to talk to each other whether they're white, pink, yellow, brown or black, because either they're too afraid of each other or, in many cases, they're so pig headed they actually think they're superior to each other. Secondly my parents and many Asian families actually came to this country because at one time there was a major shortage of labourers. In fact, this country ended up inviting foreigners for their own advantage. Leaving that aside, there was a time in great British history when Englishmen entered the Indian sub-continent and decided to take over by force, making the natives almost slaves in their own country. Ghandi had to fight to free the people of India, which my country was a part of at one time. Unfortunately, people like you forget these tragedies caused by such acts and so in a way this country is perhaps paying for those colonial mistakes of long ago by playing host to so many people of colour. I hope you've got the picture, Graham." Shazia had spoken fiercely because she was really pissed off with him. He was racist as plain as day.

"Yes, I hope you've got the message, Graham. And I hope it's as clear as crystal to you," said Ayesha with a frown on her face.

"I think my brother has had the best history lesson since his school days. And I think Graham knows exactly what Shazia said. He just needs time to absorb it," Vivien observed.

"Did you understand that, Uncle Graham?" asked Jamie as though he thought Graham needed an interpreter. David was scowling at Jamie because he was playing piggy in the middle and having a hard time at it and his son was not helping. So he decided to intervene.

"Um, what about the sunflower then, Mum?"

"Drink your tea and have a somosa," she replied with a stiff face.

"Okay, then." David knew when not to say anything and helped himself to a somosa. They tasted delicious; the lady next door certainly knew how to cook.

Ayesha and Shazia helped themselves to cakes, cookies and tea and Susan helped herself to a cookie while Vivien, Mrs Peters and James ate a somosa. They made small talk with each other and it seemed Shazia had taken Mrs Peters words as a form of apology. In fact she was proud that her elderly white neighbour had not ignored her son's words nor expected her to ignore them as well. She understood how hard it had been for Mrs Peters to stand by Shazia against her son and understood that for years she had been a white woman who had found it easier to hold the Bangladeshi community responsible for all the ills in the East End. She had been ignorant and had misunderstood many aspects of the social problems in the East End and on a wider scale. But she had been human enough to look beyond and find different answers.

Graham sat as if immobile in his chair for he felt humiliated at the way his family had shown no support for him and the pathetic moral understanding displayed by them towards two Paki girls. Didn't they understand that if people like these girls were not in Britain, there would be more homes for people, more jobs and a better education system. And that crap the Paki tart came out with about Englishmen taking over, as far as he was concerned they had done a favour to all the Pakis, niggers and chinks in the world by making them bloody civilised. Without white men to guide them they would have been like animals, like monkeys, like their forefathers. These were the thoughts that ran through his mind and he decided his family needed to be re-educated in who they were, especially his mother and Vivien.

After tea, Shazia and Ayesha helped the other women to clear the tea things and complimented Mrs Peters' baking. She was extremely pleased and made it a point to explain to Shazia that she had used vegetable margarine to bake the cookies and cakes and Shazia felt touched by her thoughtfulness. She had not expected Mrs Peters to make such an effort. The two Bangladeshi sisters found it very easy to relate to Vivien, who talked to them vividly about the many countries she had visited, and at the same time was interested in how the two Bangladeshi girls had grown up and in their family background. On hearing about their older brothers in higher education at degree level Susan had suddenly looked jealous.

"Did your brothers get some sort of sponsorship to get into university, or did they take some sort of different test?" she remarked.

"No, my brothers got in through their A Level results which were of a very high standard. They both work part time and study just like me, because our parents want us to stand on our own two feet and take advantage of opportunities offered to every student in this country. Educational opportunities are only offered in other much poorer countries if you have the money to pay for it," said Shazia directly to her.

"I'm going to be a nurse because my big brother said I can work with him when he becomes a doctor," Ayesha said to Susan hoping to impress her.

"I'm sure you will." Susan could not help but soften her tone when she looked at Ayesha, noting her big black eyes and curly hair framing her olive face.

"Right now David, Ayesha and I are going to take you round to her garden aren't we luv?" Mrs Peters stated.

"Yes, that's right, David," agreed Ayesha through a mouthful of cake.

"Come on then," Mrs Peters said as she held out her hand to Ayesha, and David followed with the sunflower in his hand. Shazia said, "I best go now."

But she really didn't want to go, because she was having such an interesting conversation with Vivien. Even Susan had contributed a little as well and Jamie had tried very hard to impress her throughout. David had said that the somosas were delicious and he had wondered if Shazia's mum made meat or chicken somosas too. Graham had watched the football without looking at the spectacle before him during that time because he felt disgusted with his family and he could not believe Susan and David's mellow attitude.

"No, Shazia stay a little longer," insisted Vivien.

"I suppose you probably have got to help your mum cook," said Susan knowingly.

"Yes, I do help my mum cook as much as I can and contribute to the housework. But then my mum expects us all to contribute to the running of our household, the boys and the girls. She expects us not be laid back and use our studies as an excuse."

"Well I used to get my kids to do the same, you know helping with the ironing, washing, getting the tea on," Susan replied, getting a little touchy.

"Yes, Susan you did, but I think your daughter is a lot more reliable than your son," said Vivien. She could not understand why Susan suddenly got all touchy and said irritating things to Shazia, who gave a good reply in return.

"Okay, then, I'll stay until Mrs Peters returns."

"Why don't we go outside in a little while and see what your brother did to Mum's garden and we can watch David plant Ayesha's sunflower, as it's such a lovely day. I don't know how people can sit in front of the telly in such nice weather," Vivien said, shaking her head at Graham.

"Well some people might not be able to tolerate hot weather as others do. Their bodies might not be built for such climates," interjected Susan defensively. She was feeling sorry for Graham, well he was her brother and these were strangers. It was like a tug of loyalty and morals for Susan and David and they could not balance their feelings or principles.

"Is that why some of us love going to Spain and baking our bodies in the sun on the beach?" asked Vivien sarcastically. Shazia was well aware of the hidden tension that Vivien and her mother had tried to camouflage with the earlier confrontation. The only way for Susan to feel comfortable was to be extremely nice to her because Shazia felt that there was a softer side to her, which just needed encouragement to come out.

"Susan, you must enjoy living outside London. It's so much fresher than the polluted air we breathe here," said Shazia smiling at her.

"Yea, it is. I wanted my kids to have a better life outside London rather than being banged up in tower blocks all day. I feel sorry for the kids with no garden and nowhere to play. It's not natural for them to be indoors all day," said Susan, for she truly meant it.

"I understand the feeling as there's not many parks around here for the kids to play in. All the spare land around gets snapped up by property developers from the city."

After Shazia had spoken, they sat there, the three of them and bitched about the local council, tax increases, housing problems and the appalling state of schools. A bloody good bitch united people and Susan found herself forgetting that she was supposed to hate Shazia and she started to come down from her high horse, and most of all she found she was enjoying herself. This did not go unnoticed on Graham while Jamie stared at Shazia smiling all the while.

****

Mrs Peters and Ayesha knocked on the Ali's front door with David behind. Yusuf opened it and smiled.

"Hello Mrs Peters. Has Ayesha caused some trouble?"

"No, luv. We've come round to plant the sunflower. As I promised Ayesha, my son David has come round to help out." Mrs Peters proudly showed off the fat, burly man behind her who managed a weak smile but looked as though he was in an uncomfortable predicament.

"All right, mate," said Yusuf to David.

"Yeah, all right, mate," answered David, a little shocked at the way Yusuf's voice sounded so English, for he almost sounded like a white man.

"Well, come in," Yusuf invited and they all trooped in to the Ali's sitting room.

Mrs Ali was in the kitchen and Mr Ali was watching the football, while Hamza was reading a book and they all looked up to see the unexpected visitors in their home. Mr Ali stood up and greeted Mrs Peters who introduced David to him and they shook hands and David smiled tightly at Hamza who nodded his head as a greeting.

"Mr Ali, We've come round to get to your garden to plant Ayesha's sunflower," said Mrs Peters.

"Fine. It will be nice to have a sunflower in the garden. Your son's going to plant it isn't he?" asked Mr Ali as he led them all outside.

"Yes that's right," said Mrs Peters. "Mr Ali and Yusuf cleared the garden and laid out the patio," she said to David.

"Yea, you done a good job here, mate," David remarked to Mr Ali as he admired the neat work in the garden. There were a few minor mistakes but that didn't mean the garden didn't look good. For first timers and since they were Asians who didn't really know about gardens, they hadn't done a bad job, thought David.

"Where do you want it planted sweetheart?" David asked Ayesha. He was softening up a bit, especially as he wasn't under the racist glare of Graham. Blimey, she's only a kid; Graham didn't have to hand it out to her in front of everyone like that, thought David. David had forgotten the times when he and his mates, after a rowdy Sunday afternoon in the pub, had often called out racist names to children of colour for the fun of it. Something had mellowed him this afternoon; perhaps the fact that the woman he called his mother had an effect on him for becoming friends with children from another race. He still saw her as the person he looked up to most in his life, even though, he was a man in his prime with grandchildren of his own, or was it he still feared her wrath that had been felt from the time he had been a child.

"Over here, David," said Ayesha showing a corner of the garden which had being neatly tidied up with a border round it. This was the corner which people would look at and admire, thought Ayesha. Her sunflower and her dead brother, for guilt was such a burden to bear. Mr Ali got out a trowel for David and he set to work with a small crowd watching him. Mrs Peters talked about the weather to Mr Ali and Yusuf went over to stand near Ayesha and watch David. Mrs Ali came into the garden and saw David planting the sunflower. He looked up and saw her and gave her a smile. She smiled back and thought he looked so big in her small garden. David was thinking what a tiny woman, almost fragile and so much younger looking than her husband.

"Mrs Peters, please sit on the chairs. I get everyone tea," Mrs Ali said.

"That'll be nice, luv, so as long as you join us," thanked Mrs Peters. Mrs Ali went back in to organise tea and some snacks as Yusuf looked on at his mother and smiled thinking how Bangladeshi women loved to make sure their guests had something to eat before they left their homes.

"Yusuf, how are your studies going?" asked Mrs Peters as she shielded her eyes from the sun. She could feel the heat on her face and was a little worried in case she became red. She did not tan very well, unless one counted the times on Brighton beach when she turned a lobster colour.

"It's going fine, Mrs Peters. I've got an essay coming up to do about the NHS and other aspects of health associated with older people and I was wondering if I could do an interview with you, to collate some information," said Yusuf.

"'Course you can. Just tell me when you want to come round and I'll have lots to tell you," Mrs Peters promised excitedly. She was looking forward to having a chat with Yusuf about the good old days, not that the new days were that bad…now.

"Mum, do you think this hole is deep enough for the sunflower?" asked David, wiping his forehead as he was feeling very hot and sweaty and he could do with a cold beer.

"Well, I don't know. Why don't you ask Mr Ali? I think he might know better than me," said Mrs Peters as though she was talking to a child. She winked at Ayesha as she talked to David. She wanted David to converse with

Mr Ali for the awkward silence needed to be broken and a common ground needed to be found - she had learnt a few things from Ayesha.

"Eh, what do you think, mate?" asked David as he looked at Mr Ali. The man had a bald head and was darker than the rest of the family but there was something honest and decent about him which reminded him of himself.

"I think that's big enough. You can plant the sunflower now," replied Mr Ali. He had understood why Mrs Peters had made her son ask him whether the hole was big enough or not. She wanted her son to acknowledge Mr Ali's presence, to ensure they spoke to each other as a sign of, if not friendship, but tolerance.

Yusuf looked at the fat white man planting the sunflower for his sister. When he had been a child, many fat white men had screamed racist comments at him - taxi drivers, builders, dustmen, officer workers and even people in authoritative positions. He now looked beyond that experience.

"It's very good of you to make such an effort," he said.

"Least I can do, mate. I think you or your brother sorted Mum's garden out and that's real generous of you. Nice to have neighbours like that," David added.

To offer something like that of one's own free will was 'real decent' in his book and he appreciated this from the Ali family. Vivien had heard the commotion from next door and knew her mother had made her way into the Ali garden with Ayesha. She wanted to meet the rest of Shazia and Ayesha's family and she also wanted Susan to meet them as well. The older girl was very intelligent and the younger sister was an angel in disguise. Without looking at Graham or considering asking him Vivien repeated her suggestion that they now go outside.

"Why don't we all go out into the garden and see what David's getting up to. I'm sure you, Susan wants to see what Shazia's brother has done to Mum's garden. Give it a little inspection... although I'm sure he's done a great job."

"Vivien, I'll go to the garden 'cause I'm sure that's what you want all of us to do."

"You read me like a book, Sis," laughed Vivien.

"Come on then Aunt Vivo, Aunt Susan and Shazia," James added excitedly. It gave him a chance to check Shazia more closely standing up.

"Yea, go you lot, get in the garden. Go and enjoy the sunshine, get yourself a tan while you're out there. Ooops, I forgot, some of us don't need a tan 'cause some of us have already got a tan." Graham sneered almost biting his words out. The situation was getting more and more cosy, Graham thought in disgust.

"I think Uncle Graham's trying to crack a joke," said James almost angrily.

"It's a pity his jokes are a little bit outdated," said Vivien tersely. She was pissed off. Susan observed the situation, she was embarrassed by Graham's behaviour, but she still could not bring herself to say anything against it. It was the tearing dilemma of loyalty and common principles that prevented her from speaking out against Graham.

However Shazia did not stay silent as she knew exactly where she stood. Her principle stemmed from the demand of being accepted by people whether they wanted to or not. She looked at Graham like he was filth.

"I suppose you're a bit jealous of my tan, especially as you're encouraging everyone else to get one while they're out in the sun. It's a pity God didn't give it to pale skinned people naturally. You must really look up to people like me."

With that Shazia walked towards the back door where James was already opening it. She could feel the glare from Graham almost digging into her back.

"Fucking Paki bitch," Graham swore in the slightest of a whisper, but enough for Susan to hear, yet she dared not look back at her younger brother. She wasn't as feisty as Vivien.

As Vivien went into the garden, the spectacle that met her was something she had never seen in her parent's home. Her mother and father had never had black or Asian friends, or even foreign white friends. They had lived their lives in a simple but boxed in way. Not making trouble for anyone, expecting no trouble from anyone, but never making their way to see beyond their own way of life. Susan looked at the gathering in the next garden and wondered how long this would last. Was her mother going through a stage in her life when older people think they can become young again, by doing something out of the blue, something out of character? Yet she felt looking at the picture in front of her that perhaps there was something genuine, something honest about it. That perhaps her mother was determined to be friends with these people and maybe make her children share her friendship with them. David was talking to Mr Ali who insisted he call him by his trust first name. He found that he had things in common with Unus Ali. Not exactly the same things but similar enough to share. They were talking about Mr Ali's future plan to build a small conservatory in his garden.

David was telling him which would be the best sort of conservatory for the Ali garden, he had considerable expertise in building and home improvements which Mr Ali found very interesting to listen to. He felt very important explaining his ideas to the Bangladeshi man, who was respecting him for his knowledge. He never really gave it much thought and nor did his wife or family. So to find Mr Ali appreciating this made it easier for him to relate and develop a friendship with the man. People often failed to find common ground to start positive communication due to their negative perceptions of each other, a great human failing. It was Ayesha who introduced everyone to each other as she provided the opening for those who were afraid to enter the unknown. She made it a point when her mother and Hamza joined them in the garden with refreshments to introduce Susan. Mrs Ali had smiled humbly at her guests but almost felt Susan's uncertainty as to whether she would understand her or not. So she thought she would show Susan that somehow, in her broken English, she could communicate with her.

"Susan, you not mind I call you Susan?" asked Mrs Ali.

"No, no, go ahead," Susan said with eyes wide at the Bangladeshi woman's broken English.

"You have children?" continued Mrs Ali.

"Yes, I've got two children, a boy and a girl. Your garden's looking nice," said Susan politely. She actually did not know what else to say, so she waited for Mrs Ali's next question, which was more of a polite demand.

"Susan, you share tea with us and nice snack. Nothing too hot but spicy," Mrs Ali said.

Susan smiled and looked at the small table Mrs Ali had laid and noticed that David had already tucked into the food with Mr Ali. They were in a deep conversation which men often got into when they had found something manly to talk about, whether they were black, white or Asian. Graham wasn't around and she could sense a lessening of the tension which his presence seemed to create.

So everyone joined in eating and talking, they laughed at odd things together, agreed on things together, avoided things which each thought the other might take offence at. Whatever English they spoke in, whether broken, Cockney or posh, the group were communicating with each other and making an effort to understand that they were all people, all humans and that there could come a time when each could talk about things which they thought might offend each other. For David and Susan, it was a great step to take, to talk with the Ali family on a one to one basis. As though the Ali family were white neighbours and they were enjoying a barbecue together. Mrs Peters had made it easier for them, by showing that they were already her friends, children could still look up to their parents no matter how old they became.

For the Ali family, especially for Mr and Mrs Ali, it was a change in their lives. It was the first time they had white people in their lives as guests. They wanted to live in peace and acceptance with all people in the country they had made their home. They wanted them to understand their way of life just as they wanted to understand Mrs Peters and her family's way of life. It was called give and take.

Graham was quietly watching his family and the Ali family chatting away. He saw how Susan and David had relaxed their hostilities towards Shazia and Ayesha and now it seemed they were becoming friendly with the rest of their family. His mother was obviously the ringleader, making sure everyone was talking to each other, along with that little Paki girl. What a scene to feel ashamed of. This had never happened in Graham's parents home when he had been growing up. He had been brought up to be proud of his white, cockney heritage, almost possessive of it. It was his lifelong identity to his self-esteem, dignity and pride. Graham found it almost painful to look at the garden scene before him. He felt somewhat betrayed by his mother for allowing herself to mix with these dirty coloureds.

She seemed to have forgotten that because of them so many white families were suffering in the East End. Graham's anger was increasingly vented against the fact that his mother had apparently forgotten that she was the one who had never encouraged them as children to associate with children of a different colour. Each to their own was what Graham's mother used to say. So why did his mother suddenly have a change of heart, a change towards strangers so different from themselves. A change, Graham could not comprehend, let alone accept.

Graham decided he would watch whether his mother and his siblings became closer with the coloured family. He would note the changes and see how their attitudes differed from his and then he would say his piece to them. Graham was going to make sure he put a stop to this kind of behaviour, for the sake of his father's name. His father had never had coloured friends although he had worked with them. He hadn't often spoken ill of the coloureds but now and then, when things went wrong, Arthur had pointed a few things out to the family, especially with regard to the housing and unemployment situation in the East End. Now and then Graham's father had taken a stand in the past and his mother had completely forgotten about this. She was failing to respect his father's memory and her loyalty to her husband, his father. Yes, Graham would ensure his family remembered a few of his father's words when he put his foot down and handed out a few words of his own f( ) each of them to remember. Even if Vivien gave him lip, he'd make sure he got through to her with a few thumps if necessary.

He h d made sure, in the last few years of his marriage, that Sharon had got a few t umps now and then, just so she would understand he was the boss in the hou e. Stupid cow, she'd become loose in the last few years and finally he had los control over her. She had thrown him out of their family home, along with h belongings and a police presence after an aggressive and violent argume t.

Grah m needed to ensure that his family did not become loose like his ex-wife an become increasingly alien to their own culture and their own kind. Graham would ensure that he took control over his family's developing relation hip with the coloured pigs who were taking over Britain, for he saw it as his d ty. These were Graham's thoughts as he watched the mixed spectacle outside nd reflected on his future plans. He would save his family from being betraye by these strange people who wanted to benefit from a white family's friendsh p. His family did not understand this but he did.

Outsic , Susan was surprised to find out that Mrs Ali wanted to know how to bake birthday cakes. Mrs Ali was very interested in learning different recipes, ll the more for her to serve guests who turned up on her doorstep and to make sure her daughters practised them as well. Susan found she could explain he recipes to Mrs Ali in simple English that she could understand and, wh re it wasn't clear, one of her children explained further. Susan had never imagined a Bangladeshi woman wanting to know about English cooking, but then she really wanted to know how to make somosas, especially as she found Mrs Ali's ones delicious.

Vivien was talking to Yusuf and Hamza about a variety of different things from her travels to where she worked and Hamza was very interested. He was desperately looking for work experience in famous financial institutions and Vivien worked in one of them. She had much experience in the financial field, certain aspects of which Hamza could use as material in his essays and course work. Vivien suggested that she visit during the middle of the week with materials and she would go through some important aspects of Hamza's syllabus with him at her mum's flat. Hamza agreed straight away.

Shazia was chatting with David and her Dad about buying a car; she had just passed her driving test and Jamie was offering his knowledge to Shazia. It seemed David had a friend who dealt in cars and maybe he could help her to buy one at a reduced price. He had long finished planting the sunflower, but found he could not stop speaking to his avid listeners. They were interested in what he had to say and responded to his opinions positively, more than his siblings and his family ever did. Mrs Peters and Ayesha sat near the sunflower having a private chat about a few things Ayesha found she could tell her.

Mrs Peters loved listening to Ayesha chat about her school, friends and family. Ayesha found Mrs Peters talked about the good old days like an adventure that she could only imagine. She was storing some of Mrs Peter's information away for when she wrote stories in school. Mrs Ali was thinking to herself, how confident she felt speaking to people whose first language was English. Maybe in a few months time they might learn a few phrases from her language, it might make communicating with them easier. But then friendship had a language of its own, a language anyone could learn if they were willing and brave enough to look beyond. Mr Ali was thinking to himself, what luck finding David as Mrs Peters' son. He had experience in fields which he had little knowledge of and was willing to share this experience. So there they were, the two families talking to each other, an East End Bangladeshi family and the other a white cockney East End family. So different from each other but brought together through the planting of a sunflower, through the dreams of a child, and her guilt in memory of her brother who had been born and died in one day.

CHAPTER SIX

After the ceremonious planting of the sunflower, the Ali family and Mrs Peters, David, Susan and Vivien crossed a stepping stone towards a mutual understanding of each others' differences and similarities. Mrs Peters started popping round to her neighbours' flat for tea, milk, sugar, or when she fell short of something or just for a visit. She found herself asking a member of the Ali family to help her out when one of her children was unavailable… things like replacing a light bulb, or checking her washing machine. Things independent people took for granted.

However it wasn't just Mrs Peters asking the Ali family to help her all the time without her helping them. Mrs Ali came round to her flat when she had someone calling and speaking in English which she could not understand. Mrs Peters simplified such conversation, making it easier for her. Mrs Ali had also learnt how to cook a few English dishes from Mrs Peters and Susan. These included recipes such as Cheese and Onion Quiche, which traditionally would have been served with salad and potatoes as a lunch meal. However Mrs Ali innovatively served the quiche as a little snack for guests with tea, along with somosas. For her it was the culinary fusion of two distinct cultures.

There was one particular incident when Mrs Peters had asked Mrs Ali to sit with her while a council plumber carried out some work in her kitchen. He was a white man who had found it strange at first to find an elderly white cockney woman and a Bangladeshi woman so friendly and had got in a friendly debate about communities with Mrs Peters. Mrs Peters had at first thought, due to his appearance, he would rather be prejudiced against the local Bangladeshi community but she had been pleasantly surprised for it re-affirmed her belief that one should not judge a book by its cover.

The worker had left, forgetting his tools, but had come back late in the afternoon to collect them and had ended up having a cup of tea with Mrs Peters. His name was John and she had enjoyed herself talking to him, even though she had found his tattoos rather distasteful at first, but he had been very well spoken and polite.

Shazia, Hamza, and Yusuf often made time to visit Mrs Peters. Yusuf used her experiences of the National Health Service for one of his coursework essays. Mrs Peters felt very important when Yusuf came to see her about this aspect for she had the chance to talk and express her concerns about how to run the country and about the golden days. However it was Ayesha who Mrs Peters bonded to the most because the child made things so much clearer, making sense of things that seemed unreachable. One afternoon, Ayesha had been watching East Enders with Mrs Peters in her home when she slyly made an observation.

"I know Mrs Peters you like us a lot and are our friend. Vivien likes us a lot but Graham does not like me or my family. He probably hates us and as for Susan and David, they didn't like us but learnt to like us. They don't know whose side to take, yours or Graham's."

It was a proclamation which shook Mrs Peters off track. Ayesha had an uncanny way of observing things and suddenly announcing them as though she should. Even if people concerned about the issues fell into a hushed silence.

"No, no, luvie. You've got it wrong," Mrs Peters began lamely. She knew she had made a mistake in trying to cover up the situation from the look on Ayesha's face.

"No, I haven't. You know very well Graham doesn't want you to be friends with me and my family because we're Bangladeshis," Ayesha affirmed forcefully. "Susan and David can't understand why we're all friends. They can't understand what's got into your head but they are trying to understand though in their strange way. And I know they're a lot better than when I first met them."

Mrs Peters looked ahead of her and shook her head.

"You're right, but I don't know what to do? I don't blame them because I never encouraged them to be friends with anyone coloured until now. Never saw the point?"

"Well why now?" asked Ayesha as she sat closer to her friend and looked at her with inquisitive eyes.

"Ayesha you were very persistent and you kept asking questions and forced me to answer you," laughed Mrs Peters.

"I don't think it was just me. I think you were lonely especially as Vera had died and she was your best friend," said Ayesha. "I also think my parents and brothers and sister could have made more of an effort to talk to you instead of feeling afraid and getting all touchy about anything you said because you didn't understand. Don't think bad of them; it's a bit hard when you get people calling you horrible names."

"I understand it's hard to make the first step to be friends with someone, especially if they're not the same colour as you. But your family meant well and I would have missed out a lot if they hadn't been so good to me," said Mrs Peters appreciating the fact that Ayesha recognised both sides of the story. It also dawned on Mrs Peters that Ayesha was right for she had felt lonely, terribly lonely. There had been days when she had had no contact with another person, another living soul, apart from the phone calls from her children. She had even started to skip meals, the void in her life made eating a burden. She had felt a lonely ache deep within her when she first saw the Ali family move in. That was nearly five months ago and it would be Christmas next month and she eagerly looked forward to it. There was something different about Mrs Peters as a person recently. The change showed in her face and the way she smiled at other people who lived in her building.

Over the past five months Mrs Peters had grown closer to the Ali family as she spent time talking and enjoying their company. Shazia had even taken Mrs Peters to her cousin's wedding along with an eager Vivien and a not so eager Susan. It had been a different experience from an English cockney wedding, but yet there was something similar about it all. The similarities were the nature of how humans were, in actual fact, in tune with each other through the basic passages in life - birth, marriage, family kinship and death. She had seen the rich colours, the fine jewellery, and the delicate materials worn by all who attended the wedding and most obviously the bride herself.

Mrs Peters had seen how the bride had wept when it was time for her to leave with the groom. Shazia had explained through the words of a wedding song....

"Now, our daughter you go,
From the castle of your father's love,
From the garden of your mother's tenderness,
To start a new beginning in,
The haven of your husband's home,
Forever to become apart from us."

Mrs Peters had in a way understood the words of the song by making comparisons to her married life. Yes, a woman began a new life when she got married for she not only married her husband but also the politics of the family from both sides. A married woman learnt to become a player in the politics of the family as she learnt things that politicians could never learn, balancing the demanding roles of mother and wife while trying to keep part of herself for herself.

She called Mr and Mrs Ali by their first names, but they called her Mrs Peters, not as a formality but due to the fact that for them, culturally it was their way of showing respect for her age and experience. Even David had a friendly chat with Mr Ali when he came round and the past few months had moulded the two families together although there had been many crossings along the way. Susan had somehow managed to come down from her narrow shelf and talked to them when she came to visit her mother and a member of the Ali family was there as well. She had even managed to swap housework and cooking ideas with Mrs Ali, because she had actually felt rather interested in the Ali family's lives. Susan had recently joined a middle class woman's club in Essex and she was airing some of her new found knowledge of other people's lives in one of the clubs projects.

However, Graham would still not even acknowledge the Ali family if he saw them, let alone change his racist feelings towards them. He was watching his family's changing attitudes and their developing friendship and he deeply resented it. Graham was still unemployed, drinking too much and beginning to build up debts and most of all, his mother did not listen to his 'woes'. She had told him sternly to straighten his life up and had even said Sharon may have left him, due to his drinking, late nights and laziness. Graham felt his mother didn't know what she was talking about as she had become soft because some Pakis had cleared her garden up.

So what if they did a few chores for her. They should do, they were living in her country and his dad had fought in the war to save that nation. Graham felt that the Ali's were supposed to help out and do what his mother asked. They were like servants or slaves, inferior to the white man. Well that's why the British had ruled them, made them from animals into civilised people. His mother was a good woman, she felt sorry for them and was being kind to them, and they were taking advantage of her good nature. His mother and siblings soon would not be calling Mr and Mrs Ali by their first names but through his 're-education' they would be calling them Pakis.

"Mrs Peters, are you angry with me?" Ayesha asked bringing her back from her thoughts.

"No, no, I'm not angry with you. Yes, I was feeling lonely and I needed the contact of other people, even strangers. I wanted that horrible emptiness to be filled up so I wouldn't feel lonely," Mrs Peters said with a stark look of emotion in her eyes, for her soul had almost been screaming for human contact.

"Well, don't ever feel lonely. We're here and we're your friends, even though we're strange. We'll look after you," said Ayesha squeezing the old hand with her small childlike hands. She carried on trying to make Mrs Peters feel better.

"You're very brave for living on your own. I know you want to live here because you feel your Arthur's here."

"No, I don't feel lonely and scared. I feel safe, secure now my neighbours are no longer strangers," Mrs Peters said.

Together they sat and watched television. The white old woman and the little Bangladeshi girl, generations apart, creeds apart, race apart but united in the need for human friendship. They sat together and watched East Enders as though they had known each other all of their lives.

Over Christmas the relationship between Mrs Peters and the Ali family gradually became closer. The various obstacles of prejudice, stereotypes and the lack of understanding were overcome by their conversations, clearing various misinformed ideas each had of the other. When people talked to each other they tended to make more sense of reality. It paved the way for less conflicts and confrontations and evoked a sense of unity. Unity, sewn together by the simple fact that Mrs Peters and the Ali family were no longer strangers but friends who looked out for each other, who cared for each other.

There had been one particular incident just before Shazia had taken Susan, Vivien and Mrs Peters to her cousin's wedding. She had come to visit Mrs Peters and found Susan, David, Vivien and Susan's daughter Martha were also there. The family had been looking through Mrs Peter's wedding photos which were very precious to her. Shazia had joined them and was chatting to them, well more to Vivien, because she had many things in common with her. Martha had been watching her and had taken in Shazia's stunning looks which the girl herself was oblivious to. Shazia had not made an effort to talk to her too much because she was uncertain of Martha's attitude towards people of colour. Martha had misinterpreted her behaviour as being very vain, especially as her cousin Jamie had raved about her so much.

Martha had waited, watched Shazia for a while and then spoke almost bitchily, like her mother had at the beginning when she had initially met Shazia.

"I suppose your kind of people have arranged marriages and not love marriages."

The remark suddenly made the whole air in the room thick and there seemed to be an awkward silence, but Shazia was not deterred.

"Well, it depends on how you interpret arranged marriages and how you view love marriages," Shazia had said slowly. She had a feeling that Martha had an unsure attitude towards her, just like her mother had had at first.

"Arranged marriages are arranged by parents for their children and they marry not out of choice. We fall in love and marry out of choice," said Martha as though summing up Shazia's life for her.

Shazia looked at her, at her blonde hair and blue eyes and the way the girl looked back at her. To Shazia it seemed Martha's attitude towards her had been shaped by myths floating around in society, by the irresponsible mass media and the wrong information distributed through schools and professionals who worked in public services. Martha had learnt to expect something of her people through this information and was willing to accept and not question whether it was actually true or false. It did not occur to her that none of the information came directly from the people in question but from others who assumed they knew everything about another culture and another way of life.

"Fortunately it isn't as simple as the way you've just explained, Martha, otherwise I would have been married by now," corrected Shazia, as though she were talking to a child.

"Well, Shazia, why don't you explain to Martha who seems rather mis-informed?" Vivien added, looking dryly at her niece.

Mrs Peters was waiting for her to explain further and Susan was beginning to look rather uncomfortable about the situation.

"In our way of life based on the teachings of our religion, Islam, parents take an active role in the arrangement of their children's marriage. They help to find a suitable match by selecting through a number of prospective candidates, based on similarities such as age, education, interests, family background and looks. An introduction is made if a suitable candidate is found and the courtship begins if the couple in question feel suited to each other. Our religion does not force people to marry someone they wish not to marry, a man and a woman have the choice to say yes or no to a proposed marriage. However our religion also recognises that people can fall in love and if they do, then they must marry. The point of an arranged marriage is that it is not just about the romantic notion of being in love …"

"Why isn't love allowed in an arranged marriage?" interrupted Martha.

"Yes it is and if you let me finish, you might be able to understand how it works. An arranged marriage is based on a partnership between two people. A partnership based on respect, trust, understanding, the reality and the responsibility to each other through the good and bad times together. It's a commitment to work together and appreciate each other's efforts. Then the passion and a deep love gradually develops that binds those two people ever closer. That love only comes because it is based on a strong foundation so it won't crumble at the first sign of trouble. Arranged marriages aren't something found in just my community but Italian communities, Red Indian tribes, in English aristocracy. It was dominant in England just a hundred years ago."

Shazia knew she had made an impact on the audience in front of her and so she continued. "Many people in love enter marriage thinking it's a bed of roses. How very wrong they can be. It's hard work especially after having children. I think many people don't understand the importance of each others' faults and when you're in love, you don't always see these faults until later."

Shazia saw they way they had listened avidly to what she was saying and appreciated the fact that they were listening and trying to understand. She continued.

"However, Martha, there are people who misinterpret our religion and use it to their advantage. That is why there are those parents who force their children into marriages that they are not ready to accept. There are those men in arranged marriages who are wife beaters and men in love marriages who are also wife beaters. That means there are wife beaters and child abusers in all communities and not just in one community. The religion lays down good morals but the fact is humans often misinterpret the religion for their own selfish reasons."

Shazia had spoken words of someone older than her age, of someone who wanted them to understand that good and bad existed everywhere, regardless of which community it was. Martha smiled at Shazia, it was a sincere smile and she accepted it with another. Mrs Peters spoke very carefully as if she wanted to find the right words, not for the benefit of Shazia but for Susan, David and Martha.

"You are right in some ways about arranged marriages. When I was growing up there was more stress put on the reality of living together than love itself... like finance and accommodation. Yes, there was passion, but my mum and dad almost wanted Arthur from the beginning because he was honest, responsible and hardworking. To them he was the right match for me. It was what Shazia said about having things in common and whether the fella you married could be a breadwinner. His family would size me up on whether I could cook, run a house, do housework and really do the things necessary for a family. What counts is that each understands the other and can compromise around each other's faults," reflected Mrs Peters as an afterthought.

"I was just gonna ask though, Shazia, if you don't mind that is. Some of your blokes, Moslems, get married about four times. That's not really fair on the women," said David. Shazia had had a feeling that particular issue would come up in due course and she didn't find it offensive for David asking such a question. He had a right to ask about aspects of other people's cultures which looked strange and odd. She smiled at the big burly man who had learnt to call her father by his first name and looked at him differently now from the first time she had met him. Shazia understood that people often did not mean to ridicule her culture and way of life. There were white people she had known in her life who found her way of life strange, different from theirs and the distorted knowledge that had led them to contradictory conclusions was not entirely their doing.

"Yes David, our men are able to marry four times. However there is a history behind this aspect of polygamy. In the early days of Islam, there were many wars which left many widows with children and many orphaned young women. These women needed sanctuary from the evil intentions of enemy men. With their permission, many good Muslim men married them and extended their protection, to feed, clothe and shelter them. However a man under our religion can only marry if he can view his wives equally, that means also from the heart. At the same time he needs the permission of the first wife on whether he can marry another or not. Some women agree for their husbands to marry a second time because maybe they cannot have a relationship with him due to physical problems or because they cannot have children." Shazia wanted the people in the room to absorb what she had said for a minute and then carried on.

"However there are Muslim men who don't comply with these religious rules and go ahead and marry several times. That's because they want everything to their advantage and abuse our religion."

"No Shazia, it's because they can't keep their dicks in one place," commented Vivien sarcastically.

"It's like sometimes when a married man working in the city keeps a mistress in a flat near his office for his pleasure. At the same time he has a good time and shows what a good family man he is," said Shazia.

"But a lot of men would probably not abide by your religious coding?" Martha injected.

"It depends on how a person interprets and practices the teachings. For example you can have a cardinal who is forbidden to have sex because of his religion and yet he might have a mistress or quietly abuse a choirboy. You see there are people who are truly committed to their religion and culture and there are those who are not. People like to believe and do what they want to, the aspect is whether a person can be true to their heart."

David seemed to understand, he nodded his head as Shazia spoke and the others agreed with him. Susan was very quiet and asked Shazia,

"While we're having such a heart to heart, I want to know why is it some of the women in your community always stay at home and don't bother learning

English? Your mum made an effort and learnt English. If they're living in England they need to learn it." As far as Shazia was concerned, Susan spoke as though she thought she was Margaret Thatcher and that was one person Shazia really disliked.

"My mum wanted to learn English like so many of the Bangladeshi women who don't speak English as it would make life so much easier and to become more independent. But like many women, she felt scared and not confident about learning it. She thought people would make fun of her from her own community and from yours. My dad and we children encouraged her to learn and feel confident enough to learn and practice it. There are women like my mum who don't speak English, but would learn it if they had the right kind of support and encouragement. There are those women of my mum's generation who have gone further than learning the language and have learnt how to drive. Staying at home and looking after children is not just in our community but in yours as well. You stayed at home and looked after your children and so did your mother before you. There's nothing wrong with women wanting to stay at home to look after their children." Shazia stated and almost ran out of breath.

Susan smiled because she knew Shazia was pointing things out which were obviously true. The fact was she realised certain communities got mislabelled when facts about their way of life became distorted. One had to know and understand all aspects of a person's life to understand the full picture. Martha had then asked about Shazia's family back in Bangladesh and she had told them about the reality of living back home. She was far more prepared than her mother to understand about other people's lives and it seemed she was more like Vivien, although she had given Shazia the initial impression that she was more like her mother.

Susan listened to what Shazia said about the poverty back home in Bangladesh and finally asked, with a tinge of bitterness,

"Is that why so many of your people have come over to Britain to earn money? Because there are a lot of poor white people here too."

Shazia understood what Susan was saying. There were already many problems in Britain and the influx of newcomers made it look to many hardworking white people as if foreigners seemed to get better treatment than them.

"Susan, my father came here legally and ended up staying. He settled in this country and sent for my mum and brothers later on. Ayesha and I were born in this country and as far as I am concerned I am a British Asian. Many people in Bangladesh think that to come to England is like Dick Whittington finding his fortune in London. That's because the gap between the quality of living and life here and over there is so wide. Many people come to this country because they might be fleeing persecution or war and many people enter illegally to escape the cycle of poverty, which is a killer as well. At the same time there are many people migrating to other countries like Canada, Australia and Sweden to make a new life. People always want to improve the quality of their lives especially if they have hungry children. A person in Bangladesh might just want a well of clean water and a family here might want to live in a house with a garden to escape from living in a small flat on the twentieth floor of a high-rise tower. Everyone has needs and dreams but most people want peace."

Shazia desperately wanted Susan to understand that her people did not want to take away her country. They wanted to be part of this nation and share in its glory. They wanted to live in peace but the conflict of differences, hostility and insecurities made living in harmony with each other hard to achieve.

Vivien had being listening and then said to her sister,

"Susan, I've travelled in many countries apart from visiting Spain, not because I wanted to flaunt my money in your face but because I wanted to see how other people lived. I wanted to see other people's cultures and customs, but I also saw the sufferings of so many people along the way. I found poor people in other countries have a generous heart just like poor East Enders. I found that just like our cockney community there was a lot of friendship and loyalty amongst people in these developing communities. People suffer terribly but they don't want charity, they just want the tools to help themselves. They're proud just like the East Enders."

That particular incident helped David, Susan and Martha understand Shazia and her community a lot more. It also helped Shazia to realise that many white people needed to talk to people from her community to understand their needs and the issues in their lives. It was the foundation of a bridge to friendship.

However although Mrs Peters had grown very close to her Bangladeshi neighbours her children had mixed feelings about the situation. David and Susan were still relaxing their hostility which was always ignited by Graham's presence or remarks. It was more their torn feelings between what they had thought was right and proper and the changing circumstances which they now faced. Vivien thought that if her mother was happy knowing her neighbours and being close to them, then she should carry on for she didn't care whether the neighbours were black, Asian or white. Graham's anger was turning increasingly into poisonous venom which he was keeping under control until the right time approached. In his opinion his mother should take a stand and show the Pakis whose territory they were walking on. He was pissed off about Mrs Peters' cosy relationship with the Paki family as she was losing sight of her white heritage and her sense of patriotism.

Mrs Peters was very much aware of David and Susan's uncertainty towards her Bangladeshi neighbours. But they were trying to understand and come to terms with the fact that what they had learnt as children had been misguided and what they were learning as adults was a better way of living. Their mother recognised this and she encouraged them to understand just as she had, although she was also aware of Graham's hatred towards the Ali family. She almost felt ashamed of his feelings. Vivien was the only one who seemed to understand her mother's feelings. Having such neighbours made Mrs Peters feel safe, secure, and so much less lonely and her younger daughter had recognised this straight away. She had seen how much the Bangladeshi family had done for her mother in the sense of their friendship. Whenever her mother forgot the milk or she was short of something and could not go out because it was too late, the Ali family helped out.

Vivien had noticed her mother looked healthier, more rosy and lively. It was the company she had and Mrs Ali's cooking which she seemed to be eating on a regular basis. Mrs Peters laughed more and she seemed to read much more widely. Vivien had found a book by Maya Angelou instead of the usual Virginia Andrews woes in her mother's bedroom, given to her by Shazia. Life seemed to be getting better than it had been for Mrs Peters for a very long time. Maybe even so far back as her husband's death.

David and Susan recognised the difference in their mother, but it seemed they did not want to admit it openly. Graham on the other hand was in complete denial of the whole situation although he knew his mother looked better and healthy. However, Graham put it down to her getting over her mourning of his father. Even David and Susan could not manage to agree with him, although they didn't tell him their real thoughts.

Vivien did and Graham became very heated and began an aggressive argument with her one Sunday afternoon when they had all gone to visit their mother. After nearly nine months of watching the scenario in his mother's home, Graham had exploded.

"What you trying to say Viv? Some Pakis done a better job of caring for our mum than us?" Graham had said to her when his mother went to the bathroom.

"Yea, those Pakis as you refer to are Mum's friends. They're her neighbours who really care about her welfare. They probably do more for her than we've ever done, in a long time," replied Vivien.

"You're such a Paki lover, Viv. You're not loyal to what we stand for as a family, as a white family. Some Pakis come over here in the East End, settle down next door to Mum and con her into becoming their friend. You need to accept that you're an unmarried white woman with no children who's desperate to be anyone's friend, especially to a bunch of Pakis!"

Vivien looked at her younger brother with cold venom and spoke with an icy voice.

"Listen to me carefully, Graham. You're right. I am an unmarried white woman with no children and I'm happy. It's better than being a divorced, wife beater whose kids are scared of him, a drunk, unemployed, ignorant, middle aged white man with nothing to look forward to in his life. I have a lot of living to do and a hell of a lot to look forward to. And one of them is getting on with people whatever bloody colour they are. The point is Graham, you're a lonely, frightened man wanting to control your mother's life through your racist attitude. You'll never enjoy your life because you always feel sorry for yourself and you want others to feel sorry for you too." Vivien finally spat out. She had almost clenched her hands into fists and her eyes were flints of anger.

Susan and David sat silently watching their two younger siblings argue. They felt they were in the middle and were not willing to take sides. Family was something dear to both of them and they did not want to see a split due to outside people. At the same time, they knew deep down inside, what Graham was saying was wrong. It was David who felt he ought to speak first and he did, softly and gently.

"Listen Graham, Viv is just trying to say let Mum be happy because she's lonely here and the people next door keep an eye on her. That's really important to her. She wants to feel safe and secure. Viv, I think Graham's just looking out for Mum in his own way and you two are getting all fired up over nothing."

Graham looked at David and almost wanted to laugh in his face. He had always been a simple kind of man who didn't want too much trouble and now he spoke like a fool.

"Bruv, you really haven't caught on. The point is, we whites don't mix with coloureds, we stick together and we don't let Pakis rule our lives..." He spoke as though David had a learning difficulty.

"David," Vivien interrupted, "you mean well when you speak, but our little brother's too thick-skinned and too damn ignorant to even understand what you're trying to say. Yes I want Mum to be happy and I'm happy now she understands all people in society are people and not dirt off the street. Graham isn't looking out for Mum, he's looking out for his prejudiced ideas which he gets a kick out of. Graham's practising what the thinks is right, he thinks he's the next Enoch Powell, only in the working class form...."

"Shut up, you bitch. Fuck you with your fancy talk," snarled Graham at Vivien. Mrs Peters came in as he spoke and she quickly snapped angrily.

"What in heavens name has got into you, Graham, yelling at Vivien in that kind of language?"

"Right, Mum. Since you've come in, we best have a lot of things in the open then."

"Yes," said Susan. "I think we best clear the air because I'm getting tired of playing piggy in the middle."

Susan wanted to clear the issue of her mum's friends with Graham because she realised she had also become friendlier with them. That meant Susan did not want any embarrassing scenes with Graham's tantrums being aired, but she still found it difficult to acknowledge Graham's deep racist attitude. It did not occur to her how dangerous his attitude was and how intense it was becoming.

"What did you want to clear with me, Graham?" asked Mrs Peters. Secretly she knew exactly what he wanted to say to her and the others. Graham could not accept Mrs Peter's friendship with people from a different race, but she was going to hear him and then give him a piece of her mind that he would not forget.

"Mum, the Pakis next door ain't the same as us. They eat different, speak different, and dress different. They ain't like white people. They're dirty, for God's sake, you see them chewing something disgusting and making their teeth bloody looking. They're lazy and are taking advantage of our country's hospitality. We can't mix with them because the more we do we encourage a load more newcomers into the country. They'll come along and take our jobs, our homes and even our education system. Our kids are gonna be taught about Paki and nigger history. Look at the number of Paki doctors and nurses in jobs that's meant for white people. The British Nation is falling apart by playing host to a bunch of losers. I want you to stop talking to the lot next door and make it clear to them where we stand as a family. Yeah, use them when you need them, they need to know living in our country means they owe us favours. Don't forget my dad fought in the war and they bloody well shouldn't forget it. What do you think Mum?"

Graham spoke to Mrs Peters as if he had just opened her eyes to the mistakes she had made in the past few months. Vivien thought Graham was Hitler reborn.

Mrs Peters looked at her son in disgust, she was so angry and appalled with his Hitler speech. Who did he think he was laying the law down to her because she was his mother and she was going to make sure he did not forget that.

"Graham, brace yourself 'cause I'm gonna say a few words and you best give me all your attention. The people next door are different, I'm white and they're brown." Mrs Peters paused for a moment and saw Graham smiling with encouragement as if she was going to say the things he wanted to hear.

"That's why I didn't speak to them when I first met them. In my life I hadn't ever been friendly with people from another colour. I saw them as outsiders and I never encouraged my husband or my children to talk to people of another race. Then one day, the little girl next door spoke to me and wanted to be my friend. She reached out and touched something in my heart, my loneliness poured out of me and I reached out for her and then her family. I paused many times along the way daunted by my old bitterness of who was better off and who was not when I became friends with them. Then it dawned on me they were people like me and that you can become friends with strangers whether they're Pakis or niggers." Mrs Peters paused again for Graham was very, very quiet. His mother was not saying the things he wanted to hear. She continued.

"You talk about Paki doctors and nurses. Has it ever occurred to you that the reason there are so many Paki and nigger doctors is because many of the white people in this country are unemployable as doctors, like yourself. That's why the government encourages nurses and doctors from abroad to work here. The education system is never going to be run by coloured people because we were never taught about black or Asian history, or their sufferings and it will always be kept shrouded unless you bump into it accidentally. We were always taught how great the British were when they ruled Indian people and turned black people into slaves. You were never taught that Indians fought in the war just as the British and Americans did, which you were taught about so readily. You say about your dad talking about the war or how people suffered. You can't be half the man your dad was. My Arthur was a simple, honest and hardworking man committed to his family. A lot like the man next door, the Paki you hate." She paused again taking in a long breath and again she continued.

"I'll be friends with whom I like and I'll do what the hell I like. The family next door have done for me what you couldn't do in a lifetime. They've been there for me when I've been in need. I've stopped feeling so lonely in the place where I was born and lived all my life. I put demands on them like I've never put on you and I do things in return for them. It's called give and take - something which is alien to you. You don't know anything about friendship. You only know about yourself and your needs. Now I'm telling you once and for all, you will not order me around and place rules on me. If you want to come to my home then you stop using that foul racist language and you start giving the family next door respect. Have you got the message?"

Graham was almost trembling with rage at his mother for he had expected her to be with him. But she was willing to compromise Graham, her son and the important things he had said, for the coloured family who were now her friends. He knew he was on dangerous ground when he asked his next question.

"What about if I don't accept what you say?"

"Then, Graham, you ain't coming in my home, got that clear?" replied his mother, very clearly so Susan and David also understood.

Graham was not going to argue any further with his mother. For the time being he needed her for his own personal and selfish reasons. Graham needed to have a good dinner every week as it cut the cost of buying food, he needed to have his clothes washed and ironed and he needed a bit of extra cash now and then. He wasn't going to let that Vivien get the better of the situation so he relented for the moment.

"What you say goes, mum,"he said brightly. And with that Graham put his hands in the air as though he was surrendering to his mum and the rest of the family. Vivien was taken by surprise by his relenting attitude and was very suspicious of Graham and secretly wondered if he was up to something.

"Yes, mum. I'll do what you want," said Graham even more brightly. He really needed his mum especially as he was in debt. She always helped him out in every way she could and he really could not afford to lose that commodity.

Mrs Peters was also taken aback by Graham's readiness to accept her new friends. She knew she had spoken sternly to him. Perhaps, she thought with pride, she hadn't lost her telling off touch with her children. She did feel a little guilty with the way she had spoken to him but even as a child when Graham got a telling off, he got frightened and she always felt guilty afterwards. Maybe Graham was attempting to understand what she was trying to tell him because she was his mother. The aspect of understanding the needs of others was a difficult matter and for Graham it would be a great step. Mrs Peters felt suddenly proud that her son with his ignorant attitude was going to try to change and she appreciated that of him.

"Graham, why the sudden change?" Vivien could not resist but ask.

"People change when they hear something decent. I thought you of all people understood that Viv," said Graham, a little edgy.

"Give him a chance now, Viv," said David feeling relieved things had got cleared up between Graham and his mother. He hated feeling tense as it dampened his appetite.

"Yes Vivien. Graham understands a bit more and it's more mum he listens to than us," agreed Susan, also relieved that the difficult issues were out of the way and she hadn't needed to get her hands dirty.

Mrs Peters spoke sternly to Vivien.

"Vivien, I think you ought to realise that Graham's not all bad but there is a softer side to him than he likes to show. Don't you luv?"

"Yup, mum, spot on. I'm not into being a big softie but I still got a soft side and only you know that," said Graham smugly looking at Vivien.

"Yes, we ought to give little Graham a chance, like we always do. Let's just hope nothing backfires here," said Vivien.

"Oh, Vivien give in," scolded her mother gently.

"Yea, Sis, give us a chance," said Graham as if he was being victimised. "I'm trying real hard here and you're not exactly being encouraging."

"Okay, Graham. I'll encourage you. This folder," said Vivien taking out a black folder from her bag and showing Graham, "needs to be dropped off to Hamza. So if you don't mind, can you drop it off to him? He lives next door."

Graham really hated Vivien for she could be such a bitch. No wonder she'd done so well in her job. But he wasn't going to give into her sly way so he smiled.

"Sure, I'll take it round now." And he got up and took the folder off her and went out through the front door without looking at anyone else. They watched him, his family, as he left.

"Vivien, I don't think you're being fair on Graham," said Mrs Peters.

"Yes, Vivien, you're being really hard on him," agreed Susan.

"Yeah, Viv, ease up a bit," chorused in David.

Vivien looked at the three of them. They really believed he was willing to change his attitude but she was very suspicious of Graham and thought he was really putting on an act.

"Graham said he wanted to change, so he can start from today. I didn't do anything mean to him. I just asked him to pop a folder round to Hamza. Was that being hard on him?" Vivien asked looking at the three of them.

It was Hamza who opened the door and he nearly had a shock when he saw Graham there. He was very much aware of his attitude and the way he behaved towards people of colour. Hamza's parents went to great trouble to avoid him because they didn't want to cause a scene. However Hamza, his brother and sisters could not care when they went to visit if he was there or not. They knew this infuriated Graham.

"Is there anything I can do for you?" asked Hamza.

"No, it's what I'm doing for you," said Graham gruffly.

This did not go unnoticed on Hamza.

"Well what are you doing for me?"

"Are you Hamza?" asked Graham.

"Yeah," answered Hamza.

"Viv, sent this round," said Graham almost roughly and handed the black folder to him. Hamza took the folder from him and was about to thank him but Graham had by then just walked off. Hamza looked at him in anger and thought what a piece of shit Graham was. He wondered why Graham had come round in the first place to give him the folder which Vivien could have popped round herself. What was the point of thanking him? Graham popped back to his mum's flat and Vivien was quick to speak.

"That was fast Graham. Did you talk to any of them or did you leave the folder outside their front door?"

"No Vivien, I knocked on the door and Hamza opened it and I gave him the folder," said Graham, getting touchy.

"Leave it now, Vivien," Mrs Peters warned sternly. She wanted to give Graham a chance.

"All right, mum, let's leave Graham alone," said Vivien.

It seemed to Mrs Peters that on that afternoon Graham had finally understood why she wanted to be friends with her Bangladeshi neighbours. She thought she had made many issues very clear to Graham. Issues which as a child growing up years ago he had been misguided on. Mrs Peters felt as though Graham, for the first time in many years, had achieved something positive by trying to acknowledge her friendship with her coloured neighbours. As far as she was concerned her younger son and youngest child was endeavouring to put his racist beliefs aside and broaden his horizons. Graham was trying to change his way of thinking and the ignorance and arrogance he was steeped in.

****

Every Tuesday Mrs Peters went to the Post Office to cash her social security. On this day she paid her various bills, did a large part of her weekly shopping and always bought a fish and chip dinner from her local chip shop.

95

However, this Tuesday, she was collecting a little of her savings to give to Vivien to book her holiday somewhere nice and exotic as Vivien put it. Vivien would go with her. She'd been on Mrs Peter's back for ages to go away with her abroad for a long time. Vivien had even offered to pay for her trip but Mrs Peters still liked to pay her own way if she had the capabilities to do so. Someone watched Mrs Peters in the post office collect her money, go and pay her bills and do her shopping. That same person followed and watched her buy her lunch and then walk home. That same person watched her go into her flat and come out an hour later to pop into her neighbour's home for a visit. By then it was very late afternoon. The same person watched Mrs Ali open the door to Mrs Peters and smile and invite her in. Gradually dusk drew near and the person watched and waited and planned their move.

She was teaching Mrs Ali a crochet stitch she had learnt as a young girl, which Mrs Ali had seen on one of Mrs Peter's shawls and had insisted on being taught. Mrs Ali knew much about needlework and was always looking to improve her skills and she found her neighbour such a good teacher. So Mrs Peters sat for ages with her friend and together they enjoyed each other's company and did not realise how late it was until Mrs Ali got ready to do her prayers and that was when she took her leave.

****

The person now stood there in the shadows, waiting like a vulture… evil, preparing for its attack. The person heard the front door open and the old woman came in and shut the door behind her. It was dusk and the night was not far away. Outside the streetlights gradually came on one at a time. The intruder was worried if the old woman noticed their shadow from behind the wall unit so the person adjusted their standing position and waited. The woman was singing to herself, singing an old hymn. She was religious just like her neighbours. Their different faiths had paved ways for them to understand each other where others had failed. She sang…
"Morning has broken,
Black Bird has spoken,
Like the first morning,"

Yes, a black bird will speak and the morning will break with the act of what will happen, thought the person in the shadows. I'll just hurt you a little, thought the person, enough to achieve my goal.

Mrs Peters continued singing as she took off her coat and put her keys on the tea table. Quietly the intruder approached from behind the wall unit and crept up behind her. The person lifted the wooden bat he had found in Mrs Peter's flat and brought it down against the back of her head. The impact and shock sent Mrs Peters on her knees as if kneeling before God. She fell gradually to the floor with a dozen images floating in her head. The person grabbed her handbag but, as he did so, Mrs Peters saw the hand that had struck her. More than the pain of being physically hurt, Mrs Peters felt pain, like a sharp object plunge through her into her heart, for she had seen the colour of the hand which picked up the handbag near her. The ultimate betrayal of the trust she had in that person was so painful and shocking, enough to send her reeling into an unconscious sleep where she could run away from her painful knowledge. She could feel her whole world collapsing around her. The person looked at Mrs Peters and stood silently for a moment as though giving her a mark of respect.

Silently as the person had entered, he left for home. Outside a traffic warden was waiting to be collected by her pick up bus. She saw the person leaving Mrs Peter's home. She noticed how he huddled his body and hurriedly walked near the dustbins to dispose of something.

The traffic warden found the person's behaviour strange, constantly looking over his shoulder and walking fast, almost sprinting. The person disappeared then into the distance and the traffic warden didn't give it another thought. All she was interested now was getting home and eating her dinner, she was hungry and tired.

CHAPTER SEVEN

. It was Monday morning when Hamza was walking past Mrs Peters' front door and noticed it had not been properly shut. He looked inside and called out her name but no one answered. Strange, thought Hamza, his neighbour never left her door open and went out. He knew how she hated going out in the dark and opening doors to strangers. He had often sat with her when workmen had come to fix something, so he walked in, calling her name. No-one answered and he carried on walking into the sitting room. He was shocked as he found the elderly woman lying on the floor with her face down. She looked as though she was sleeping, but there was a gash on the back of her head and the blood had gradually dried up.

At first Hamza thought she had fallen, but when he noticed the back of her head, he knew something was wrong. Mrs Peters seemed to have been attacked, especially as the contents of her handbag were strewn everywhere. For a good few seconds Hamza was rooted to where he stood, shocked and horrified at what he gathered had happened. Slowly and shaking, he retreated and ran back to his home. Hamza banged on the door and shouted in Bengali for his parents to hurry up. It was Mrs Ali who opened the door looking annoyed with her son.

"Hamza, what's the matter with you? You're always in a hurry."

"Shh, there's something wrong with Mrs Peters. I think she's been attacked. Where's dad?" Hamza ranted.

"What are you talking about? Mrs Peters doesn't go out that early in the morning. If she does, she sometimes takes me with her." Mrs Ali could not comprehend what her son was talking about.

"No, you don't understand, she's been attacked in her home."

By now Mr Ali had joined them in the sitting room and caught the last of what Hamza said.

"What's going on?"

"Come with me, both of you," said Hamza.

Mr and Mrs Ali followed Hamza out of their home and through the front door of Mrs Peters' home and into her sitting room. Like their son, both were equally horrified at what met their eyes.

"Oh, my God!" whispered Mrs Ali in a frightened voice.

"Call the police and an ambulance, Hamza and hurry up. Tell them to be quick," said Mr Ali. Hamza ran into his home to call the police and to get away from the terrible scene.

Mr Ali went closer and touched Mrs Peters' hand; he could just faintly feel a pulse so there was hope that Mrs Peters was still alive. He called his wife to check urgently whether Hamza had called the police and ambulance. Mrs Ali went to look for Hamza and found him on the phone. He was speaking fast and she could tell the urgency in his tone. She hurried back to Mrs Peters' flat and informed her husband that Hamza was on the phone, then looked at Mrs

Peters and felt numb.

"It's serious isn't it?" she said in Bengali to her husband. His eyes spoke his answer.

Hamza was getting annoyed with the woman from the police department. He was trying to tell her the seriousness of the situation, the bitch wanted to know how he had managed to get into the flat without a key. The policewoman on the line was more interested in trying to find out what ethnic origin Hamza was when he had told her his name. She then went on to find out what kind of friendship or relationship he had with Mrs Peters, especially as he was a Bangladeshi and she a white woman. Hamza had never felt more pissed off in his life than with the bitch of a woman on the phone. He was torn between trying to make her understand the dire situation in hand and getting into a debate with her bloody prejudices. Finally the conversation ended with the policewoman sending a couple of police officers and the ambulance to the scene.

Hamza had slammed the phone down and rushed back to his father's side. His mother had covered Mrs Peters with a blanket. There was a dreadful silence in the room because the family had to face the police who were as unpredictable as the British weather - sometimes sunny, sometimes grey and sometimes icy cold. The screaming of the police sirens and the wailing of the ambulance could be heard racing towards their building. Mr Ali and Hamza looked at each other and together they went outside to face the police while Mrs Ali stayed with Mrs Peters.

Mr Ali and Hamza stood outside Mrs Peters flat. Already there were a few people standing around and staring; there were both white and coloured faces amongst the gathering. They had mingled together as they heard and saw the approaching police cars and ambulance. The police car stopped and two white policemen got out, they straddled towards Mr Ali and Hamza.

"Right, which of you lovely boys is Hamza Ali?" asked the older officer without introducing himself.

"I am and this is my dad," said Hamza. His heart was sinking; the police officer looked more like a Nazi officer than part of the British Police Constabulary.

"Right, you best show me what's happened to the old lady, the paramedics are here."

The ambulance crew had already jumped from their vehicle and were pushing a stretcher towards Mrs Peters' flat. They looked much friendlier than the two police officers and the older paramedic spoke to Mr Ali.

"All right, mate, you best show me the way and tell me what happened."

Hamza started explaining as he and his father showed the ambulance crew where Mrs Peters lay with the policemen following behind.

They found Mrs Ali still near to Mrs Peters on the floor and the paramedics smiled at her when they entered the sitting room. The older paramedic knelt down to start an examination while the other paramedic prepared the medical equipment.

"What time did you find her like this then, mate?" asked the younger paramedic.

"Just under half an hour ago," said Hamza as his parents nodded in agreement.

"I see you tried to warm her up a bit. That's good thinking," said the older paramedic.

"It was my mum who covered her," Hamza said. "Is she going to be all right?"

The paramedic was about to answer when the older police officer abruptly interrupted.

"That's enough questions and whether the victim is going to be all right or not, you'll know later. Right let's get you out of here so I can ask some questions and get some answers as to what's happened."

Mrs Ali ignored the police officers and turned to the paramedics.

"Mrs Peters, my friend, please take care of her."

"I said get out of the room or don't we understand English here," the older officer almost snarled.

"Listen, mate, the lady's a friend. She's just showing some concern for the injured person. Just chill out a bit," said the young paramedic angrily to the policeman.

"By calling us quickly the family have done a lot for the old woman's chances of living," added the older paramedic. Mrs Ali smiled at them almost in gratitude for their encouraging support. They smiled back as the Ali family filed out of Mrs Peters' flat.

The small crowd forming in the streets watched the Ali family and many of the spectators were white.

"What's going on mate?" asked a tattooed white man.

"Some old lady's got attacked in her home. Looks like she knew who it was," the younger police officer volunteered, glancing at the Ali family in front of him.

"She was a white old woman," added the older police officer quietly. The same black traffic warden who had seen a person leaving Mrs Peters' home the night of the attack also heard this piece of conversation as she stood with the rest of the crowd. She was working on this patch of the estate this week. She was good at her job and she mentally noted the conservation she had overheard.

"We'll ask you a few questions in your home," stated the younger police officer and the older one nodded his head in agreement.

Mr and Mrs Ali humbly showed the police officers into their sitting room, while Hamza felt dismay at their obnoxious behaviour. Mr Ali asked them to sit down. The officers settled themselves down and the younger one got out his note pad.

"The council has done a hell a lot of decorating for you especially for a council flat," said the older police officer.

"No, I own the property. My sons and I done the decorating. We worked hard on the flat. The council paid for nothing. It was our own hard work," Mr Ali replied quietly. He hated the way the police officer assumed things.

"Oh, you own your property. I suppose you think you're living in some kind of mansion and you're some sort of king," the police officer remarked rolling his eyes and his colleague smirked. "Well, mate I'm Sergeant Blakely and this is PC Woods. We'll start asking the questions. I see you don't need an interpreter. Who found the old lady next door and what's her name?"

"Her name is Mrs Peters and I found her. Shouldn't you tell the paramedics her name and contact her children?" asked Hamza.

"Don't tell me how to do my job, sonny boy," said Blakely. Mr Ali indicated for Hamza to be quiet. "Paul, get round there and find out what the paramedics are doing and start getting the old lady's details." PC Woods went off to do what he was told.

"Right, you," said Blakely turning his attention back to Hamza, "how did you get into an old lady's home?"

"I was on my way to uni and I saw her front door wide open and she doesn't usually leave it like that so I went in to find out what had happened…"

"You see, mate, what I don't follow is how you just went in as if you knew her…"

"That's because Mrs Peters and my family are neighbours, close neighbours. We're all friends; we know each other, help each other out. I mean Mrs Peters just came in yesterday and spent the afternoon with my mum. We're almost like family now," Hamza interrupted.

"So how long have you all known Mrs Peters?" Blakely asked. His eyes suggested that he did not believe a single word Hamza had said.

"Since we moved here about nine months ago," said Mr Ali. The police officer was goading his son and he prayed that Hamza would not let this attitude get the better of his character.

"That's a bit short notice to declare you're all family. Nice cosy picture you're trying to create here," Blakely added as if he had discovered some kind of important evidence.

"Look, we know her children as well. I can give you their phone numbers so you can at least inform them of what's happened," said Hamza.

"No, need to, Sarj. We got one of the old lady's sons next door. He dropped by to see if she needed anything," said PC Woods as he walked back into the Ali family's home. He had left the front door open when he had gone to Mrs Peters flat.

"Ah, this will be interesting. We'll see how much everyone's all close and family," Woods added. "Come along with me."

Hamza wondered who it could be - David or Graham as he and his parents walked behind Sergeant Blakely. His heart sank as he saw Graham follow the stretcher with Mrs Peters lying on it, an oxygen mask covering her face.

Graham was obviously distressed and the mainly white spectators outside the flat, noting his distress, were quietly in sympathy with him. A few were gently shouting out.

"She'll be all right mate, you hang on there."

Hamza had a dreadful feeling things were not going to work out in his favour. Graham turned around and saw the Ali family with Hamza.

"You filthy Paki bastard. You done her in," he shrieked. It was enough for the crowd to hear and work out what could have happened. It was obvious Graham had been informed who had found Mrs Peters and who he suspected of the attack. To the Ali family's dismay, the two police officers almost encouraged the crowd to turn their angry discovery on to the Ali family as Blakely shouted out to Graham in support.

"Don't worry, mate, we've got him in hand and we won't let him off the hook that easily. It don't matter if he's an ethnic minority."

"Yea, mate, just rely on us, we'll do him in," said Woods.

Hamza felt numb hearing this and he suddenly felt his father's protective arm around his shoulders for his face must have shown his emotions.

The paramedics were the only ones who had the courage to say to Graham,

"No, mate, you got it all wrong. He did your mother a favour. In fact he saved her."

But somehow their loud and clear voices seemed to be ignored by the white crowd and by the two police officers who quickly beckoned for the paramedics to go. The crowd was aware that Graham was not getting into the ambulance but edging towards Hamza. The paramedics were calling him to get in but he turned around and said,

"No, you lot go on with me mum. I'll catch up later 'cause I've got unfinished business here."

The paramedics wasted no more time and sped off wailing through the streets and Graham proceeded towards Hamza ensuring the crowd saw his anguished face. Hamza wasn't sure what Graham was going to do but PC Woods was walking towards him with a sympathetic look.

"Why the fuck did you do it?" he screamed at Hamza. The young Bangladeshi man looked at him in bewilderment and saw his accusing glare, but his mother had watched and waited and now she stepped quietly in front of her son.

"My son done nothing wrong," she said firmly. "My son is innocent. He find your mother on the floor and called help."

Her voice was clear and strong and it rang through the crowd, but in vain. The senior police officer looked at her and said sharply,

"If you don't mind can you keep your trap shut? This man's upset and your lip ain't helping." He was actually shocked at her behaviour, for the petite woman sounded so strong and fearless of the situation around her. Most of all he found it a surprise she spoke English.

Mr Ali echoed every word.

"My wife is right, my son do nothing wrong."

"We'll decide that," said Sergeant Blakely pointing a finger at him. Graham was angry and wiping his tears and repeating "Me mum, me mum."

"Shouldn't you call Viv, Susan and David?" Hamza asked loud enough for the crowd to hear. He wanted the crowd to know that he and his family had been friends with Mrs Peters and her other children. He was desperate for them to be aware of this.

"I'll fucking call them in my own time," Graham said gritting his teeth. He was well aware of Hamza's intentions.

"We'll give them a ring," said PC Woods.

"I can ring Viv, if you like?" volunteered Hamza.

"Are you taking the piss?" screamed out Graham.

"No, I'm trying to help," Hamza said.

"Help out? You nearly fucking murdered her," said Graham with an incredulous look and loud enough for the onlookers to hear.

"No I did not," Hamza shouted. He was not going to be accused of something he had not done.

"Yes, you fucking did." With that Graham tried to punch Hamza, but the punch fell on Mrs Ali who went reeling to the ground. Hamza seeing the violence against his mother tried to push Graham away, but the two police officers, noting Hamza's attempts, immediately grabbed Hamza against the wall. Sergeant Blakely said with relish,

"Right, you're nicked. You'll have ample time to answer our questions down at the station."

"What are you talking about? What have I done?" Hamza said helplessly. Mr and Mrs Ali were protesting along with their son, but their protests fell on deaf ears as Blakely and Woods handcuffed Hamza and walked him to the police car. The crowd booed at Hamza and his parents and cheered the officers and Graham along. Blakely radioed for extra officers explaining the situation and Graham stood by while a few people came up to him and patted his back.

Graham looked over at Hamza in the car with almost a look of triumph on his face. Hamza stared back and felt Graham's twisted feeling of triumph. It was as though he was taking advantage of the white crowds' sympathy in his time of tragedy. He looked on at his father arguing with the police officers for his release and his mother crying. Hamza called to her in Bengali and Mrs Ali walked over to the police car.

"Don't worry. Just tell Bhai and Shazia. Try to ring and tell Vivien as soon as you can. She'll help. She knows her brother well," Hamza suggested. He saw Vivien as a way forward in seeking the truth about what had happened to her mother.

"Yes, my son I will do that," Mrs Ali said in a trembling voice. She touched her son's head and went back inside her home to phone Yusuf and try to contact Vivien. There would be a way forward with their help.

Graham, in the meantime, was stirring up a heated feeling amongst the crowd, a feeling of hatred towards the Ali family, especially against the colour of their skin. He was enticing and encouraging racial hatred amongst the often peaceful white people who lived on and around the estate. He was using his mother's attack as a way of centring attention on his deep-rooted prejudices.

"Yeah luv," Graham was saying to a middle-aged woman wiping his tears, "me mum took that Paki family under her wing. I warned her, I told her not to be so generous. But she did and that bastard just waited for his time and pounced. These Pakis, they live off our British goodwill and smack us in the back."

"I didn't think some of them were that bad. I mean I don't know that family very well, but you never know these things. Anyone can stab you in the back. And like they are different from us. They haven't got no morals. Do you wanna cuppa, luv 'cause I can get you one? It'll help you," the woman said, giving him a warm hug.

It was the old fashioned East End tradition coming to the surface, of rallying round someone in a time of need and distress and Graham was revelling in it. It was part of his character to be the centre of sympathetic attention which was something his mother had sadly shaped into his personality. The crowd continued to debate about how British whites were suffering and who was to blame. Issues about housing, health, crime, unemployment, education and asylum seekers, were all covered by the crowd and the final conclusion was that the rich got richer, the poor got poorer. The Pakis, niggers and Chinks and anyone who was not a true white got the advantages of getting a better deal. Graham helped to steer the debate in that direction with off beat comments here and there, his eyes full of tears.

To the two police officers who smiled at Graham, he was doing nothing wrong. They obviously didn't want to arrest him for encouraging racial hatred since they were indirectly encouraging it as well. However, all did not go unnoticed by the traffic warden who had witnessed what had taken place the night before and saw what was going on now. She had been standing and watching from afar for the last two hours. She had later been joined by her colleague, a middle aged white man who was also shocked at the behaviour of the two police officers and the crowd and most of all, Graham. It was the traffic warden who had stopped her colleague from commenting on the officers' actions because she had wanted to show him how white police officers could treat people of colour with the authority they held.

However, even she now wanted to go and scream at the two police officers. She disliked what she saw in front of her and believed she could help them to find out who had attacked the old white woman. Her name was Jackie Simmons and she went over to the officers, followed by her colleague.

The two police officers were smiling in silent agreement with Graham about something he was saying to the crowd. The surrounding crowd started mumbling in agreement and slowly their voices rose in a need to find a scapegoat for the betrayal that was presented to them. Graham was using their emotional sympathy to bring out any problems they had, be it a pent up grudge of their social or economic situation. He was goading them into a different walk of life, an extreme prejudiced walk of life, which he knew could bring out the worst in a human character. And all the time Hamza looked on, seeing the bleak and bitter future, which the day's twist of events, would bring. He knew when a group felt they had been attacked by a different group - a different race - it was only natural to cling on to each other and become stronger and also to seek revenge. Hamza suddenly remembered the naturalist Charles Darwin's words.

"When two races of men meet, they act precisely like two species of animals. They fight each other, eat each other…"

Hamza watched how Graham was manipulating the crowd and knew instinctively, the stench of danger that would come in the near future. He knew it like he had known the smell of racist danger as a child, of its poisonous fumes, which could engulf the very best of natures.

Mrs Ali had by now informed Yusuf on his mobile, who said he was on his way back from a class. She also found Vivien's mobile number and phoned her leaving a message on her answer phone. It had been a panicky sort of message with broken sentences but somehow Mrs Ali had made it clear it was urgent that Vivien contact her as soon as possible. She looked out of her kitchen window watching the crowd talking loudly with Graham. Her son was in the car and Mr Ali was telling the police officers about his son's innocence. She knew the crowd was feeling anger towards the attack on a white elderly woman and understood. She felt their growing resentment towards her son and her family and the rest of the Bangladeshi community. Mrs Ali saw another police car approaching towards her home, but at that moment the phone broke into her thoughts.

She ran to answer the phone. It was Vivien.

"Hello, is that Mrs Ali?"

"Yes, yes. Is it Vivien?"

"Yes, it's me. I got your message. What's going on?" Vivien asked apprehensively. She hadn't quite understood the message Mrs Ali had left on her phone but she had understood the urgency.

"Vivien, your mum got attack and in hospital. Hamza found her and now Graham and police blame Hamza for the attack," Mrs Ali said all in a rush.

"Oh, my God!" Vivien cried out. She felt shocked for she had always imagined getting a call that her mother had been taken seriously ill. She had never foreseen her mother getting attacked and a friend of the family being blamed for it.

"Oh, God!" Vivien repeated again.

"Vivien, please my son, we stay with your mum and hold hand. We call ambulance and police. Ambulance takes her away. I pray for her. Hamza get blame. We no wrong do," Mrs Ali was crying as she spoke.

"I'm coming down, I don't believe Hamza hurt my mum. Graham, where is he?" Vivien asked. She did not believe for a second Hamza or any member of the Ali family would hurt her mother. Vivien would find out what the hell was happening and she would find the answers.

"Graham outside now with lots of white people. He hates us and he make people and police hate us. Hamza in police car with hands tied," Mrs Ali replied tearfully.

"Christ! What the hell is Graham playing at?" Vivien almost screamed, partly out of anger and partly distress. "You're telling me Graham's outside having his fucking racist debate and my mum's alone in hospital. Do Susan and David know what's going on?" Vivien had never spoken in such a manner to Mrs Ali.

"No, I not think so," said Mrs Ali, her senses alert to the facts that Vivien had pointed out. How could Graham not be at the hospital with his mother when she needed her loved ones near her in her darkest hour?

"Mrs Ali, are you still there? Are you telling me Mum's alone in hospital and Graham's listening to his own voice?" said Vivien dangerously.

"Yes, yeah… right, right." Mrs Ali assured, noting Vivien's tone.

The phone went dead; Vivien was on her way down to the East End and Mrs Ali felt relieved, hopeful that things would be put right. She went back outside and saw that the police car Hamza was in was no longer there. However there were other officers going into Mrs Peters' flat and a large part of the area surrounding the flat had been sectioned off.

Mrs Ali saw Graham taking phone numbers from the crowd and giving his number out. He had finally made a few more friends than Scott and Daniel, but what a way to socialise. She noticed her husband looking ahead, a look of despair on his face, desperate to get his son home. Mrs Ali walked over to him and spoke gently in Bengali.

"Vivien is coming. She doesn't believe Hamza attacked her mother. She's angry why Graham's not in hospital beside his mother." She spoke as though it was some sort of consolation for the way Hamza had been taken away.

Mr Ali looked at Graham and then his wife as if he was analysing the future and said just as gently,

"Even if Hamza comes home, I don't think we'll be living in peace till it's made clear who attacked Mrs Peters. And God help us, if it's one of our people. From now on we have to be careful, we have to watch over our children more closely and hope that they remain safe. We have to ensure we all avoid any confrontations. Especially, our sons."

His face showed the signs of a father planning the future survival of his family in the face of extreme predatory danger. In that moment Mrs Ali remembered her early years of racial abuse and she realised from her husband's words that it would soon be coming back to haunt her and her family in the future. It was only a matter of time. Rokiya Ali's heart beat fast and she felt as though her dreams and her world were collapsing around her.

She knew she had to be strong, for she was a woman.

****

Vivien pulled up on the kerb near to where Jackie Simmons and her colleague were standing. She got out of the car and said almost irritably. "My mum's just been attacked and I have to talk to my neighbours and the coppers, so let me leave the car and don't give me a ticket."

"Yeah go on. I hope you have better luck with the police than I did. Your brother seems to be the only one in everyone's good books apart from your mum."

"What do you mean? You haven't had much luck with the police? And as for my brother I'll sort him out."

"Look, darling, me and my colleague went over to the police to ask if we can have a word in private. I have some information that may be of interest to you and the coppers, about who attacked your mum."

"They didn't give you a chance to speak to them in private," Vivien stopped in her tracks and her comment was more of a statement.

"Darling, I am black and they didn't even bother looking at me, even though I'm in some kind of uniform. I think you know what I am talking about. I wanted to help out, but the law ain't listening especially scum coppers like those two over there," Jackie continued as she pointed to Blakely and Woods. They were engrossed in a deep conversation with a senior police officer.

"Yea, Jackie's right. Those two think this is some kind of holy war especially as your brother's trying to be a martyr." Peter Smith, Jackie's white colleague added.

"Your brother should have gone in the ambulance with your mum, but he's got no feelings left in him. He said he had a few things to sort out and I reckon the Bangladeshi boy's going to be the one who'll be sorted out soon," Jackie Simmons said ominously.

"Listen, let me take your name and number or I'll give you mine. Which ever way, I've got to talk to you and I'll find a decent copper, one who listens and doesn't act the big boy," Vivien said. "I need your help and I'd really appreciate it."

"Darling, I'll give you my name and number and we'll have a chat. But find a bloody good copper though, especially with what I've got to say," Jackie replied warmly but at the same time her tone held a warning. And so Vivien took Jackie and Peter's details and told them to hang around for a bit.

Vivien walked over to Graham who was with Blakely and Woods and the senior police officer. She looked a stark difference to her brother in her expensive city suit and the authoritative manner in the way she walked. Graham saw her approaching.

"Sis, Mum's been attacked and it's that bloody Hamza," he cried out.

"Shut the fuck up. You're talking a load of shit. Why the hell didn't you go with the ambulance crew since you turned up when Mum was discovered by

Hamza? You didn't even bother informing me or Susan and David. Hamza's mum had to ring me and let me know. I'm going to the hospital and you're not coming with me. You've just stood around and wanted some attention from this lot so you could ram your racist philosophy down their throats. You shouldn't be accusing people of things they haven't done, but then I suppose you had enough encouragement to do so. I'm going to find out what the hell's going on and why the hell those two bastards arrested an innocent boy?" Vivien finished off nodding her head towards Blakely and Woods. Her face showed her determination and her stark intelligence.

Graham was completely taken aback by his sister's attitude and the crowd had become subdued. Blakely and Woods suddenly became interested in their notebooks but their senior police officer smiled as he took their notebooks from them. The crowd and the two police officers had not expected such an outburst and it really was not going down too well. They had all assumed the rest of the Peters family would have the same attitude as Graham Peters. Perhaps if David and Susan had turned up, they might have reflected a little of Graham's attitude.

Vivien walked over to Blakely and Woods.

"Now, if you two gentlemen would be kind enough to give me the details of where my Mum's been taken to I'd like to be with her. And I'd also like your names."

"Yes, Madam." The younger of the two police officers said. "I'll write everything down for you."

"We can always take you there if you'd like," Blakely smiled as he made his offer and continued, "we still need to talk to you about your mother's attack."

"No thanks, I'll make my own way. And well, you'll know where to find me then won't you. You can ask your questions, or are you going to get that all mixed up as well?" Vivien said icily. She hated Blakely and then she turned to the other police officer and said, "I presume, you're a senior to these minors. I'd like to talk to you in private when you have the time. It's important; you might be interested in what I have to say."

Detective Sergeant Brown obliged and gave his details. As he did so Mrs Ali came running out of her flat with Mr Ali behind.

"Vivien, Vivien," she called out in apprehension pronouncing the V as a B in her haste. "You come. At last someone to your mum."

"Hello, luv." Vivien called back warmly, aware the crowd, the police and her brother were watching the interaction with mixed thoughts. "I'm going to the hospital."

"I go with you. I see your mother. She my friend. Mr Ali, he go police station. Yusuf already at police station." Mrs Ali said taking Vivien's hand, who, in turn hugged the woman.

"Viv, give us a lift," whined Graham.

"Fuck you," Vivien gritted through her teeth. "You should have been there at the hospital with Mum from the start, but you were too busy airing your voice." With that Vivien walked towards the black traffic warden who was still waiting for her with Mrs Ali. She heard what Graham said and ignored him as though he was a spoilt child.

"Fuck you, too," snapped Graham aggressively. He had had just about enough of Vivien's high and mighty attitude and he was pissed off with her as well, because the crowd in turn were beginning to become a little too quiet. Graham was desperately trying to keep them in the spirit which he had created. So he turned around to the crowd.

"This sister of mine ain't married, got no kids and most of all she's a Paki and nigger lover. Get the picture. Anyway I was wondering, could one of yours give us a lift to the hospital?"

There was a little bit of mumbling amongst the crowd, but everyone suddenly seemed to be wondering whether or not they should give Graham a lift. He looked around at the crowd and waited for someone to respond but no one seemed to want to offer him a lift. They were all wondering what they should do and questioned Graham's words inside their heads, each with their own private opinion, fearful to voice them in case others did not agree. Graham still waited, an anger building up inside him. These people were his people and they should not be taking such a time to offer their assistance or help. They should be standing by him just as they had done earlier.

Suddenly a man appeared from the back of the crowd. He'd been watching the crowd and their response to Graham and wondering if anyone would offer a lift, but no one had. The man would have offered help immediately, but he had wanted to see who else would stand by Graham and his words. None had offered and he had quickly stepped out to ensure that the feelings Graham had created earlier were not lost completely on the crowd.

"Yea, mate, I'll give you a lift. You need all the help you can get at a time like this. Your slag of a sister ain't much of a help." With that, the man put out his hand and shook Graham's hand. "My name's Derek George Benton. Come on, we'll go straight away. We're all by you, mate, you ain't alone."

Graham looked at the man before him, a bearded bald man wearing tight jeans and boots. He had a white T-shirt with the flag of St George on it. He had two gold teeth in the front and had a slight beer belly. Both his arms had the Union Jack tattooed on them. The man was in his late thirties. He was the kind of person Graham admired and would respect. And he smiled in appreciation. "Thanks, mate. You're doing me a great favour."

"No, it's no favour. It's what we should be doing for each other. Looking out for each other, our own," countered Derek, looking at the crowd. Graham smiled for Derek and he were going to get on just fine. Graham's face was all lit up with the knowledge he had someone on his side. He followed Derek to his worn out brown fiesta. They both got in and drove off.

****

Vivien and Mrs Ali had now got into the car and were heading towards the hospital. A police car followed them. Mr Ali had already left to go to the police station. The crowd gradually dispersed with the seeds of patriotic thoughts gently sewn in through Graham's words and the man who had suddenly appeared from the crowd. They went home to contemplate what should be done in response to such an attack on a frail old white woman. Some thought of the old fashioned East End theme of a collection, or a prayer at the old lady's local parish church. However, others had more serious and harsher approaches in response to such an attack. An eye for an eye was what some wanted to keep white honour in place. But an eye for an eye made the world blind voiced others quietly.

The Bangladeshi families, looking from behind their curtains at the scene, were wondering what lay ahead in the coming week and what would happen to their lives. They could feel the tension the crowd felt over the attack. It was something their own community felt from time to time when one of their own got attacked. Families found it hard to contain the younger generation, hell bent on seeking revenge, for they were so much more volatile and quick to act than the older passive generation. Generations change over the years and the passive attitude of the older generation was almost hated by the younger one. To them it was a sign of weakness.

On the way to the hospital, Vivien called both David and Susan to tell them what had happened. They were both shocked, David almost started to cry. He had always been soft but they were both on their way to the hospital. She hadn't told them about Hamza. Vivien would tell them when she saw them face-to-face. The hospital staff were very helpful but they seemed to find it surprising that Vivien had a Bangladeshi woman with her as a friend of the family. Mrs Ali and Vivien had reached the hospital before Graham and his new friend. They had found out Mrs Peters had been admitted to the Intensive Care Unit. The doctor there greeted them and before he allowed Vivien and Mrs Ali to see her, he explained to them her condition.

"She's had a terrible blow to the head and she's lost a lot of blood. Mrs Peters has lapsed into a coma because of her head injuries. However her vital signs seem stable at the moment, obviously that could change any minute. I must stress to you that until she breathes on her own, I'm not in a position to say what the future holds for her. I'm sorry you may find me a little straight forward but it's best you get the full picture. Otherwise your version of the reality might be a little cloudy."

Vivien understood and as much as she could, she explained to Mrs Ali about her mother's condition. Mrs Ali understood and her tears indicated her feelings. Together they walked into the room where Mrs Peters lay; a ventilator, pipes, tubes and monitors were in operation to keep her alive. Together the two women stared at the woman who was causing tears to flow. That was when Vivien prayed for her mother to live and be able to enjoy more years of the life she loved. Just as Vivien and Mrs Ali went in, Graham and

Derek arrived. The doctor explained the situation to them and added that Mrs Peters could have only two visitors at a time. He also added Mrs Peters already had two visitors with her. Graham knew who they were and his eyes became cloudy. He waited until Vivien and Mrs Ali came out and looked at them as though he wanted to kill them both with his bare hands. The doctor was shocked at his reaction but said nothing. He would warn the nurses that there might be trouble with this family and security should be warned beforehand.

Vivien and Mrs Ali left the hospital and drove back home. The place was still taped off and a lone police officer stood watching the scene. Shazia was standing outside the flat as they approached. She came up to Vivien's car and smiled wearily. Shazia had already been told what had happened by other Bangladeshi families.

"Vivien, how's your mum?"

"She'll be all right. I know she's going to pull through. She's on a ventilator but if she can breathe on her own, then there's some definite hope."

"Mum, you stay at home because someone has to collect Ayesha from school. I'm going to the police station," Shazia said.

"I'll take you there because that's where I'm going. Come on let's go. I know about Hamza and it's all bullshit. I'll clear that for him"

"Go, Shazia. Go with Vivien but careful," Mrs Ali said smiling and touching her daughter's hair. She felt afraid for her, for all her children. Mrs Ali went home and Shazia got into the car and again Vivien drove off from where her mother had been attacked. They both wondered what was happening to Hamza.

Vivien and Shazia walked into the police station and found Yusuf arguing with the police officer behind the desk about wanting to see Hamza. It almost broke Shazia's heart to see her older brother fighting to have the right to see Hamza who was being detained there for something he had not done. She saw how easy people in authority could manipulate their powers over the ones they governed, especially over people of colour. Such people thought it was so easy to walk all over the people from her community. Shazia promised herself she would not let them talk to her as though she was some slave girl imported from abroad for their services, nor would she let them get the better of her.

"Look, mate, we'll let you see him when we want you to, not when you want to," said the police officer.

"We've been here for nearly two hours and we're still being told to wait until you're ready. This is worse than going to casualty. Hamza has rights and you lot are abusing them." Yusuf usually a calm and placid person was feeling increasingly angry as time went by.

"Don't lay the law down to me 'cause I am the law," bellowed the officer.

"Well act like the bloody law and not a Nazi police officer."

"Listen, Boy, you trying to accuse me of something. 'Cause if you are, you best spit it out 'cause I don't like people who beat around the bush," said the officer darkly. Shazia thought, he thinks he's such a big man with his attitude.

"I'm accusing of you of something. I want to know what crime my brother has committed and why he's being held here. I want to know if my brother's rights have been made known to him and why it's taking so long for my father to see him. Have you actually charged him with anything?" Shazia spoke her words softly with a hint of danger. She must have struck a chord in the officer, for he replied at once.

"We, young lady, we can keep anyone whom we suspect of having or withholding information, for questioning in our cells."

"And after that you have to release him." Yusuf smiled at his sister and Vivien, feeling relieved to see them. Mr Ali stood up when he saw his daughter and Vivien. He had been sitting down and was feeling suddenly old and tired.

"And perhaps Hamza may have a few words to say about the manner in which he was arrested," said Vivien smiling at the police officer.

"And are you their solicitor?" mimicked the officer back.

"No, I'm Mrs Peters' daughter," Vivien replied registering the shock and embarrassment on the officer's face. "I've come to see a Detective Sergeant Brown," she continued.

The officer looked surprised at the woman's words. He looked at the group in front of him, Mr Ali, Shazia and Vivien. He could not comprehend why Vivien was with the Ali family when he had heard from the other officers that the Paki in Cell B was responsible for the racist attack on a white, elderly lady, his neighbour in fact, whom he had been harassing for a long while.

"Yes madam, Sergeant Brown has returned to the station and I'll tell him you're in reception," the officer said very tightly. And with that he went to a phone on the far left of his desk and quietly told someone that there was a Vivien Peters in reception for him. He came back and said that Detective Brown would be out shortly.

"Yusuf, don't worry about Hamza. We'll get him out soon. He has done nothing wrong," Vivien comforted.

"Thanks for the help. I haven't even asked how your mum is."

"She'll be all right, but someone gave her such a whack she's lapsed into a coma," Vivien said sadly.

Shazia put an arm around Vivien.

"I don't know who could have done this to Mrs Peters. Whoever did it is sick minded. My brother didn't do it, but if I hear anything in my community as to who it might be, even if it's one of our own people, I'll never stay quiet. We've been taught to speak the truth and not be afraid to do so. We'll get through this together and find out what happened to your mother."

Just as she said those words, Graham, Susan and David walked through the door. Their faces did not look as though they intended to find out what happened to their mother. David and Susan looked very much as though they had taken Graham's version of what happened on board. It was David who spoke first, which was very unusual in such a situation.

"All right, Viv. We went up to see Mum and she looks pretty bad. I think there's a lot more going on than what you told us."

"Yeah, Viv. I think you ought to give us a bit more insight into what happened; Mum's lying in a coma and you're up here." Susan did not finish off what she wanted to say, what Graham wanted her to say, what he wanted to hear.

"Well Viv, you better tell her who the coppers are holding responsible for Mum's attack. You best spit it out 'cause I think Susan and David don't want any beating around the bush," Graham said smugly. He made Vivien sick. He was using Mrs Peters' attack as though it was a game of chess, a small battleground for his beliefs.

"Susan and David, you are good people. I will tell the truth. My son, Hamza, he was walking to go to uni and he saw Mrs Peters door open and he went in her flat and found her on the floor. Hamza called his mum and me. We came and called the ambulance and police but when they came, the police started thinking that Hamza did the attack. Graham came along suddenly and he also accused Hamza of the attack. He tried to make Hamza angry but he became very angry and tried to attack Hamza, but instead he punched my wife. Hamza has been taken into a cell, but what for, I still have to find out? Whether you believe me or not is up to you." Mr Ali spoke before Vivien did. "I cannot believe the horrible attack on my neighbour and friend. My family are in prayer with you, for her wellbeing."

He spoke softly and there was sincerity in his voice that was not lost on Susan and David, but Graham seethed.

"Your son beat me mum up and that's why he's in a police cell."

"No, there is no evidence for the police to arrest my brother. This is a made up fantasy of Graham's and he's probably getting moral support from some of the great law leaders in this station," said Shazia.

"If there is evidence that Hamza has done something without our knowledge, then we would not hide Hamza. My parents would say to the police, punish our son, but there has been nothing brought forward to even suggest he had anything to do with Mrs Peters' attack, apart from Graham's version of events," Yusuf added.

"I think we ought to tread carefully here. There's a lot of logic in what Mr Ali, Shazia and Yusuf are saying," said Vivien looking at her siblings.

CHAPTER EIGHT

"Yes, Ms Peters, you're right. We have to tread carefully until we have enough evidence to find out what really happened and who is responsible for the attack on your mother," Detective Sergeant Bill Brown stated as he walked through the doors.

"Who the hell are you and what you talking about? The other coppers at my mum's flat said they'd bang up Hamza Ali and get him," Graham bit out his response.

"Mr Peters, if those officers did say that, they had no right to. Perhaps you misunderstood what they said. Anyway, my name's Detective Sergeant Brown and I'll be carrying out the investigation into Mrs Peters' case," replied Brown as he started flicking through a folder in his hand.

Shazia and Yusuf noted how swiftly the officer had politely tried to rectify what Graham had said while at the same time making things clearer to everyone else. Coppers stuck by each other, not always because they were loyal, but to ensure the institution they worked for never looked bad to the public. If the police institution seemed unjust, then the people would never trust any part of what it stood for. In particular, Detective Brown knew how Asian, black, Chinese and homosexual people were reluctant to talk to the police. He knew the Met was not perfect, he knew how certain officers could treat people differently according to their social background, the way they talked, their jobs and social standing and most of all, their race. Detective Brown was not blind to the Met's hidden faults.

"So, do you intend to charge my brother or let him go home today and most of all, when do you intend to let us see him?" Shazia coldly asked.

"If you don't mind, Shazia, but seeing your brother isn't as important as telling us what leads the police have come up with as to who attacked Mum. And if a couple of officers and Graham suspect it's Hamza, then it should be looked into," Susan added bitchily.

She knew deep down inside that Hamza was innocent but she wanted to lash out her feelings of despair and Hamza was unfortunately her 'lashing out target'. And anyway Graham and a couple of police officers thought it was him. Susan just could not believe what had happened to her mum. It was so unfair, her mum, an old helpless woman had not deserved such a horrific attack and there was Shazia whining about her brother. It wasn't Hamza lying in a coma but her mum. As if reading her thoughts, Shazia spoke directly to Susan.

"Hamza was not the one who attacked Mrs Peters. He was the one who found her. Mrs Peters suffered terribly and she's the one in a coma and not Hamza but he was not the person who caused her suffering and your pain. You must surely feel that it's not Hamza. You know how he became close to your mum. We all did. We looked out for her and she looked out for us. We cared for each other and we, as a family, want the truth and not just for

114

Hamza's sake, but for Mrs Peters' sake."

She spoke passionately as though to reach Susan's heart. Trying to show another view to the terrible tragedy that had occurred as the evil of a person's mind was sometimes unexplainable.

Somehow, just a few months ago, Ayesha had touched Mrs Peters' heart. Shazia's words now had a similar effect on Susan. Susan's eyes showed her unshed tears and slowly the tears that she had held back stung her and then gradually flowed, along with her whimpers of hurtful uncertainty. Vivien held her sister and David hung his head. He knew his mother would not have wanted them to fight with her friends without a solid reason. She would have wanted them to seek the truth. It was easy to find a scapegoat for something when one needed answers.

"You bitch," Graham hissed like a snake. "Look what you've done." He wanted Susan and David to carry on blaming Hamza, but the two weaklings were giving way to pathetic moral doubts.

"Graham Peters, I advise you to refrain from becoming aggressive. This is a very emotional time for your family. However, I think you brother and sisters are handling this in a much more mature and responsible manner. I suggest, Sir, you take note of that."

"Oh, don't give me that," Graham said.

Every time Graham managed to make people listen to him whether it was the crowd at the scene of Mrs Peter's attack or whether it was Susan and David, the Ali family or other Pakis always managed to come and burst his bubble. He was the one trying to give them the truth and it was being kicked in his face, yet again by Pakis and his Paki loving sister, Vivien. For God's sake, I've sacrificed so much for people to understand the importance of why this bloody country should be white and my family still don't get it, thought Graham. Well fuck them, I'll find people who'll support me to put the scum away. He laughed to himself because Graham had a new friend called Derek who was going to introduce him to a group which helped people like him to get their stories out in the open whether people wanted to hear them or not.

"I'm going now 'cause this cosy scene makes me sick. I got mates and they'll help me and I'll see Hamza in hell." And with that Graham walked off with Brown looking at him thoughtfully.

David must have seen Brown's face and quickly added,

"Graham loves Mum a lot and he's the youngest. Don't mind him, he's letting off a bit of steam."

Detective Brown looked at him; he knew David was justifying Graham's underlying racist behaviour. He could almost feel Graham's racist beliefs and his need to blame someone, in particular a coloured person; he had had a taste of it earlier in the day.

"I was going to talk with all of you. Just to get some insight into your family and whether Mrs Peters had any enemies or someone who might have a grudge against her. And Vivien did say earlier that she had some information that might be of interest to this case. I'll arrange an interview room and some tea for everyone." He then turned to Mr Ali. "I'll find out why it's taking so long for you to see your son."

Brown went back through the swing doors to sort things out. He was, to both families, a beacon of hope. He was honest and wanted to get things done properly. Brown, although he did not say much or give anything away, was the sort of police officer who was quick to question other officers and colleagues over their actions and behaviour. He was what cockneys and Bangladeshis would say, "A person with a big heart." They just hoped he lived up to it.

Behind the swing doors Brown was completely taken back when he learnt that Blakely and Woods were with Hamza in his cell. The two officers had been told that Hamza should not be interviewed without senior police officers present. However that had not been the case and they were currently below with Hamza. Brown told one of the administration staff to organise an interview room for the Peters family. In the meantime Brown went down to the cells to find out what Blakely and Woods were up to.

****

Blakely and Woods had been with Hamza for almost half an hour and they were not exactly being soft with him. They had entered the cell with a smirk on their faces. Blakely had begun.

"Hello, sonny boy, what have you being up to then?" Hamza had not answered and looked straight ahead. He would not say or give away anything. He knew his rights even if they had not been made known to him.

"You clobbered that old woman didn't you? How much cash did you take from her?" Blakely accused.

"Did you need it for your uni fee?" taunted Woods.

"Or was it because you got a kick out of beating your neighbour 'cause she was white?" Blakely said almost perversely.

Hamza carried on staring ahead while he listened to their racist jokes. He could not believe the two officer's taunts and the way they were trying to goad him into giving way to pent up aggression. Hamza would not allow them that opportunity. He remained silent.

"So, we're acting the silent victim are we?" Blakely said.

"We could remedy that very simply, couldn't we, Sir?" Woods carried on. "Pakis like him need a bit of extra attention."

To Hamza, Woods sounded like a dog and he wanted to tell him to lick his master's hand. But he didn't, he carried on staring ahead. Then suddenly Blakely sounded as though he was clearing his throat, belched and spat at Hamza's face. Hamza's face was covered in Blakely's saliva that ran down the side of his cheek. Blakely stared as he waited knowingly for Hamza's reaction. Hamza's deep anger burned inside him and his face showed the rage that ran through his body like a forest fire. With all his might Hamza spat back at him and found that Blakely's face turned into twisted disgust. Very gradually Woods came nearer and a sneer developed. Without warning, Blakely punched Hamza in the face and he went flying against the cell wall. The force of such a punch brought blood from Hamza's nose and mouth.

When Hamza lifted his face, Blakely and Woods realised what a mess the lad had become. There was already puffiness developing around his mouth and under his eyes. Woods looked a little unsure of the situation and wanted to see if Hamza was all right. This was not because he was concerned about Hamza's well being, but because Woods was afraid of any consequences that he might face as a result of his and Blakely's "little interrogation" with Hamza. As he stepped forward to Hamza, he froze at Blakely's words.

"No, Woods, he can clear his own mess up. You feeling frightened, Woods 'cause you think we'll get the can for his bloody face?"

"Well, we might, um, have to just cover our backs a little, Sir," stammered Woods. He really didn't want any trouble. This had got a bit out of hand for he had only wanted to show the coloured boy a thing or two about who was boss.

"You, Woods, you're gonna say that you tried to stop Hamza from attacking me and as a form of self defence I had to throw a punch," Blakely said coldly. He was a liar and a manipulator.

"But, but I don't think the seniors are gonna take that story for real," Woods argued.

"Well, what other story do you want? 'Cause whether you like it or not we're in this together. So if you, Woods, want to be seen as a decent copper you best do what I want you to," Blakely said through clenched teeth. "Anyway there are other senior officers who have minds like us and see things the way we do," he added.

Hamza was feeling dazed, he could taste his own blood and his face felt as though it was blowing up like a balloon. Blakely's punch had come like a shock to him. He had heard in the past from other young Bangladeshi men who had got into trouble with the law, that coppers often gave beatings. It was a white thing, the master in place with a whip in his hand and beating his slaves into control. That's what the other Bangladeshi young men used to say. They always found a way of getting out of it. Jamal, a young man Hamza was acquainted with had often commented on this fact.

"The police, man, they can get away with a lot if they want and no-one will ever question them. They'll easily say, hey these Paki yobs are so short tempered and we have to be careful, look out for ourselves, that's why they need a few beatings now and then."

Hamza understood now what Jamal had been talking about at the time. It was happening to him. Blakely and Woods were still talking when Brown walked into the cell.

"What's going on here? And what's happened to Hamza Ali's face?" Brown asked in a dangerous voice. His face gave nothing away of what he thought happened. Brown was a person who took in detail very quickly, peoples' faces, gestures, body language without showing his reaction.

Blakely suddenly faked pain in his right arm and sat down on the cell bed breathing hard.

"Look, mate, that boy came on to me like a dog on fire. I tried to push him away and so did Woods. But by God, he's got some strength in those skinny arms. In the end I had to punch the piece of shit off me," Blakely said and he carried on moaning and whimpering.

"Yea, that's how it was. That's how Blakely and I had to put a stop to Hamza's aggression."

Brown then turned to Hamza and asked quietly betraying nothing of his thoughts.

"Was that how it happened, Hamza?"

Hamza looked at Brown and said with sarcasm,

"You can believe what you like, but whatever I say won't get me anywhere. If you did believe me, I wouldn't be here in the first place. Now, I need to clean my face. If you'd be kind enough to get me some ice it would really help."

"I think you've had a rough time but this won't go under the carpet. Blakely and Woods still need to put everything into a report about this incident and why they were in your cell in the first place. Especially as they knew that I would be doing the questioning," Brown said without any emotion. The man really did not want to reveal anything, thought Hamza.

Blakely and Woods were about to explain themselves but he cut them off.

"I suggest you two get out of here and start typing the report." His voice was cold and empty towards them as they left the cell without looking at Hamza; they were too busy thinking what kind of report to write.

"Hamza, I'm going to get someone to help clean you up and then I want you to tell me exactly what happened in this cell and then put it into a statement."

"Are you sure you want me to do that? Can you handle the truth or would you hide it? You should be getting a statement of what happened today, how I discovered Mrs Peters."

"Yea, I do want a statement about that, but I want a statement about what happened between you, Blakely and Woods - your side of the story. And yes I do want the truth, that's what my job is about. Sometimes the truth is hard to accept," Brown said and then added, "not all coppers are like Blakely and Woods."

Hamza was confused, he really didn't know whether he should trust Brown or not. The confusion played on his bloody face and Brown saw it.

"Your family are waiting to see you. They've being waiting a long time because of Blakely and Woods. I think you should talk to them and tell them what happened and what I've said. Maybe they could help you go in the right direction."

Brown then left to send a policewoman in. Hamza was alone in the cell and he suddenly felt an overwhelming sense of loss. All of his life he and his family had fought against odds to ensure they all managed to walk the tight-rope between the barriers racism created and the goals they wished to reach. But still Hamza had managed to end up in a police cell through no fault of his own and get beaten up. Was all the tightrope walking he had done worth the humiliation he had suffered at the hands of two white men? He had one of the white men's saliva all over him and he felt vomit in his throat. Hamza wanted to scream and shout his words of revenge, that he would find Blakely and Woods and return to them their act of humiliation, one hundred fold. He laughed bitterly to himself as he remembered his father's words that an eye for an eye makes the whole world blind.

The deep rage that curled and uncurled in the pit of his stomach was driving him towards chaotic thoughts. Thoughts which he had being taught to hold in check in case those thoughts lead to his own downfall - a downfall which many Bangladeshi young men had gone through, leaving their families in tears. In that emotional moment Hamza realized how many Bangladeshi families could fall apart through a racist police officer's actions. Brown had taken several photos of Hamza and taken them away with him. He then organised Mr Ali, Shazia and Yusuf to be taken down to the cell to see Hamza. When the cell door opened and Shazia walked in, she took one look at Hamza and gasped.

"Oh, my God! What happened to you?"

Hamza did not say anything. He just stared at them. Mr Ali and Yusuf's mouths dropped when they saw the state of him. Mr Ali walked over to his son, touched his shoulder and spoke gently in Bengali.

"Tell me, my son, what happened."

Hamza did not say anything. He sat quietly staring and again Mr Ali asked gently.

"Hamza, my son, who has done this to you?"

Hamza looked at his father like a lost child. He felt terribly distressed, partly due to his physical pain, his anger, his humiliation and his sense of helplessness. The eyes that had often got into trouble and had to be guided by his father and brother looked broken. It hurt Mr Ali's heart to see his younger son in such pain. Then without saying anything, Mr Ali took his son in his arms and finally Hamza started crying. Shazia and Yusuf stood at either side of their father and brother and quietly waited with their own unshed tears held in check. They both guessed what had happened to Hamza and both felt the old anger unleashed by the acts of racism.

"Hamza, you must tell Brown the facts. You've got nothing to lose," Shazia was saying after Hamza had managed to tell them exactly what had happened.

"Hamza, I think you should give a full statement to Brown and find out what the hell he's going to do about it," Yusuf said. They were all talking in Bengali in case they were overheard by police officers who had a dislike for people of colour.

"Hamza, what do you want to do?" his father asked.

"I want to kill those bastards with my bare hands," Hamza replied.

"Hamza, that's your anger speaking to me," said Mr Ali.

"Hamza, you don't have to kill them with your bare hands. Kill them; get them through the opportunity Brown has offered you. Get them by getting rid of their jobs and get them through the law they work for and abuse," Yusuf said.

"That's right Hamza. Get them through the law they work for. They want you to use violence so they can get the better of you," Shazia said. "You need to get the better of Blakely and Woods."

"But, say Brown turns out like the other two," Hamza lamely protested, although he felt as though he could trust Brown.

"I think you may be able to trust Brown. He's not like the others. He seems a lot more honest and down to earth," said Shazia.

In fact Shazia had never met a police officer like Brown. The ones she had met had a habit of stopping and searching whether it was herself or one of her family members.

"Come on Hamza, give it a go. We'll stay with you when you give the statement to Brown if you want. Give a full account of what happened. Include everything from the way the officers behaved and the way they ignored Graham's enticement of racial hatred amongst the crowd," Yusuf said.

"Yes, listen to them, Hamza. You have nothing to lose if you tell the truth," said Mr Ali.

Hamza stared ahead and thought to himself, I have everything to lose if I speak the truth and am not believed because of the colour of my skin.

****

In the interview room with Susan, David and Vivien, Brown was putting a picture of the family life of Mrs Peters together. Her three children in front of him were ordinary, respectable people who got on with their lives fairly and squarely. They were not perfect by far but they were decent people. Brown wanted to know if Mrs Peters allowed anyone in her home without checking their details thoroughly. Mrs Peters' children were clear about her carefulness towards any strangers or anyone who knocked on her door unexpectedly. They explained they all had a key to the flat dating back to when they had been teenagers. Brown laughed.

She must have a hard wearing door then."

"It's Mum, things do last a long time with her," said Susan smiling tenderly through foggy eyes at the thought.

"I suppose Graham's got a key too," enquired Brown thoughtfully.

"Yeah, 'course he does, just like us," said David.

"Why do you want to know about the keys so much?" Vivien asked.

"Because, whoever attacked Mrs Peters was already in the flat, there was no forced entry anywhere. Our Scene of Crime officers reported this. Is there anyone else who has the key to Mrs Peters flat?" Brown said.

"Yes, the Ali family do. They're neighbours and Mum took a liking to them through their little girl. She made friends with them and eventually became very close. They look out for each other and do things for each other, things cockneys would know about," Vivien said.

"So, you don't think Hamza or any of his family members had anything to do with it?" Brown was quick to ask.

"No, I don't," Vivien clearly stated believing every word.

"What about you two, Susan and David?"

"No, I don't think so," said David slowly.

"Nor me," said Susan.

Brown agreed, although he said nothing aloud to them. Instead Brown asked delicately.

"What about Graham?" They were slow to respond.

"Well..." Susan began, looking at the others. David flushed and Vivien was stone faced. "Graham's the youngest member of the family and Mum did tend to spoil him a bit when he was growing up. She didn't mean to but he was the baby of the family." Susan looked at David to carry on.

"He's not in a job at the moment. Lost his job a while back but Graham is trying to get another one but you know his age and everything, well he's on the dole at present. Mum's been on his back to get a job. We all have in our own way. But he isn't bad, just a bit mixed up at the moment. I suppose 'cause he's split up with his wife and all," David said.

"Was he keen on your mum being friends with the Ali family, an Asian family, a coloured family?" stressed Brown.

All three understood what he meant but none of them spoke. David cleared his throat.

"Well, he had mixed feelings about Mum and her new friends. We all did..."

"I never had mixed feelings," corrected Vivien.

"All right, Viv, you didn't. Me, Susan and Graham have never had coloured friends before, only Viv has. But we weren't brought up in that manner so to speak, you know being friends with coloured people. Our mum and dad never had coloured friends. Then Mum suddenly makes friends with a coloured family and Graham found it a bit strange. Me and Susan did too but we understood afterwards."

"Is that why Graham accused Hamza Ali of the attack on Mrs Peters?" asked Brown slyly.

"Well, you know, he thought that it might have been him. You know what it's like, new people and all," said David trying to find words to defend his brother.

"Graham believed Hamza had attacked Mrs Peters because he's a non-white person," said Brown.

"Well, at last we're getting to the point," Vivien exclaimed and she went onto enlighten Brown even more.

"Graham hated the fact Mum was the Ali family's neighbour and friend. He wanted Mum to keep to herself; he didn't want her to be friends with an Asian family. He had racist beliefs, all bred on deep-rooted prejudices, and it suited Graham to take advantage of the situation earlier today. He should have been with Mum right from the beginning, but she went alone to the hospital with no family because my dear brother was too busy collecting votes from people as to who believed Hamza had smacked Mum and who didn't." Vivien paused for a moment watching Brown's growing interest.

"In fact," Vivien carried on, "on numerous occasions Graham was very rude to members of the Ali family. When he was around Mum's place he was always slagging them off to us. Then last night, he took it to a point when he emptied it all in front of Mum. They had a row about it and then to my amazement and disbelief, Graham went suddenly soft. He promised he'd try to be friends with the Ali family. Just like that in the middle of a row, he suddenly went soft as if he had thought about something. It was important to Mum that he was friends with her neighbours. They were good to her and she appreciated little things like that. It didn't take too long for Graham's true colours to come out today though did it?" Vivien said accusingly to her brother and sister who sat quietly listening to her. They had found it difficult to believe Graham would be friends with a coloured family and for him to give it a try had sounded rather unbelievable, but then they didn't like to argue with Graham.

Their silence spoke their agreement. Susan and David then asked rather agitatedly about the investigation into their mothers attack.

Brown had sighed and then sensitively carried on talking about the investigation, explaining that they had been looking into the facts surrounding the scene of the attack. Brown was wondering why Mrs Peters was attacked in her home and only her purse had being taken and all the other items in her flat had being left untouched. Nothing had been overturned or put in different positions. The person had gone to great lengths to enter the flat without any forced entry. The person had also carried a large object with them due to the fact that Mrs Peter's head injury had been caused by the use of a cricket bat, baseball bat or a wooden club. Brown found it extremely difficult to understand why a burglar had not touched anything else but his victim's purse.

"Would any one of you be able to tell me how much money was in Mrs Peters' purse?"

"I think Mum had collected her pension today and some extra money. About a grand," said Susan.

"What did she need a grand for?" Brown's ears were alert.

122

"Well, she was going to go on holiday with me. She's never been abroad. I thought it might be a nice change for her," Vivien said.

"Who else knew about the money?" Brown asked.

"All of us of course," said David.

"Including the Ali family. They knew Mum was supposed to go on holiday with Vivien. Mum probably told them anyway how much she was picking up. She's either at their place or one of them is at her place a lot of the time. I don't know if she told them when she was going to pick up the money or not though," said Susan.

"That doesn't mean anyone of them attacked Mum for a grand," said Vivien.

"I'm not saying any member of the Ali family attacked Mrs Peters because she had a grand in her purse or any of her children attacked her. But the point is there are a lot of people out in the world who would attack an old woman or a vulnerable person for a five-pound note. You must bear in mind there is no evidence to suggest that Hamza Ali attacked Mrs Peters, other than the fact that he was the one who found her. Vivien, you said you had some important information," Brown said

"Today at Mum's place, there had been two traffic wardens watching what happened. One of them told me she had wanted to talk to the police officers privately as she had some important information to give them. They had both refused to listen. The traffic warden was a black woman. However she and her colleague wanted to help me when I came on he scene. She gave me her details and so did her colleague. They'll only speak to you in private. Do you want me to phone them to arrange a time to meet you?" Vivien asked.

"Yes, that will really be helpful. Look you all go home now and freshen up and take it in turns to stay near your mum. I would like to talk to Graham so please tell him to contact me," said Bill Brown.

Susan said she would tell Graham and they got ready to leave. Sergeant Brown watched them from his window. The three of them were close and their affection for each other was obvious, but the strongest was Vivien. Graham was another story, Brown thought to himself. The three of them had not mentioned the fact that Graham had a record for physical abuse against his estranged wife, Sharon. Brown was a fast worker as he liked to know a bit more than people told him. Brown touched his head and then rubbed his forehead. He wanted to go home early today but he still had to deal with Hamza. Work for him never stopped.

Bill Brown went back down to the cell and found the Ali family talking quietly amongst themselves in their own language.

"I hope I'm not interrupting, but I do need to talk to Hamza alone and take a full statement. If that's all right with you all?" Brown said kindly.

"Yes, Sir, please, go ahead. Talk to my son. We will go in the waiting area," Mr Ali said. He smiled at Hamza and then saw himself out with Shazia and Yusuf. Another police officer took them back to the waiting area.

"Right, Hamza, let's start talking," Brown said. "You ready?"

"Yes, I am," Hamza said confidently. Brown took him to the interview room and Hamza started talking. He spoke in detail of everything that had happened from how he had found Mrs Peters, the behaviour of the two police officers and Graham's encouragement of racial hatred amongst the crowd. He also told how Graham tried to punch him, but his fist had found Mrs Ali instead, how he had tried to protect his mother and then got arrested for it. Hamza talked about the interrogation from Blakely and Woods and how Blakely had laid a punch on him. He talked in detail of the racial abuse he had suffered and the way he had been treated. Hamza gave an insight into the way his family and Mrs Peters had become friends.

Brown found Hamza to be a very intelligent young man with a stark honesty that was apparent in the way he spoke. Hamza did not really strike him as the kind of person who attacked his elderly neighbour for a thousand pounds. He really didn't fit the picture. Hamza was at university studying Economics and had a part time job. Why would he want to attack an old woman? Unless of course he had a private drug habit that there seemed little evidence of, or Brown thought cynically, could it have been for an Economics experiment. In Brown's policing experience the young man did not look like a violent burglar or mugger.

Brown had decided beforehand that Hamza Ali really was not the suspect. Firstly there seemed no concrete evidence to point the finger at him and secondly Brown had no gut feeling. Brown always had a gut feeling if he had his suspect. Bill Brown smiled at Hamza.

"I've got your statement now. I'll get it all typed up quickly and you can read it and sign it before you go home. I want you to request a hearing on the behaviour of Blakely and Woods after I make your statement into a formal complaint against them." Brown grinned as he said it.

For the first time Hamza smiled and it reached his eyes. Brown really was not that bad, Hamza had a liking for him.

"All right, can I wait with my family?" asked Hamza.

"Of course you can," said Brown and together they walked out of the interview room. Hamza finally realised that not all policemen were aggressive bastards, but they could be a friend. Hamza felt Brown was a friend in an institution which he had learnt long ago to hate. Perhaps there were friends amongst the strangers one walked with. Brown had not judged Hamza on the colour of his skin, but as a person. So he waited with his family for the statement to be written up and wondered was it worth really signing. Only the future would tell. Hamza looked forward to going home to see his mother and younger sister.

****

Ayesha had come home happily from school with Mrs Ali, but when she learnt from her mother what had happened to Mrs Peters and that the police

124

had taken Hamza away, Ayesha started crying and the tears flowed from the very core of her heart. Ayesha cried not only because her brother had been taken away, but also because her elderly friend whom she had grown close to, had been hurt and was now in hospital. She wept in her mother's arms and Ayesha repeated over and over again, "Why? Why?" As she held her daughter in her arms, Mrs Ali thought what a difficult question to answer. Why would a person carry out such a brutal act and why had her son being pointed out for it.

"Amma, I want to go and see Mrs Peters," Ayesha cried.

"We'll see about that," Mrs Ali said for she had been afraid the little girl would ask to go. She knew Ayesha would want to see Mrs Peters and she was very unsure of the situation herself. Vivien would understand but not her brothers and sister. Anyway the hospital staff had stressed about Mrs Peters having limited visitors.

"No, Amma, I am going to see Mrs Peters," insisted Ayesha.

"Okay, we'll see," Mrs Ali repeated. She did not want to make any promises to Ayesha in case she could not keep them. She was very unsure whether Ayesha would be able to see Mrs Peters or not.

Ayesha hugged her mother and could feel the uncertainty in her. Why was it her mother would not say yes to her? What was wrong with going to see her friend in hospital? Ayesha young as she was had a very determined spirit. She would go and see Mrs Peters. Ayesha got out of her mother's arms and went to the bathroom to wash her face. When she came out, her mother was in the kitchen making a sandwich. There was something inside her telling her to phone Vivien as that would be the way to visit Mrs Peters in hospital. So Ayesha quietly went to the phone and dialled Vivien's mobile from the phone book which still lying open on the V page. The answer phone came on and Ayesha whispered.

"Vivien, it's Ayesha. Come to my home, I want to see Mrs Peters." She then quietly put the phone down again.

"Ayesha your sandwich is ready," Mrs Ali called out. She had finished her cooking earlier in the day and looked anxiously out of the window for the rest of her family to come home. She wondered what Hamza was doing in the police cell. She had heard stories from other Bangladeshi mothers whose sons had been arrested in the past. Prison was a terrible place especially if you were not white. Mrs Ali had a friend whose son had been arrested in the past and beaten up by two police officers. They had stopped him in his expensive car, seen he had a white girl with him, and had pulled him out claiming he had being drinking and driving. He had got out with them and the two officers had beaten him up laughing and making racist jokes about the situation. Mrs Ali shuddered as she remembered.

Mrs Ali left Ayesha eating her sandwich and went to do her prayers. She would pray for her son and for the future to bring good tidings. When nothing was left, there was always prayer, the solace for peace and a sense of hope to the hopelessness that could easily submerge people into waves of darkness. For dark days were to come, Mrs Ali felt it deep within her especially as she had seen the way the crowd had gathered around Graham, agreeing with him in his racist rhetoric.

It had been half an hour since Ayesha had made the phone call to Vivien and suddenly there was a knock at the front door. Mrs Ali ran to open it hoping it was her son. It was Vivien. Ayesha came running from the garden and shouted out.

"Vivien, you came."

Mrs Ali looked bewildered for she had no idea what Ayesha had done. Vivien smiled at Mrs Ali.

"Someone phoned me to say they wanted to visit their friend."

"It was me, Amma; I want to see Mrs Peters," Ayesha admitted.

"I'm sorry I can't take you, Ayesha. No one is at home and I think not good idea. I'm sorry Vivien, she bad for phoning you. You have so much worry and she be naughty."

"No, Mrs Ali, Ayesha wasn't naughty, all she wanted was to see her friend and neighbour. She loves my mum and my mum loves her. Mum always talks about her more than anyone in this family. I think Mum would be so happy if Ayesha went to see her." Vivien said. She had heard from way back that a person in a coma could hear the voices of those they felt close to and sometimes that helped them to come back to their loved ones. Ayesha was close to her mum and one never knew what a child's presence or voice could do.

"Mrs Ali, please let Ayesha go with me. I'll only be half an hour with her. You never know, my mother might hear her voice if not ours," said Vivien.

Mrs Ali felt torn. She felt afraid to let her daughter go because of Graham and another part of her felt she owed it to Vivien and her mother. It was true, children often brought a sense of change in a sick person and perhaps Ayesha might be able to do something. Her daughter was so determined to go and even if Mrs Ali said no, she would keep pestering her about it. Ayesha could be very stubborn so Mrs Ali sighed and relented.

"Yes, she can go. But you can only be half an hour, Vivien."

"She'll be back in no time Mrs Ali. I'll make sure of that, thanks very much," replied Vivien.

Ayesha wasted no time and she went to the garden and came back with some of the sunflower petals in a tissue. Both Vivien and Mrs Ali stared at her and asked what she planned to do with the petals.

"I'm going to leave them for Mrs Peters near her bedside, so when she wakes up she'll know I went to visit her."

With that, Ayesha held hands with Vivien and walked with her to the car. Passers-by watched them; they were wondering what was going on. One minute one member of the family of the old woman who had been attacked was accusing her neighbours of murder and the next minute one member was taking the little girl out for a walk. It was, to outsiders, a parody of affairs. Families usually stuck together over certain issues but Mrs Peters' family seemed to have differences naked to the public.

Vivien drove to the hospital with Ayesha comforting her all the way.

"Vivien, Mrs Peters will be all right. She told me she's got a very busy year ahead of her. She has to do all her spring-cleaning before she goes on holiday with you. I was supposed to help her with her spring-cleaning. I'll still help Mrs Peters when she comes out of hospital. Don't look so sad, hopefully she'll wake up and tell you all off for being silly," Ayesha had said.

Vivien smiled to herself, almost having to hide her chuckle. Ayesha had a way of talking that could put a smile on many a glum face.

They walked hand in hand to the ward Mrs Peters was in. They met the doctor from earlier in the day. He was standing in the doorway and Vivien went over to him.

"Doctor Mackenzie, I'm going in to see Mum, and Ayesha, here, wants to see her as well."

"Ms Peters, I don't think this is really appropriate for a young child…"

"I am young but you see Mrs Peters is my friend and when she wakes up and finds out I wasn't allowed to see her because of you, she'll be mad with you." The little girl interrupted the good doctor. She looked at him for a response. Her black eyes shone as she pushed a black curl behind her ear.

"Are you trying to frighten me?" the doctor asked smilingly.

"No, I'm just giving you a warning about Mrs Peters' bad temper," Ayesha answered solemnly.

Vivien looked at the doctor.

"Well, doctor, what now?"

"All right, go on in, but only for a little while."

"Thank you," said Ayesha politely.

They walked into the room where Mrs Peters lay. Ayesha let go of Vivien's hand and walked over to the bed; she was oblivious to all the medical equipment that Mrs Peters was attached to. She put the tissues with the sunflower petals on the bedside cabinet. She then held the frail old hand in her soft child hands and spoke very gently.

"Mrs Peters, I know you can hear me, so don't pretend you can't. I know you can't speak because you've got a big tube in your mouth, but that doesn't matter, I'll do the speaking. You just do the listening. I want you to get better and come home. You're making everyone cry especially me. You wake up and come home and see my sunflower. I won't watch East Enders until you come home. Anyway you best get home because Graham's been picking on Hamza."

Ayesha turned around to see Vivien watching and listening. She leaned closer to the white old woman's face and whispered ever so quietly.

"You can't go to the place where my brother and where your Arthur are. It's not your time yet. Come back and let's have a bit more fun. I love you, you're my friend and you remind me of what it would be like to have a granny."

Then Ayesha moved her face away and stood watching Mrs Peters for a moment and gently kissed her hand. Vivien watched touched by the child's gentle gestures. Her mother and this child were truly close. She turned around and walked back to Vivien and together holding hands they both left the room. Big fat tears fell from her eyes and she sniffed and clasped Vivien's hand tighter. It was so unfair that Mrs Peters had been attacked and her brother had got the blame. Grown-ups were so blind sometimes, thought Ayesha. She just wished they could view the world like she did.

Vivien took Ayesha home and found Mrs Ali had some dinner ready for her. Mrs Ali insisted she eat when Vivien had said she didn't have the time. Mrs Ali had scolded her

"You need food in you to walk and have strong mind. You have a lot of sadness."

So Vivien had ate her dinner and felt better afterwards. Vivien suddenly felt tired and she accepted Mrs Ali's offer of a cup of tea and they both sat together. Ayesha sat in the garden near her sunflower and read a book.

"Have you heard anything about Hamza yet?" Vivien asked.

"No, no-one phone me," Mrs Ali said sadly.

"Oh, he'll be home soon," Vivien comforted.

"Are you sure?" Mrs Ali said with a tinge of bitterness.

"He will be home, don't worry," Vivien insisted.

The front door suddenly opened and Mrs Ali rushed to see her husband, Yusuf and Shazia walk through the door. Then Hamza walked in and Mrs Ali just stood rooted to where she stood staring at son's face.

"What has happened to my son?" she whispered horrified.

His mother then put her arms around him and gently took him to the sitting room. She sat him down and took his face in her hands and spoke in Bengali.

"Who did this to you?" Vivien instinctively knew what Mrs Ali had asked and she also knew the answer to the question.

"Hamza, the police did this to you," Vivien said sadly to him. Ayesha hearing voices in the sitting room had come in from the garden. When she saw Hamza's bruised face she ran to her brother and threw her arms around him.

"Who hit my brother, who hurt him?" She kissed his face and Hamza held her as she cried for his pain. Vivien could not believe what she saw. How horrendous could the police really be? She finally understood what Shazia and Hamza meant when they stated if you're coloured you have to be twice as good at everything.

In the quiet sobbing of the room Shazia spoke.

"You know what happened, don't keep asking him. They won't get away with what they did."

"Shazia, stop talking about revenge all the time," Mrs Ali snapped in Bengali.

"I'm not talking about revenge. I'm talking about the unfairness of what happened to Hamza and how another police officer has given a chance for Hamza to say his side of the story," Shazia snapped back.

"Shazia, your Mum's feeling scared, that's all. Come on relax, love," said Vivien. She did not understand Bengali but knew there was a lot of pressure on the family as a whole.

"Listen, everyone, there is a lot of trouble brewing out there. I could feel it coming home. It's in the air. Hamza and all of us are not in many people's good books at the moment. The damage has already been done earlier this morning. Now we stick together and hope that we can pull through this with no more serious trouble," Yusuf said imploring his family to keep calm. He spoke in English for Vivien's benefit.

"Hamza Bhai, don't worry. I went to see Mrs Peters at the hospital and she told me she was going to get better. When she wakes up she's going to put everything right. I know she will. Mrs Peters has the key to lots of secrets," Ayesha said touching her brother's face very tenderly.

Ayesha's voice brought hope to all of them in the room. She seemed to be so optimistic about everything that had happened. She always looked ahead and hoped for the best. The child believed in miracles and the adults in the room wondered would her hopes be dashed. They all looked around at each other. Perhaps there could be a way ahead and things could come back to normality. If only they could look at the world through Ayesha's eyes, oblivious to the reality of the kind of conflicts that lay around them. In the midst of the thoughts that went around in the Ali family's room, there were suddenly a number of bangs on their kitchen window and they heard someone screaming.

"Fuck you, Paki; we'll get you and the whole bloody lot of your tribe."

CHAPTER NINE

Graham and his new friend Derek were on the way to the Isle of Dogs, to meet up with a certain group. Graham had discovered his new friend was more of a brother than David had ever been - A brother who understood the pure heritage of British race as they had common beliefs, loyalties, an understanding only a true white heart could have. Derek was going to introduce Graham to people who were fighting for a cause for the white people. He was a patriot but there was a thin line between patriotism, nationalism and exclusion and Graham was making that journey.

They came to a large tower block and Derek led Graham up to the thirteenth floor, to flat fifty-five. Derek knocked on the door and it was opened by a clean-shaven headed man with a moustache. He was dressed in tight jeans and wore a T-shirt, which read "Rights for whites." He smiled at Derek and then at Graham.

"Come on in. I've been expecting you both."

They walked in and Graham smiled with pleasure when he saw the décor in the flat. It had white washed walls and the floor was covered with navy blue carpet. The walls were decorated with all types of pictures, flags, and symbols showing the Union Jack. In the sitting room, a massive swastika had been engraved on the wall and there were pictures of Nazi Germany, Hitler, Mussolini, Stalin and other well-known fascist leaders. There were books on the shelves on fascism, racism, the apartheid system and many other books depicting white race superiority. St. George's flag was pinned to the ceiling and hung like a canopy as though there was some perverse holiness about the room. On one wall hung the crucifix and Christ had a clear white face, with blue eyes and blond hair. There was a picture of the holy Mother Mary holding her baby and again she was portrayed as a fair, blue eyed, blond haired woman. The man smiled at Graham's obvious admiration of the flat.

"My name is Malcolm King. You must be Graham Peters." Graham took the extended hand to shake it, but the man embraced him and said, "We're brothers." Graham felt a sense of belonging, a sense of closeness he had never felt with his family.

"Graham, sit down," Malcolm said as they both sat down on the settee, which was navy blue and had small red crosses all over it.

"I know what happened today. Derek has updated me on all the events that have taken place. My sympathies are with you for your mum. But she is a victim to the loss of our identity. We now, with you, have to fight back." Malcolm was well spoken. Graham thought he sounded very intelligent and well learned. He must be quite a brain box, especially if he reads all the books in the room, thought Graham, whose usual read was the Sun, in particular page three.

"Thanks, mate, for your sympathies. I want to get those Pakis and all the other fucking Pakis, niggers and coloureds who are destroying England. I

130

want the true English identity to come out," Graham said. He felt as though he was in an interview.

"I'm going to tell you all about our group, what we believe in and what we are fighting for. By the time I've finished, you tell me if you want to be a part of it or not?" Malcolm said. His eyes bored into Graham and Graham could feel the power the man had over the people who belonged to his organisation.

"Go, on tell me. I'm listening."

"Our organisation is called the Nation for White British People. We are believers in racism and fascism. We hate black, Asians, half-breeds, gays, people with Aids and we don't believe disabled people, whether they are mentally ill or physically disabled, have a place in the society we seek in Britain. We are followers of Hitler and others like him. Oswald Mosley for example, a man from our own East End, was a hero for what he did in 1936. We need to stand together with all our white brothers and sisters and beat the outsiders back to where they came from. Look around, there's no jobs for white people, white people die on the NHS waiting list, our white kids don't receive proper education. There are no decent homes for white families. Do you know why this is so?" Malcolm's voice was rising. Graham was about to answer but Malcolm carried on.

"There is a conspiracy amongst all non-whites in this country to take it away from us, the native whites. Do you know in 1905 a document called the Protocols of the Elders of Zion was published in Russia. The protocols were secret papers revealing a Jewish conspiracy to take over the world. Then twenty years later the great man, Adolf Hitler wrote in his book, Mein Kempf that the Nazi party did not believe that all races were equal, but there was a duty to promote the victory of the better and superior race. Do you know which race that is, Graham?"

"The white race," Graham answered quickly. He wanted to get something right in front of Malcolm. He did not want Malcolm to see him as a fool.

"The Aryan race," roared Malcolm. "We, Graham, are the Aryan race and we must guard our racial purity. Even God has said the black man is the white man's slave. We are the superior race but our people do not realise this and until they come to understand and accept this, their woes will not diminish. Do you know that a British white leader in the past has admitted that white people are superior? Arthur Balfour, a conservative British Prime Minister from 1902 to 1906, once told the House of Commons that to think the races of Africa were equal to the races of people of European descent was an absurdity. And today we have fools like Tony Blair ramming equality down our throats." Malcolm paused for a moment.

"Yea, I hate Tony Blair. He's a right puff. Personally I think the Conservatives have all gone soft as well. There ain't no real politicians around these days. That's why I don't vote," Graham offered a thought proudly.

"You're absolutely right. We need politicians like you and me, Graham. The white British people need an alternative party 'cause the Lib's are in bed with Labour and the Tories are in bed with anything that opens its legs," Malcolm said flaring his nose.

"Right on the dot," said Derek with a perverse look on his face. Graham nodded in agreement.

"Graham, even in America, politicians have gone soft in the past. In 1939, the all white Daughters of the American Revolution refused to allow the black opera singer Marian Richardson to perform at their concert hall in Washington DC. Then that bitch of a wife of the president at the time, Eleanor Roosevelt, arranged for the singer to give an alternative concert on the steps of the Lincoln Memorial in the centre of Washington DC. These, Graham are examples of barriers we have to overcome and make sure never happen again." Malcolm almost looked sorrowful at the incident he had just spoken of.

"Graham," Malcolm carried on, "the Ku Klux Klan, were a powerful force and still are and it is this force we have to look up to. If I could, I'd lynch every single non-white in this country. But that won't help our cause because we'll frighten our white people away. We have to reach out to them and achieve compassion amongst them for our cause. And Graham, your mother is the key to that compassion. Now my friend, do you wish to become part of the Nation for White British People?" Malcolm asked.

"I sure bloody do," said Graham eagerly.

"Then come forward Graham and take this folder. The folder contains leaflets, posters, and articles of interest of white history. All this information is vital for every member in this organisation to read and remember. By reading this information you can use it to win the support of other white British people. We, as a political party, must look professional at every moment we come into contact with potential supporters. But we have another side to our party. It's called SWAT, Superior White Active Threat. They are specially trained white members who carry out certain acts of interrogation, assaults and acts of violence where it is needed, special forms of harassment and any act which needs to be carried out, instructed by senior members." Malcolm then showed him his arm, which had mainly Union Jacks and Swastikas tattooed on it. Malcolm advised Graham to get a few done on his arms and back. Graham said he already had one on his backside. Malcolm insisted Graham get a few done where they could be seen.

Malcolm then started to explain to Graham how he intended to use Mrs Peters' attack to the party's advantage. Just as Hitler had shrewdly exploited Germany's apparent need for a scapegoat, the Jews, Malcolm planned to use Hamza and his family as their scapegoat. Gradually pointing out that all the ills in the East End were due to the fault of coloured people trying to win over as many decent white people as possible. Their ideas would be simply put forward to the increasing number of people who would start to listen, get rid of all the coloureds, starting with a repatriation system, the half breeds would

132

be put on a different program. Malcolm explained that the party would bring in ideas of dealing with gays, Jews, disabled and misfits. The people who were not truly white and weak in white history would have to be dealt with gradually. Along the way, the party would show how there would be more opportunities in terms of employment, housing and the quality of health would improve.

Graham listened with all his heart as Malcolm talked and talked. He was finally fitting into an organisation which he understood completely and where he was being looked up to. Graham's greatest desire had been to be in an authoritative position, with people listening to him as though anything he had to say was important. He had found something fulfilling that he related to. Justice for his mother, Malcolm had said, would come from the very heart of the white British people who stood for everything dear to him.

Graham, along with Malcolm and Derek would campaign against Hamza Ali and stir up the frenzy of racial hatred by using the volatile tension between the white community and the Bangladeshis. It would be simple to use peoples' high running emotions of fear, retribution, hatred, ignorance of the truth, to the advantage of the fascist and racist organisation which he now was part of.

Hitler had managed to win the ignorant masses through his in doctrine of the belief of one superior race, "Aryans." People need answers, someone to blame for the cowardly attack on an elderly white woman who now lay in a coma. A woman people were now going to see as a saint. Graham would see to that, because he planned to tell people how his mother had befriended a Paki family against her family's wishes to show how charitable the British people could be. As a consequence of her kindness one of the sons had taken advantage and mugged her for her savings, because she was a white helpless woman.

Graham and Malcolm talked on and on into the evening, while Derek went out and got some food and beer for their supper. Malcolm talked about how forms of racial segregation existed in all colonial societies, especially during the British occupation of India. He glorified to Graham, the history of past white leaders who had taken England to great peaks in history and how that history had now been thrown into white peoples faces. Pakis and niggers needed to remember who had been their masters at one time and how they had been made to become more civilised through their rule. For example, the British had taught the Indians how to play cricket, a great mistake, as now the Indians sought to humiliate the English at their own game.

Malcolm talked fanatically about his theories, which was undoubtedly his obsession and he was collecting dedicated followers along the way. He then revealed to Graham that his grandfather had been a colonel in the army. His parents had died in a car accident and he had then been cared for by his grandfather. Malcolm had had a top-notch education in Graham's opinion and now he was using it to help the white British people to regain a hold on the country they were unconsciously losing to non-white people, people of colour. It had been Malcolm's grandfather who had taught him his racist views; he had almost been weaned on the fact the white race were the greatest in God's eyes and damn the person who thought otherwise. In that time, Graham had never felt more at ease with another person. Graham connected with Malcolm and the organisation, Nation for White British people.

****

It had been exactly five days since Mrs Peters' attack and she still lay in a coma, but her vital signs were stable. The doctors believed now it was just a matter of time. However, the atmosphere in the East End was not so stable. The tense sense of conflict between the white community and the Bangladeshi community was being played out on full stage. The days since Mrs Peter's attack had led to the racist organisation, Nation for White British People to take to the streets of the East End, to demonstrate their anger against why the suspect Hamza Ali had not been charged with Mrs Peters' attack. The lead campaigners were Graham and his new friends.

It had gradually started off with a small march in one of the local markets, led by Graham and Malcolm with a few St George's flags in their hands. Graham had made a tearful speech on how his innocent and frail mother had made friends with a coloured family living next door to her and how the son had attacked her for her savings. How the police had let him go because he was a coloured boy and the police were afraid to carry out their duties in case they were seen to be racist. Graham had cried and asked the growing crowd where had the British system of justice gone. It was then Malcolm had taken over quietly and spoken with charisma about the losses white people and their children were suffering. The crowd had got larger just as Malcolm had anticipated and finally Malcolm had managed to get a number of them to join his organisation. Those who did not join had a burning hatred towards the Bangladeshi community with whom they lived side by side.

The Nation for White British People repeated this performance in places where there were large groups of white residents. The effect of these performances had led to the reaction Malcolm had hoped for. The words which he had carefully chosen to win the sympathies of white people trapped in the poverty cycle, had an intoxicating effect on them. Many cheered and clapped their hands at Malcolm and had gone home debating all that he had said along with membership forms for the organisation stuffed in their pockets.

There was suddenly a dramatic rise in the number of racist attacks, incidents, harassment perpetrated by whites against the Bangladeshi community in the East End. Bangladeshi women were spat on when they went shopping, or when they collected their children from school, girls with headscarves had their scarves pulled from their head and young Bangladeshi boys found walking home alone were set upon and beaten. Even in the hospital, staff had had to ask a white patient to move to another ward. This was due to his racial abuse against a Bangladeshi patient in the bed next to him. Hospital managers had had to warn him that his behaviour warranted an arrest. The patient had left the hospital by discharging himself from their care. He then told the white community that the hospital had thrown him out because he had stood up for his rights against a Paki doctor.

Mosques, community centres and supplementary schools that Bangladeshi people and their children used as resource facilities, were targeted with racist graffiti written on the walls. A Mosque had several bottles of cheap alcohol thrown at its walls. Bangladeshi shops were vandalised and even owners of stalls in the large market in the area, which was used by a cross range of communities, felt afraid to open for business.

Little Bangladeshi children at primary schools, in areas where the majority of the residents were white, had to be escorted to and from school with police protection. White parents who had often seemed placid towards the Bangladeshi children in the past, now appeared to barely tolerate coloured children and their parents. The East End had gone blind and was unleashing silent conflicts wildly brought to the surface by manipulative aggravators. But many schools, against all odds, still worked within their walls to try to make sure that white and Bangladeshi children played together and expressed the importance of friendship without going into the issues of racism. The teachers knew, as children grew older, the wider the divisions between them became.

Bangladeshi young people now grouped together for their own safety and, because many wanted revenge on other white people, often an innocent white person was hurt either physically or verbally as a form of revenge. Malcolm, with his organisation, and Graham had unleashed a can of worms. They had opened silent wounds, conflicts that would have gradually mended, if only they had not spoken their racist, persuasive words. Malcolm was terribly pleased and proud of what he had managed to create within a matter of a few days. He had planned it that way, to react quickly so as to tune into peoples' anger and turn it to his advantage.

Many people from the white community saw the Bangladeshis as a peril to their way of life, their chances of survival and chances of leading a better quality of life. Just as the German people had seen the Jews as a threat to their potential success - as a barrier to their social and economic development. In particular, just as Hitler saw the Jews as the 'final solution', Malcolm and his party saw people of colour as their 'final solution'.

Many Bangladeshi groups and gangs saw themselves as campaigners for Hamza's cause. They walked around in large groups shouting slogans against the police and the way they had racially abused Hamza. They were championing a much deeper cause and the fact was, whether Hamza wanted to be or not, he was a hero in their eyes - someone who had suffered a great injustice at the hands of white perpetrators for a crime he had not committed.

135

Just as there were white people like Malcolm who manipulated and used situations for their personal benefit or the benefit of their chosen organisation, so too there were Bangladeshi people working to promote their views.

There were those amongst the Bangladeshi people, in powerful positions and with social standing, who tried to use Hamza and his family as a publicity stance to seek support for their own private cause, but showing on the surface they were in solidarity with the family. However above all this, there were genuine people who worked voluntarily in the community of various races - white, black, Asian and other origins - who truly wanted to help the Ali family by supporting them. Their sole purpose was to find a way of living in peace with each other in a harmonious manner.

Such groups realised that there was more to the truth than the half truths that were floating around, whether it was through the Nation of White British Peoples' speeches, local Bangladeshi groups, mis-informed newspaper articles, leaflets and community gossip. They realised that there were divisions in the Peters' family itself and that in reality the elderly woman had been a close friend of the Ali family and that there was no evidence to accuse Hamza of her attack. These truths needed to come out into the community as a whole. People, in particular people from the white community, needed to understand what really happened and come to their own conclusions, whether they wanted to fight their neighbours or live amongst the strangers they had lived with for so long. The distorted truth had to be unravelled for people from all communities.

Community leaders, workers, religious leaders, councillors and many well known figures called for a sense of understanding and peace between both communities. But their words seemed to fall on deaf ears. No side wanted to listen to words of peace and normality. The madness that engulfed them was rooted in the anger they felt for each other - an anger which was reaching a peak and waiting to climax with a thundering shudder back to its original form. Malcolm knew full well that until that anger found a place to halt, it would carry on like a whirlwind. He would in that time harness and bring from its crazy dance, the support and strength he needed for the party which he so reverently wanted to push forward. The Nation for White British People was his dream, his religion and his future.

Amongst the chaotic violence, the Ali family, the focal point of such violence, remained aloof from both white and Bangladeshi. They were horrified at what was happening around them. Six days ago they had been an ordinary Bangladeshi family, living their life as best as they could. Then like a creeping volcano, a burning laver had erupted and their world had changed forever. The Ali family's home had become subjected to various racist violations. Racist graffiti had been sprayed on their front door and swastikas stuck on the window, their kitchen window had been subjected to eggs being thrown as a daily routine and small rocks threatening to kill them had been put through their letterbox.

One occasion they had animal faeces put through the letterbox. Mrs Ali had been threatened whilst taking Ayesha to school as two white boys had pulled out a knife and waved it in front of the little girl. She had started screaming and Mrs Ali had grabbed her and run into the school for safety. The Ali family were not alone in their block to suffer such racial attacks, but they were the family receiving the worst of such harassment. The Ali family had, right from the start, called the police every time something happened. Brown had insisted that they did that, even though the perpetrators disappeared by the time the police arrived. There were no witnesses, no evidence as to who was harassing the family. They had visits from Victim Support but no one could help find out who the culprits were, or find a way to end the harassment.

Shazia was harassed on the way to school and, tough as she was, she now understood the term 'living in fear'. Shazia, who enjoyed making her own way in the world, was suddenly always darting in and around places she needed to go. She had developed a habit of looking over her shoulder. Her father had bought her a mobile phone to use in case of an emergency. She made and received many a call to and from her home during the course of the day. She felt her spirit was dying and felt helpless in spite of all her strong wilfulness.

Hamza had left the flat a few of times since his return from the police station, but he had disguised himself and been accompanied by friends. Along the way Hamza and his friends had been harassed verbally by white children. They had not said anything back in case things got out of hand and Hamza was recognised on the streets. His friends were very mature and responsible with regard to his situation and the situation as a whole affecting the community. Eventually Mr and Mrs Ali had insisted their children came and went from the flat by car.

Yusuf found it hard at his medical training; he knew his colleagues were well aware of his current problems, especially as they saw the way he was juggling his rota around them. Yet, only the colleagues of non-white origin had come up to him to offer support. His white colleagues felt embarrassed to say anything and he could often feel their whispers about him in the medical rooms. Their immaturity infuriated Yusuf and he wondered how they would cope with becoming doctors in an inner city with such a vast multi-racial population.

However Yusuf remained silent and his quiet dignity was admired and looked up to by his professors. Finally when the issues of interaction between patient and doctor were discussed, one professor spoke up.

"You all must question whether you can interact amongst yourselves and see each other as an equal in whatever you do. You must question whether the prejudices you have one of each other will effect the way you make decisions. For in the future you must question your own ethical and moral conduct with patients from all races as it will effect the decisions you make in medical treatment. Often silence itself speaks volumes to those who are uncertain of the future."

The professor's words had a great impact on the class as a whole for there was a difference in the way Yusuf's white colleagues treated him. Many felt ashamed that they had not spoken to him earlier about what he and his family were going through. Communication was such an incredible tool and listening was such a gift.

Mrs Ali felt frightened to cook because she was afraid something would be thrown at the window. She had become increasingly protective over her children wanting to know exactly where they were going and with whom. She would not put the clothes out on the washing line as someone had thrown red paint on them on one particular occasion. In fact she refused to allow her family to go into the garden. Mrs Ali felt like an over protective mother, paranoid about her children being hurt.

Mr Ali felt like a broken man, unable to offer the protection his family needed. He almost felt a failure watching the effects living in fear was having on his wife and children. He tried to help in his own way, through making sure all his children travelled in cars and did not go out alone. He prayed with his wife everyday for the peace they craved, for themselves, their children and all people who were suffering, whether they were black, white, Bangladeshis or any other colour that God had created.

But the toil of such harassment and abuse, the living in fear, was having the most tragic effects on Ayesha. Her innocent world had a few days ago, been shattered with the birth of a nightmare. Ayesha had even started wetting her bed and insisted on sleeping with Shazia in the single bunk below. She was frightened of sudden movements, sounds, and the raising of a voice and of anyone screaming or laughing loudly. Within six days Ayesha had changed from a carefree child to a bundle of nerves and had an increasing fear that she would lose her family or she would be kidnapped. Ayesha woke up from sleep in the middle of the night screaming for various family members, to ensure they were well and not hurt. She had found it so difficult to concentrate at school, erratically trying to play and finish off class work, that the teacher and head teacher had requested Mr and Mrs Ali should give her a few weeks' break from school. The school wanted her to be seen by a psychiatrist and to be treated for her increasing asthma problems.

Amongst all this, Ayesha still wanted Mrs Peters to get better because she believed, in her childish heart, that Mrs Peters could make things right. Perhaps in a way Ayesha was right. Due to Mrs Peters, the change from the usual quietness in the East End to a violence which had erupted so quickly and sharply made many wonder if the old woman would be able to turn back the storm of change.

Through their sufferings, Vivien stood by the Ali family with what comfort and support she could offer. She knew that her younger brother was responsible for their suffering and pain. Susan and David did not come to see the Ali family even though Vivien had argued with them over the issue. They did not directly blame the Ali family for anything, but they felt a deep sense of hostility and bitterness towards them. The Ali family were very much aware who was behind the various marches, meetings and frenzied protests that were taking place. Because of their respect for Vivien they never mentioned Graham's name.

****

However Vivien brought the issue up and genuinely explained that she could not understand why Graham was turning people against the Ali family and against each other. As far as she was concerned, he was a sadistic, racist bastard. But she offered the Ali family hope that eventually the truth would emerge and there would be a lot of guilt felt by many a decent white person who had been taken in by the lies her brother had fed them. Vivien wanted the truth to come out for her mother's sake, for her own peace of mind and for the fact that Ayesha's change in character haunted her terribly. She had already set up a meeting between Jackie Simmons, Peter Smith and Detective Sergeant Bill Brown.

Vivien told Shazia this and was dismayed to find how cynical she was about the matter.

"Look Viv, take a shot at it. What's a traffic warden going to reveal? That she gave a ticket to the attacker and got his details for the police. On top of that she's black."

But Ayesha who had overheard their conversation had said kindly to Vivien,

"I believe something good might happen because you're trying to help us and yourself. You're very kind Vivien and I think my God will be kind too to us soon."

Ayesha's words were enough for Vivien to feel motivated. She really hoped the traffic warden had more to tell than giving out tickets. It was the following Tuesday morning when Vivien went to visit Bill Brown at his station. He greeted Vivien at the front desk and led her to the interview room. Bill Brown got a cup of tea for them and they sat down and talked about what was happening in the East End.

"I never thought that things would escalate to such an extent," Brown said quietly.

"Escalate is not the word to describe what is happening out there and the people suffering the most are the Ali family. Their child Ayesha, she's a changed little girl," said Vivien.

"I can well imagine."

"No, you know nothing Bill," Vivien replied. It was first names now between the two of them. They had spoken often on the phone and a trust based on honesty had developed between them. They were friends, working towards the same goal.

"She wets the bed every night and she wakes up screaming. She's frightened of sudden sounds, of quick movements; she's not at school. Ayesha had a shine in her eyes at one time. In fact, just a week ago she was a happy little girl full of robust life and health. The shine's gone from her eyes and they look afraid all the time. When she holds my hand, she holds it so tightly, I feel as though my blood has stopped circulating. Ayesha's not at school anymore because emotionally she's not well enough and physically her asthma has got worse. You never knew the Ayesha I once knew. If you did you'd understand what I'm talking about," Vivien said as a tear fell gently down one side of her cheek.

Sergeant Brown touched her hand in support; sometimes a person's touch helped more than words could express. He knew the hell the Ali family were living through but his hands were tied. He had no concrete evidence who the persons were carrying out the racist harassment on the family. If only he could find one of the perpetrators then he would be able to find a couple more names. Brown knew of all kinds of ways to get names if he could just find one connected person, because the streets of the East End were not talking to any police officers.

"I didn't realise how much people could hate each other and to what extent," carried on Vivien. "Most cockneys want to get on with their lives quietly and peacefully. Now and then they have a screaming match with a coloured person but it dies down and life carries on. I grew up with cockneys that kept to themselves and lived their lives without making friends with a coloured person. But they didn't go around shoving dog shit through coloured people's letterboxes. The mums had their bitching session at the school gates and the dads had a debate down the pub on a Friday night. But that's where it stopped. It didn't get any further than that. Now, it's do any vile act people can think of to each other and to hell with the children. An eye for an eye is what's happening for every wrong felt by people against each other. I can understand how wars begin now; it all stems from ignorance, manipulation, greed and personal vendettas." Vivien's eyes now showed a hollow sadness.

Brown listened quietly and understood what she was talking about. As a child his father had had a Japanese business associate, a Japanese friend. The Japanese man had often been a visitor to their home. One day Bill Brown had come home from school after having a class discussion on Japan with a rather narrow minded teacher. He had asked his father why all Japanese people were so intelligent and rich. His father had laughed and said he'd been listening to too many silly stories. Bill had persisted on stating he was right and what he was saying was not silly. At his father's silence he had gone on to say how evil Japanese people were and how they had such easy lives.

Bill remembered how his quiet father had become very angry at what Bill was saying and had then made him sit down to listen to what he had to say.

"Listen to me very carefully Bill. By listening to what you don't want to hear, you will find a clearer understanding of the world we live in. In 1941

Japan went to war with America. Three months later President Roosevelt signed an Executive Order. Under this order more than 100,000 people of Japanese origin, including my friend Yoko Harmi who was a child at the time, and living on America's West Coast, were taken from their homes and put in camps. This was done even though they were full American citizens. At the time America was at war with Italy and Germany." His father had paused and sighed holding his hand and then continued.

"But the Americans of German and Italian origins did not have their homes taken away, nor were they put into camps. As they were 'white' in skin colour they were seen as full Americans, while the 'Yellows' - the Japanese - were regarded as different, almost alien. One wonders whether the Americans were any different from the Nazis for this degrading act. It's easy, Bill, to listen and believe in words and lies which make you hate, but you must always look further and broaden your mind to find all sides of history, stories of all cultures and people. To be able to do this is much harder than to conform to what is believed popularly - to generalise."

Mr Brown senior's words had a dramatic effect on his son. An effect that could never have been achieved through any history, sociology or philosophy lesson Bill Brown would have in his education. It shaped the way he thought and viewed people from his own community and people from other communities and races. One never really knew a person until one had walked with them in their footsteps.

"Vivien, it's so much easier for people to believe what they want to believe. No matter how much you scream for them to stop hurting each other, they feel it from their hearts to stop. Sometimes it takes a tragedy to rock the senses back into place. We just carry on hoping for the best, for sanity to return and we just keep trying."

They both sat quietly drinking their tea and waiting for Jackie Simmons to turn up. They felt comfortable in each other's company. Vivien had never felt like that with another man in all her lifetime. She felt so safe and secure in his presence. He's such a good and honest man, Vivien thought quietly to herself.

Jackie Simmons and Peter Smith turned up just as they had promised. They were led to the interview room where Brown and Vivien were waiting. Vivien greeted Jackie and the two women smiled at each other. Bill asked them to sit down while Vivien introduced Jackie and Peter to him. Bill began in his usual sombre voice.

"This is a rather unorthodox way of interviewing people but I wondered how you would like to approach this?"

"Well, I want to have an informal chat 'cause what I've got to say might burst your ears," Jackie said. She looked the kind of person who was straightforward and did not mix her words.

"Okay, why don't you speak with all of us here and I won't take any notes until we hear you out. How about that?" Brown said.

Jackie laughed at him, a deep, throaty chuckle;

"Hey, man, you're one negotiator."

"Well at least this copper wants to listen and not shout at you." Vivien joined in the banter.

"It's hard to find good coppers but then you still have to prove yourself to me," Jackie said, winking at Brown. Brown smiled, he could tell when a person had a good heart and Jackie Simmons was that kind of person. He could tell that she wanted to put things right, to put a new light on the events surrounding Mrs Peters' attack. But her lack of trusting police officers had forced to her question herself as to what she should or should not do.

"Well, I might be able to charm you into telling me. They say women often like men in uniform," Brown teased.

Jackie let out another throaty chuckle.

"You're right, about that Billy boy 'cause that's why I'm with my Peter. Vivien and Peter laughed with them as well. She really enjoyed being in this kind of company where people could tease one another without offence and where honesty was a must.

"Look, PC or whatever your title is," Jackie began seriously. "Last Tuesday evening around eight, I was waiting to be collected by my pick up van and I saw someone come out of the old lady's flat and they were walking as though they'd done something wrong. I saw that person keep looking here and there and everywhere. That person dumped something in the rubbish bin of the block of flats. If you're lucky it might still be there 'cause the bin ain't been collected yet. The council are running late as usual. But I tell you this, I did try telling them boys in blue the day the Asian kid found the old woman. You know those two coppers treated that Asian family as though they were the Ku Klux Klan and they were going to lynch the family. I thought they were going to piss on me with the words they came out with. Those two coppers, especially the older, one hates anyone coloured and mark my words, I reckon they've given enough beatings to many a coloured person in their custody," Jackie said angrily. Brown agreed with her completely but kept silent.

"Yes, Jackie's right," said Peter Smith. "The way those police officers behaved was unbelievable and despicable. Even the ambulance crew were shocked at their behaviour. You should interview them, maybe they'll give you an account of what happened. Your brother didn't look concerned about what happened to his mother."

"Yes, I gathered that from his behaviour," said Vivien dryly.

"Going back to where you let left off Jackie, you haven't described what the person looked like who you saw leaving Mrs Peters' flat," Brown said. He wanted a description from Jackie fast of what she had seen. He wanted to get to his computer with the information and find the bastard through profiling him. He saw Jackie take a deep breath and she smiled as though she was reading his thoughts and plans.

142

"Well, what is it Jackie?" Brown inquired lifting his brow.

"Brown, I ain't gonna give you no description."

"But, Jackie, this is important," Vivien panicked. "You said you'd help out."

"I know said I'd help and I'm a woman who keeps my word," said Jackie proudly.

"Then spit it out," Vivien asked impatiently.

"I ain't giving you a description, I'm going to give you the name of the man 'cause the more I think about it, the more I'm sure of who I saw.. Jackie said solemnly.

Her words sent shock waves through Bill Brown and Vivien's mind. The woman was going to give them a name. She sounded mad. Only Peter did not look shocked as he knew what Jackie was about to reveal and he sat quietly waiting for her to do so. Vivien could not help herself.

"And how the hell did you figure his name out?" she said.

Jackie looked at Vivien strangely.

"Because darling, the day your mum was discovered, I saw the man who attacked her amongst all those people and I wanted to tell the police officers there and then." Jackie paused as though she was reflecting what she was going to say.

"I'm going to tell you this because of what's going on in the East End. I live and work there and I want it to stop. There's enough damage already, with broken families, poverty, drug abuse, seven year olds smoking, alcohol abuse, kids being beaten up and child prostitution. Now we get more damage from people beating each other 'cause they blame each other for their troubles, they look at each other and see the colour first and nothing else. That damage is the hardest to mend. It roots back to my ancestors and the hell they went through. Whether you believe me or not, think deeply about what I'm saying and don't keep asking me am I sure. Because that will wind me up the wrong way. So Vivien brace yourself, girl, 'cause it's going to hit you like a rock."

Vivien was suddenly on full alert.

"Vivien, I saw your brother, Graham, leave that evening. I saw him leave your mother's flat that evening before her neighbour's son found her in the morning. He was the one who carried something in his hand and dumped it in the building bins."

The words fell on Vivien like water falling on to fire, killing all that she had thought was clear and real. She could not believe her ears, Vivien almost refused to acknowledge what Jackie had said. No, thought Vivien, Graham was a racist but he would never hurt his mother over a difference of opinion with her. Graham loved their mother, she was the light of his life, and he had a bond with her so very special. How could this woman have the audacity to accuse him of such a crime? Her brother attacking their mother, how bloody ridiculous.

"Is this some sick joke?" Vivien asked, her voice a deathly whisper.

"No, darling, I know what I saw. I would never have known who Graham was had he not turned up on that day. Don't you think that it was bit of a coincidence to turn up on the day your mum's friends discovered her?" Jackie said gently. She hated herself for sounding so full of herself, but she had to make Vivien understand that she was not fooling around. Jackie felt sure she had seen Graham Peters the evening that his mother was attacked leaving her flat.

"Why?" said Vivien. The single word spoken like a child, like the way Ayesha had spoken. Vivien was finding it hard to think clearly. Her mind was hazy and blurry from the shocking discovery she had made. This could not be happening for real. Maybe Hamza had felt like this when he had being accused of Mrs Peters' attack.

Brown had absorbed everything like a sponge, what Jackie had said and the interaction between the two women. His mind was racing to find a possible motive for why Graham Peters would carry out such a vicious act on his own mother. He realised that the person who could possible help him with this was Vivien and she looked at though she was in denial of what she had heard. However Brown could tell the black woman felt sorry for Vivien for the information she had just given.

"Vivien, baby, I've had a hard life. I came from a home where my father beat my mother till he saw blood. He then beat us if we even made a move to stop him. But my mother, she did good for us. She taught us how to be good, honest and hardworking. She taught us to live a life where God would be happy. When my father died, my mother finally felt free. She had given him the best part of her life and he had owned her lock, stock and barrel. You don't know what I've been through living the past week knowing what I know, what I just told you. I don't like lying and making up stories. That ain't me. Just like my mother felt free from my father, I feel free from telling the truth. I'm black and you're white, other than that we're fairly the same. I'm a decent woman and so are you, but girl I saw what I saw and I'm sticking to my story come all hell."

Vivien sat quietly listening to what Jackie had said. Jackie was an honest woman who had nothing to gain from making up such a story and what Jackie pointed out about Graham turning up on the day when her mother was found was a coincidence. Vivien had secretly found that strange. He was not an early riser; he had not been since the time he had lost his job. Since then Graham had always been at her mum's house in the late afternoon or evening. He did no odd jobs for her and rather got things from her like a dinner, having baths at her home, their mother had done his washing and Graham even borrowed money he never repaid. The night before the Tuesday Mrs Peters collected her money, he had known about it and had tried to prevent his mother from going on holiday, feigning worry over her ability to travel. Graham had even said that his mother should give him the money so he could invest it for her, but she had laughed and said she might not be around for that long to reap such investments.

Vivien remembered the confrontation between Graham and their mother over his racist behaviour and beliefs. She had made it clear he was not welcome in her home with those beliefs. But he had refused to acknowledge that and carried on arguing and then she had put her foot down sharply. Vivien had always found it strange how Graham had become so soft minded straight after that. Since his childhood, Graham had been a liar and a manipulator. She knew him very well. But could Graham really have hurt their mother. Vivien realised she did not know. All she knew was that people could rapidly change their emotions in the heat of the moment and carry out acts that they would have normally thought vile. People could do acts in the name of things they believed to be true and held dear to their hearts. Some times the distorted truth developed a distorted trail of thought, of vision and tragically actions.

Vivien looked at Jackie.

"I'm not saying I don't believe you. I just don't know. I feel very lost." Jackie put her arms around her.

"I'm sorry for speaking so rough but I had to make sure I was taken seriously. You have every right to doubt me. I'm a black stranger and your brother is no stranger to you."

Vivien wanted to laugh, a hysterical laugh. Jackie had spoken such a contradiction. Vivien felt that her brother was more the stranger than the black woman who was comforting her. Brown had listened to what Jackie had said and he knew he had to wait until Vivien could compose herself and carry on with the discussion. But he had more of a gut feeling that Graham was the attacker rather than Hamza Ali. He had had suspicion of him from the start but not with regard to the attack itself. The four people in the room sat with each other gradually taking in the shocking news.

As they sat together, the guerrilla side to the Nation for White British People, the SWATS, were carrying out their instructions as ordered from their senior members. A hundred SWATS rampaged through Brick Lane burning shops, destroying council property, smashing cars, spraying paint over the roads, defacing the mosque walls. They had dogs with them and made them foul as much of Brick Lane as possible, they threw beer cans at flats and put up Union Jack flags where it was possible. People were afraid to stop them and the police had taken their time to come. Even when the two police officers arrived they had retreated due to the scale of the rampage. They had then waited for back up teams which took longer than expected. By then the massive damage financially, socially and emotionally had being completed.

The Nation for White British People had finally given Graham the understanding and power to realise as a nationalist, how easily it was to exclude the minority. Graham had made the journey of his lifetime and for him there was no turning back. He had tasted the power one could have over others and how to wield that power to achieve ones goals.

CHAPTER TEN

The rampage of Brick Lane by the SWATS made headlines in all the local newspapers in the East End. It even hit the national news on television, nothing on that scale had happened since Oswald Mosley took his black shirts to Cable Street in the summer of 1978. It shook all communities in Tower Hamlets to the core and local councillors and council leaders found themselves in serious meetings on how to control the surge of racial conflicts, before something even more tragic happened.

During the week that followed local councillors called for voluntary and community organisations to come together and formulate a plan to drive out the racist and fascist influence poisoning the East End. Self help groups, community and voluntary organisations, individuals, women's groups, disabled, gay, black and immigrant groups all came together to challenge the racist and fascist poison that had developed since the attack on Mrs Peters.

The greatest fears of the councillors and people in authoritative positions had been the fact that the Nation for White British People was putting forward candidates to stand in the local elections. That meant there could be wards with racist and fascist people as their councillors. Many of the black, Asian and Bangladeshi councillors were finally realising that they needed to do some real work on behalf of the people, the people who had put them into their positions and greatly needed them.

Brown had heard and seen the carnage the SWATS had left behind in Brick Lane. He heard from residents, passers-by, shopkeepers, city workers and customers in restaurants, what they had witnessed and how they had run in fear of their lives. Brown had heard of the SWATS through the grapevine and knew what they were supposed to carry out and now he had seen what they were capable of. Brown had been told how fierce and vengeful the SWATS had looked chanting their racist rhetoric and screaming to make Britain white. For many people it was something out of a horror film. Something they had only heard about or seen on documentaries on TV. But the SWATS had come to Brick Lane and shown what racists were capable of.

Little children, both from the Bangladeshi community and the few white children who lived in and around Brick Lane, had watched in terrified fascination from their block of flats. Their mothers had often warned them that if they were naughty, 'the bogey man' might come and get them. Those little children, from their hiding places behind the windows, had been afraid that the men they had seen were the 'bogey men' trying to catch them for every naughty thing they had done.

At the time their mothers had also watched with them aghast at what the SWATS were doing and what they had done. Many of the Bangladeshi families who lived around Brick Lane were below the poverty line and the rampage the gang had shown they could create, brought home to their hearts how distant they really were from being accepted in the country they had chosen to live in.

Local businessmen whose shops, cafes and restaurants had been damaged, grouped together to demand that the local authority help them with the financial costs of rebuilding their livelihoods. They had worked day and night for their businesses to succeed and for them to see how racists could easily destroy what they had built was a blow to their self-esteem and dignity. Community groups and voluntary organisations dotted in and around Brick Lane gathered together as a forum to voice their anger at why such racist and fascist people could be allowed to even group together. They wanted the financial cost of the physical and emotional damage done to Brick Lane's community as a whole, to be met by the local authority.

The Nation for White British People saw it as a tremendous victory for their cause and congratulated the SWATS on their courageous work. Malcolm, Graham, and Derek, along with other authoritative members, planned their next move. The local elections were coming soon and it was the perfect opportunity for the party to put forward three potential candidates. The candidates being Malcolm, Graham and a woman called Margaret Hollow. They would stand as candidates in different wards populated by white residents. These three places would be a start in Tower Hamlets and gradually the party would move on to other inner city areas. The time had come, Malcolm had said to his party, for great changes to take place as he already had many people canvassing on his behalf.

****

Brown had asked Vivien, Jackie and Peter not to disclose the information Jackie had found until he had dug around to find out exactly what Graham had been up to since Mrs Peters' attack. Graham had been very busy with the party for the Nation for White British People. Brown wasn't ready to charge Graham with his mother's attack. He needed hard-core evidence. Jackie's account of what she had seen was her word against his. Brown had discussed this with Jackie, Vivien and Peter. He made it clear to them that Jackie's version of what she had seen could easily be argued down by a smooth talking barrister. He explained that there were problems with Jackie's eyewitness account as she was the only person who had seen Graham leave his mother's home that evening. She had only seen a full profile of his face once in the dark. Brown wanted Graham, but could not touch him until he was absolutely sure and that meant two things to him. Either he found whatever Graham had thrown in the bins for forensic investigation, or by some miracle his mother woke up and recognised her assailant to be him.

Brown explained very clearly to Jackie, Vivien and Peter that if he went after Graham on the strength of Jackie's eyewitness account, there was a large possibility he would fail. If he failed and Graham was released, Jackie could easily become the target of a race hate campaign. They had all understood what was made clear to them and the four of them had decided to wait while

Brown made further investigations to uncover any other leads. Brown wanted to trap Graham into slipping up himself.

Brown learned that Graham had spent every minute since his mother's attack with Malcolm King, the main man for the Nation for White British People. Graham had gone to see Mrs Peters one more time since he had last visited. Brown had been told from his various sources that Graham was now a leading person in the racist party and one source hinted that he would soon be a councillor after the next local elections as his popularity was increasing amongst softhearted white Cockneys.

What a bastard, Brown had thought, the man was busy getting himself famous by entering a political career. He showed no signs of a distraught son for his mother's critical condition. Graham seemed to be a man who was having a good time and creating a new life in racist politics. He had no contact with his other siblings other than asking how they were coping and encouraging them to join in his cause for their mother. David and Susan had declined his offer, ignoring what Graham was actually involved in. They had turned a blind eye to his fanatical racist activities and, although angry, they had not shown their anger towards his lack of concern for their mother in front of Brown when he had visited Vivien at their home and found them all discussing Graham. He had asked whether Graham visited their mother often and they had been very uptight with his question. He had asked knowing full well the answer.

However, Vivien had blurted out her fury on their behalf. She had hurled abuse at her younger brother and revealed how she had told him where to go when he had asked her to join his party. Vivien had then turned on David and Susan for keeping quiet about Graham's behaviour and his racist ways. She attacked them about their morals and the fact they always wanted to keep their hands clean. Brown had watched her and found that her anger was an added attraction. To him, Vivien had looked as though she was on fire, sweeping her arms around and walking with her hands on her hips. He was fascinated by Vivien's sense of total confidence with herself.

Bill Brown was a couple of years older than Vivien, divorced with one son who did not relate to him but loved his "alley cat" of a mother. He rarely saw his grown up son and did not exactly miss him. It was a tense affair; whenever they met Brown found his stomach ulcer always hurt afterwards. His wife had always kept his son away from him, so father and son had never bonded from the beginning. Maybe that's why he had ended things with his wife, Grace. They had been different from the start in class background, outlooks on life, hobbies, their taste in food, wine and even in bed. Yet, they had still married. There had always been an expectation by family and friends for him and Grace to get married and so they had obliged. Unfortunately the expectations had not produced an everlasting relationship.

Brown had found Vivien to be a very striking woman from the moment he had seen her stride across the street towards her brother. Her classy, short blond hair, well-spoken voice with that hint of Cockney, her confidence and her broad outlook had attracted him to her. They had had many a long conversation on the phone, over tea at his office, at her office, in her home and Brown knew inside his heart the attraction was mutual. It was just a matter of time before they decided to take the friendship forward.

Vivien, on the other hand, had not been attracted to Brown from the start. It had happened through their deep conversations and she had realised how good a man he really was when he had made his efforts to comfort the Ali family with her. She had met many men and had been hurt very badly twice in her life because she had loved too quickly and deeply. It was this that had made her mistrustful of men and she could not cope with serious relationships. But she now found herself questioning whether Brown was the same as her two other mistakes.

Meanwhile the Ali family continued to be a target for a rain of serious harassment and they continued to fight back in their own way, by trying to live their lives as normally as possible. They had decided that they would work with a couple of Brown's ideas and try to identify a couple of the perpetrators. Brown had ensured that in the evening a police car was around their estate as often as possible but to no avail and no one was caught.

Ayesha was still not at school but the Education Social Worker, Sally Wilson, had made a visit to the Ali family home to arrange an alternative form of education, until things settled down a little and Ayesha felt better. During that time Sally would organise some form of home education for a couple of hours everyday. It was the least she could do for the family in their time of such distress. But Sally Wilson had wondered to herself during her meeting with Mr and Mrs Ali and Ayesha, when things would settle down for the family and for the community as a whole. On her way to the Ali home, she had seen the eggs smashed on their kitchen window, the smell of red paint plastered on the front door. She had felt the family's sadness and anxiety; it was there behind their hollow smiles and unlit eyes. Sally Wilson was determined to give the family what support she could.

The rest of the family - Shazia, Yusuf and Hamza carried on with their lives as normally as possible. Holding onto whatever used to be normal was the only way they could get through each day. However, the carefree days of laughter, gentle teasing, the aspirations to do well in what they hoped to achieve was dampened by their heavy hearts. They all carried a great burden on their shoulders, a burden of restlessness, the lack of peace and calm, the fear and the uncertainty of the future. Each carried their burden without showing their real emotions to the others so as not to cause more worry and anxiety. Each longed terribly for tranquillity to come back into their lives and each wondered when it would come and at what price.

It was now nearly two weeks since Mrs Peters had been attacked and she still lay in a coma. The unrest in the East End carried on and now there was a focal point for everyone whether they were black, white or Asian and this was the local elections. Meetings were taking place and the different political parties were putting forward candidates - Labour, Liberals, Conservatives, Green party, Islamic party, the Looney party and the Nation for White British People party. There was a race between them all as to who could canvass the most votes - the most support to get their candidates through for their varying causes and beliefs. The elections were just two weeks away now and each party had made every effort to ensure there were enough glossy leaflets, with their smiling and confident looking candidates on the cover pages, pushed through as many letterboxes in Tower Hamlets as possible. Each party met at strange hours of the day and night to update progress, barriers, and secrets and to 'relax' in the different ways that appealed to them.

****

Bill Brown was very much aware of the future elections coming up and he felt a deep apprehension about the outcome in the light of recent developments in the borough. He hoped something would trigger the community to come together before things got any worse. Brown had also made sure Hamza Ali's report against Blakely and Woods had been processed to go on to his seniors. They were going to send a date to Hamza, within the next week or so, to hear from him verbally about his treatment from Blakely and Woods. After meeting with Hamza the Superintendents and Commanders would meet with the police officers in question and discuss these accusations with them. It was a bureaucratic process, but one Brown would not let go of as he felt a deep moral obligation. He would make sure Hamza's side of the story would be heard along with any evidence he could dig up. Brown was going to see Blakely and Woods were never police officers again.

Brown's policing experience had shown what many officers were capable of what they could do with the power they had in their hands. Brown secretly blamed it on the politicians who, in the past and present, had not exactly been great models for the police to look up to. He often remembered the Thatcher years and how her brand of 'Britishness' had rubbed on to many police officers. Under her rule he had seen many hard-line and unjust policing tactics grow almost into a policing culture - the culture in which many police officers had felt that they could do anything to keep control over blacks and the indigenous population.

In fact, particular police officers thought they could belt anyone who they thought was against the 'Iron Lady's' views because her views were for the true British people. Brown had always felt that policemen would have had better relationships with blacks, Asians and other people of colour discriminated against in society had they had positive and honest politicians to look up to. The police institution was not exactly a friendly face to the black and Asian communities in Britain. Better relationships between communities often made it easier to police areas and helped keep crime under control. Bill Brown sat in his office with his thoughts and then decided to ring Vivien and talk to her about what was on his mind. He looked forward to that.

However the people who wanted to achieve a peaceful and harmonious community gathered together under an umbrella group called Free Tower Hamlets from Racism and Fascism. They were not a political party; the interested members were from different organisations, groups, progressions, religions, races and backgrounds - ordinary residents living in the borough whose main concern was to ensure that the racist and fascist party candidates did not achieve credibility in the eyes of the voters; that they did not become councillors and that the party was subsequently pushed out of Tower Hamlets.

The group had met in a large community centre and found that amongst the people who attended were members from the local political parties. The white man who co-chaired the meeting with his black colleague had begun by emphasising the reason why the meeting was being held. His name was Nick Chambers and he was the steward of the borough's UNISON. He talked in detail of how the recent attack on a white elderly woman had sparked off the intense racial tensions and hostilities. Nick Chambers talked about how the Nation for White British People party was putting forward candidates for the local ward elections. This could not happen, he said, for if it did there would be the step backward into racist history and a step forward for racism to take its place back in history.

Nick Chambers, along with Angela Agna talked about the historical changes that had been made in Tower Hamlets and the East End as a whole, in terms of race relations, multiculturalism and the changing communities that had come and gone, but had left their marks in the borough. For the people who met, it was a time of reflection and hope, to find possible solutions to out wit the racist party that had made its presence known in the community.

Shazia and Yusuf, along with Vivien, were on their way to the meeting. They had decided to walk to the Darby Community Centre against Mr and Mrs Ali's wishes. Shazia and Yusuf had been reluctant to go to the meeting. It had been Sally Wilson, Ayesha's Education Social Worker, who had encouraged them to go and Mr Ali was asked very earnestly by his local mosque to send a couple of his family members to attend. He had at first declined but the pressure from the congregation at the mosque Friday prayers had made him feel obliged to do as they asked and so Mr Ali had given his word.

Mr Ali and his family were afraid to trust anyone who wanted their help to campaign against the racial hostilities that were currently going on. Many a person and cause from various sectors had visited his family for such purposes and they had gradually realised that those people had not been genuine. They had had their own self-interests at heart and not the interests of the people who were suffering. How selfish of them in times of crisis to seek their own advantages. However, Mr Ali had persuaded Shazia and Yusuf to attend and Vivien who was present at the time had also agreed to go.

The three of them walked into the community centre, quietly unnoticed by the panel and the large numbers of people who had made an effort to come. Shazia looked around and to her amazement she saw Bangladeshi women she would never have thought would have the confidence to attend. They had come with their buggies and children amongst the audience. There were elderly Bangladeshi men and women, Somali people, Chinese and black people, disabled people, youths and young women and other vulnerable people. Amongst them there were white Cockneys Shazia had never expected to come to such a meeting and not just middle class white do-gooders. They had all come because they wanted the racial hate to stop and were afraid in case the fascist party's candidates managed to win places on ward seats. Shazia stood looking at the people around her and marvelled at the great effort they had made in making their way to such a meeting.

They were ordinary people who lived and worked in Tower Hamlets and wanted a safer environment and a united community for themselves and their children. The black woman was speaking now and talking about her experiences of being racially abused. She talked at length how she had grown up with the violence of racism; she talked about the Brixton riots. But most of all she talked about Nelson Mandela's dream of a 'rainbow nation'. Angela wanted to see a Rainbow Tower Hamlets being created.

Nick Chambers then asked the audience if they had any questions to ask. There was a lot of whispering, mumbling and jumbling and people looked at one another as to who would ask the first question. Someone came forward, a Bangladeshi woman, who broke the common nervousness with her question.

"You no mind me but one question I please ask?" She had a little child who was holding her hand looking rather uncomfortable.

"Please, go ahead," said Nick encouragingly.

"Where your toilet, my son very need toilet?" she asked very seriously.

The audience burst into laughter and so did the panel. Shazia found herself laughing. Even in the midst of such important discussion, the need to release human necessitates never failed to cease. It was from then, one by one, people asked a variety of questions -

"What do we do now?"

"How do we drive out the fascists?"

"How do we get people to respect each other?"

And so it went on, question after question. It was when a tall middle class man in his late twenties asked a question that Shazia, Yusuf and Vivien plucked up their ears.

"What I would like to know is why the Bangladeshi family whose son was accused of Mrs Peters' attack has not made a single comment or spoken out about their views or their side of the truth?"

"Yes, that's true. They ought to come out and say a few words. They've caused a lot of the trouble," interjected a sourly faced Bangladeshi man.

"Yea, right on, mate," said a white Cockney woman.

Shazia could hear other people talking away to one another in agreement.

She was feeling angry with the audience and with the panel for not saying anything on their behalf. Then Nick Chambers did say something and it was not what Shazia had hoped to hear.

"Yes, I agree it would help if the Ali family did speak out..."

Shazia was now only half listening to what Nick Chambers was saying. Her head had so many insults to hurl at him and his meeting. She looked at Yusuf whose face was taught with anger and Vivien looked as though she was entering her Iron Lady mood. Shazia would not allow these people to use her family as a scapegoat for the backlash of violence that had come about since her elderly neighbour's attack. She would make them listen to her views and she would make sure she was heard.

Without another thought Shazia made her way towards the panel. As she walked past people they turned and looked at her, not because they recognised her but because of her youthful good looks and confidence. Shazia made an impressive figure walking up towards the panel; she looked neither left nor right and there was no sign of fear in her step. She walked with an assured confidence and there was fierceness in her eyes that sparkled like black opals.

"I don't agree with what you're saying." She spoke loudly towards Nick Chambers. He looked and saw her coming towards him. For the first time since he had learnt the gift of the gab, Nick Chambers did not know what to say or respond to the speaker in front of him. He had not expected a young, beautiful Bangladeshi woman to stand in a crowd and challenge him. Nick cleared his throat.

"You have every right not to agree with what I'm saying, but tell me and all the people here why?"

She looked at him straight in the eye and Nick felt something he had never thought possible.

"I'll tell you why and everyone else in this room who wants to use an innocent family as an excuse for the racism that has come out in the light." She looked at Nick squarely and he could feel the heat of her anger almost burning his face.

Nick Chambers watched Shazia turn and face the audience and the panel at the same time and she spoke words that he knew instinctively he should have spoken.

"My name is Shazia Ali. I am the sister of Hamza Ali, the person accused of hurting our neighbour and friend. You all stand screaming and shouting how you want the racist violence in Tower Hamlets to stop. You all stand here thinking how incredibly moral and broad minded you are. Not one of you in this room can say that you are not prejudiced or even racist. How dare you stand here and judge my family. How dare you pass judgement on my family for what is happening on the streets of the East End?" Shazia's voice was rising along with the glow on her face. Nick Chambers sat watching her mesmerised by the passionate anger in her voice.

Shazia carried on unaware of the allure she created especially in the eyes of

Nick Chambers.

"My family did not speak about the events surrounding the attack on Mrs Peters because we were worried whether our views would be put forward as the real truth. There were very few people who came to our home wanting to truly help, other than gaining something for themselves. We became friends with Mrs Peters, our neighbour. It was my younger sister Ayesha who opened the way to friendship with a woman with a skin different from the colour of ours. We became friends with her and a few of her family members. Then one day my brother walked past her flat and saw the door had not been shut properly and walked into her home. He found Mrs Peters on the floor with her handbag emptied. He called our parents for help, horrified at what he had discovered and so my parents came, sharing my brother's horror. They phoned the police; the so-called authoritative figures supported Mrs Peters' youngest son's allegations, that my brother Hamza was the attacker."

Shazia paused and looked at the audience and her face was aglow with the depth of her feelings. She carried on like a warrior.

"My brother was taken away to the police station trying to protect my mother from Graham's anger. At the police station two officers beat him up because he was not white. They let him go because there was no evidence to tie him to Mrs Peters' attack. From then on my family and I have been the victims of severe racial harassment and abuse. We have been spat on, my mum and little sister have been threatened with a knife, our home has been plastered with paints and eggs, we have been harassed outside, faeces and dead animals have been put through our letterbox. My sister was so confident and happy at one time and now she wets the bed every night. My mother looks half crazy, my father is a broken man and my brothers plan how to protect themselves and us. And me, I'm so angry and hurt at what my family and I are suffering."

Shazia's eyes were burning with hot angry tears but she forced herself to hold them back. Nick Chambers saw her shiny eyes and he could almost feel her pain. For some unknown reason he wanted to protect her and shield her from suffering. The feeling almost left him breathless. But he carried on looking and listening at Shazia as her voice intensified, and his feeling deepened.

"I hate the racists for what they are doing to us. But today I almost despise you all because, without knowing my family and the truth, you made assumptions and decided we should take the blame for what the racists are doing in the borough. Your ignorance shows that you have done exactly what the racists are doing. Blaming others when something goes wrong for you and anything that affects you. By denying the truth, by not knowing the truth and understanding and accepting it, you have accepted what racists and fascists feed people who want to believe in them."

By now Shazia's eyes sparked with tears of anger and her heart ached. All she could think was how unfair it was of these people to stand here and judge her family without knowing them. She looked on at them defiantly.

It was silent in the room, but Shazia's words had echoed through the minds of everyone present. It was incredibly silent and Shazia looked at the audience wondering whether they would now start harassing her family because of her outburst. Well, fuck them, she thought angrily and turned to leave. Just as Shazia turned, she thought she heard someone clap but she quickly dismissed the thought. Then she heard another clap, and then another and then many more. She turned back round and to her astonishment, she saw the audience standing clapping and the panel were also clapping and standing. They clapped on and on. Shazia could feel herself feeling a little heady at what was happening. Somewhere, she had heard that this kind of response was called 'a standing ovation'.

The audience were not angry at what Shazia had said. Their applause showed her their admiration for her courage to speak out and challenge their unreasoned beliefs. Their jubilant cries showed how right she had been. Shazia found herself smiling and Yusuf and Vivien joined her and stood there with her while the audience carried on clapping. It was a great feeling of people bonding together as though Shazia had lit a torch for them to find their way through the dark days.

The audience gradually settled and it was Nick Chambers who spoke apologetically.

"I must apologise to Shazia Ali and her brave family for the way I spoke earlier. I think all of you would be pleased if I apologised on your behalf for the way we all assumed the truth. Shazia Ali has shown great courage and dignity in speaking out about what actually happened on the day Mrs Peters was attacked. She has opened our eyes to a number of issues which we must take on board if we wish to unite all people to be free of the racist and fascist venom that now prowls our streets. We, as Shazia said, we must look for the truth and not blame each other for our sufferings, our problems. But look together for a better future without a racist party taking advantage of the heated emotions and mixed feelings of all the people in our communities."

People loudly agreed with Nick Chambers and before he carried on Vivien stepped in front and spoke.

"I'm Vivien Peters, the younger daughter of Mrs Peters. I want to tell you that what Shazia has said is the truth. My mother and Shazia were neighbours and close friends. I do not believe for a moment that Hamza Ali or any member of his family had anything to do with my mother's attack. I am also going to clearly state that my brother, Graham, is a person who had deep racist beliefs and it is this that has led him to join the appalling racist party in Tower Hamlets. My brother had no right to accuse Hamza of attacking our mother. It was a lie based on his twisted and racist views. My mother lies in a coma but if she knew what was happening, she would have been extremely angry." Vivien paused and then continued knowing she had everyone's attention. She wanted to explain in her own way why things had gone sour.

"My mother was a good Cockney woman who tried to bring up her family, with my father, the best way she could in the face of poverty and social hardships. She never made friends with the people of so many racial backgrounds who she lived among and she never taught us to do so. They were strangers and we lived and walked amongst them. My mother never chided Graham about his deep racist views because she thought he did not really mean them or they were not as serious as the way he spoke about them. She should have chided him." Vivien looked at the people in front of her with eyes that showed her guilt. She carried on with her efforts to explain.

"And then suddenly in the midst of loneliness and so late in her life, my mother made friends with the little Bangladeshi girl who lived next door to her. And then she made friends with the little girl's family. So, you see, my brother is racist because he was misguided when he was growing up just like me and my other siblings. However in adulthood, I chose not to believe in such racist views but my brother, for his own selfish reasons, did." Vivien stopped and looked around.

"If you really want to make sure none of the racist candidates win, then you must see each other as friends and come together to stop them. Frankly, as my Cockney dad used to say when he worked in the docks, 'United we stand, alone we bang our heads'." Vivien fell silent and looked at them hoping her words had made sense.

The words had made sense to them because the people in the centre applauded Vivien for her courage to speak against her own brother. They clapped and praised her for trying to make them see how easily her brother had taken his racist views to such an extreme.

"What now?" people were asking amongst themselves and the panel. There was a new sense of adrenaline amongst them, pumping away in their blood, since Shazia and Vivien had spoken. A sense of purpose fell amongst them, a purpose which Nick Chambers had wondered how he would achieve in their minds before the meeting had started. But Shazia and Vivien had done the job for him; the large crowd felt elated and there was a great sense of community spirit amongst them.

"Yes, yes, absolutely," said a Bangladeshi Labour Councillor who sprang from his seat and took to standing near Vivien. He had not dared stand next to Shazia; her eyes had looked as though they were throwing knives at him. Councillor Uddin really wanted to see if he could improve his popularity by sneaking in at this united moment.

"I believe as a person, standing for the people who put me in my position, that we must achieve a goal for people to vote Labour and not the racist party…"

"Well, that's rather a sneaky stroke of you to pull, Councillor Uddin, at this moment in time," interrupted Councillor Emily Ford from the Liberal Democrat party. "It seems to me you're trying to put in an old word for New Labour. I think it's safe to say most people will be liberal about new Labour

156

on Election Day."

"I think you both sound terribly selfish. Most people want to conserve the old traditional values of fairness and that's what counts on voting day," said the rather pompous Conservative Councillor Tim Hayfield. He had felt he ought to put in quiet word since the other two major parties were having a political spin off.

Nick Chambers looked at the three councillors in disgust. Only the Green party and the Loonies looked ashamed at what their political rivals had ventured. Ordinary people had come together to find ways to fight racist filth damaging their community and the three main political parties were squabbling over voting strategies. He looked at Shazia and her eyes mirrored his thoughts. And she spoke to them on his behalf.

"Shut up, all three of you. You sound like spoilt children and you must sound even worse in the Town Hall when you have debates. You," she looked at Councillor Uddin who seemed to back away from her, "stand for the people who put you there. The people being your family, extended family clan and friends that owe you favours, not the real people, the voters."

Then she looked at Emily Ford who gave Shazia a haughty look. "You are liberal and so liberal that you can't decide on your policies. And as for you," Shazia glared at Councillor Hayfield whose forehead was decorated with sweat beads, "you stand for Thatcher and lots of blacks and Asians detest her. Now the three of you get your backsides into your chairs and listen to what people have to say, hope for and want. And maybe in the process you might learn something from them instead of them learning from your lies."

Nick and Angela found it incredibly hard to contain their laughter, after all they were professionals. It didn't really matter because the audience burst into laughter with everyone enjoying the joke whole-heartedly. The three councillors wisely sat back down mortified at the insults they had received. Shazia turned to Nick and Angela.

"Now ask these people how they want to drive out the Nation for White British People."

"You're right." He smiled at her but failed to receive one back. "Please let's hear some ideas from everyone out there. The streets are yours, you'll know more than me."

He looked out at the people and waited.

A hushed silence fell on the audience and everyone fell into serious thought. What ways were there to go forward and achieve what they hoped for? Many knew ways in which they would not choose to campaign for what they wanted. A white woman in her mid fifties spoke.

"I'm no brain box, but I'll tell you this. I know ways that I would not choose to fight for peace in Tower Hamlets. I don't want to frighten people; I want them to know we ain't campaigning for any political party. All we want them to know is the truth. I don't want no fighting involved. My mum once told me that she saw an Indian man called Ghandi when he came to visit England. He

157

was someone who didn't like to use his fist to make a point. So you see I want a way in which to show people we're all about what morally is right and what is wrong. That they have choices to make if they want to face God."

People applauded the woman and a black man then spoke up. "I completely agree with the lovely lady who spoke before me. She's right; we have to convince people to make moral choices by questioning themselves, by sorting the truth from the lies, by looking deeper than a fleeting glance - that will make people sit up and think."

"I think I want people to think me nice. Not bad. In same problem as them. Just different colour skin," said a Bangladeshi woman, in her broken English.

Yusuf had been listening and smiled at the woman who spoke. It was important to consult with the grassroots people before making plans and the panel were coming to understand this aspect as each minute of the meeting passed. Anyway they stood there, sat there, but talked to each other to find the answers they were looking for. He knew that by talking to each other, people learnt to understand each other and then came to respect each other. By respecting each other, a community learnt to live in harmony. And only then did a community become responsible for its welfare and its future.

"I would like to point something out to the panel, the local councillors and everyone else," Yusuf said. "What all the people want are simple things that ordinary people facing hardships want desperately and find so hard to achieve, because the hierarchy often has its own agenda. I believe that if people campaign together whether it's knocking on doors, posting leaflets, speaking to people, the message must be loud and clear. The message being, do not vote for the Nation for White British People party. Vote for any other party of your choice but not to vote for a racist and fascist party. People must also know and understand why they should not vote for such a party. They need to realise that their problems will not disappear if they vote for the Nation for White British People party. They need to remember the German people voted for a racist and fascist party and their problems did not disappear. In fact their problems became worse and they were hated by the world who united against them." Yusuf paused.

"It should not be a campaign for, or on the behalf of, any political party but for the people who do not want racist councillors on their ward. Political parties should encourage people, when they promote themselves, not to vote for racism."

"That's absolutely the point," Angela said. "The young man is right. To free the community of the Nation for White British People party, one has to ensure people do not vote for them in the first place. That is where our starting point should be, to remove the greatest racist barrier, the political right wing, from our streets and out of our borough and then slowly to bring positive changes."

The voice of agreement rang through the community centre.

"Yes, that's right," said a tiny Chinese man.

"That's the way to go," said young men who cheered.

158

"Great, great," said the black man.

"Knock 'em out," said the white man.

"Yes, Inshalla. That is the way," said a Muslim cleric.

"Yes, just like when Moses led his people," said a Jewish Rabbi.

"Yes, when Christ rose from the dead, hope lit the world," said a local Vicar.

They spoke with the voice of reason with which sometimes great and powerful leaders of the world forget to speak. As people talked and gave each other the chance to voice their ideas and concerns, gradually a plan developed and a strategy came about. Nick Chambers eagerly started writing target points in align with a timetable of how to achieve them. He did not do this on his own but with the help of all who had made an effort to attend. Finally the councillors understood that politics was not always about talking at people but talking with them and listening.

The main points of the group's plan was to make small sub-groups in as many areas as possible, with slightly larger groups where there was much support for the Nation for White British People. Canvassing people not to vote for the fascists, through talking, sharing information and reminding them of past history was the key to persuading people to question what they truly wanted. The major flag point of the campaign would be a march through Tower Hamlets the day before the election. A march to unite as many people as possible to find the truth and to diminish the idea of, "If there were no coloured, Britain would be a better place." 'If'- so futile and hopeless. 'If' - a word for those who dreamt but had no moral vision. But now there was a vision, a vision that had emerged from the very core of ordinary people who wanted to live without the shadow of racism, prejudice and ignorance. They wanted to go forward and meet head on the challenge that lay ahead.

Years ago, in 1978, people had come together in the East End to drive out the vicious National Front and its bully boys. They had come together and challenged the local authority for the lack of a forceful response for the sufferings of people of colour from white racists. It had taken the murder of a young Bangladeshi man to make the dormant authority sit up and realise the intensity of racial violence against the Bangladeshi community. The community had come together to challenge not only the outright racist party but to challenge the so-called 'just authority' of the council and police who were supposed to protect them.

The lessons of the past had made the community stronger and the young dreamt of building better lives for themselves and of finding a self worth and to take pride in their identity, for they were now British Bangladeshis. The long ago image of the passive Bangladeshi was a part of their history, they had journeyed amongst strangers to find their dignity and self esteem and no-one could take that away now.

Just as the people who had met in the community centre were forging ahead, Brown too was forging ahead with his investigations. He had finally managed to track down the wooden club used to attack Mrs Peters, his greatest piece of evidence to place Graham as the attacker. The wooden club had fallen behind the bins and had been missed by the refuse collectors. It had stayed untouched until Brown had insisted two of his officers comb the refuse area in case it had not fallen in the bin.

Brown's instincts had proved right and the wooden club had been found. The club was sent immediately for forensic examination and Brown waited for the results to come through impatiently. The club was being examined for fingerprints and for blood and hair samples matching Mrs Peters. Brown already had Graham's fingerprints on record and did not need him to come in. He wanted to get Graham with hard evidence and he wanted to be careful to show no indication that he thought Graham was a suspect.

In the meantime, Brown had dug around for information about the two people Graham was associated with the most, just as he was digging into Graham's life. Brown had even made a visit to Graham's local pub and learnt from a rather reluctant landlord that Malcolm and Derek had also been frequent visitors to the pub as well. It was easy for Brown to get the landlord to give him information; he effectively blackmailed him with the threat of a heavy investigation into the illegal gambling that went on in the basement of his pub. Apparently Graham had never met the two there as they had drunk in different parts of the pub, which was of a rather unusual layout. But Brown had sat there for a long time observing the drinkers who came and loudly held various types of conversations. Many came to drink down their sorrows and woes.

The landlord had kindly informed Brown that Graham had often got drunk and his favourite topic of discussion had being about niggers and Pakis. Graham loved to listen to his own voice and have an attentive audience; it gave him a self-fulfilment that he lacked in other areas of his life. The pub owner had revealed that Graham had, of late, talked about his worry over his mother's Paki neighbours and his resentment of her friendship with them. He had sworn about them and had made violent threats about the Asian family in his drunken haziness.

Brown had sat there and watched the skinheads and the restless youths who were also frequent visitors to the pub. He realised how easy it was for alienated white youths to be enticed into the frenzy of racist theories and easily believe the distorted truth. Hitler had ensured that the German youth were brainwashed to believe in the NAZI party's racist and fascist beliefs, which had given them a new sense of identity and purpose. The Nation for White British People's party could easily find many eager members in the pub. People who felt excluded and oppressed through the socio-economic class system that functioned in a democratic capitalist society. The British loved the vision of a hierarchy system, a tradition that had been passed through many generations and had been such a focal point during the time of the British occupation of India.

It was a system that put people into social classes, shut away in tables and columns, so everything could be neat and tidy for statistical data to be collated for politicians in their debates. It was a neat and tidy way to line the pockets of the already rich and kept the poor poor or made them even poorer. Politicians often thought such aspects in society could be contained and ignored. Only when the container burst open did they realise that they might have a major problem to deal with. However, Brown had thought wryly, there were opportunities and chances in British society and whether individuals wanted and dreamt of a better life depended on whether they grabbed those opportunities and took advantage of them.

Brown had returned to his office contemplating what he had learnt. It seemed that so much pointed to Graham being the suspect of his mother's attack. Jackie Simmons was probably right about who she had seen on the evening of Mrs Peters' attack. He was getting ready now to bring charges against Graham. It was just a matter of time before forensics came back to him. He had told them the urgency of his request. He thought of Vivien and looked forward to their dinner together next week. Their relationship had turned a corner in the last three weeks. They could both feel the chemistry between them. The phone rang interrupting his thoughts and he lazily answered it.

"Ah, Bill, the person I'm looking for. Got some news for you about the club you sent down to me," said Jack, his forensic colleague.

"Yup, I'm listening," Bill said, sitting upright, his ears straining eagerly.

"The wooden club's got Mrs Peters' hair and blood on it, but the fingertips don't match Graham Peters. In fact it's someone completely different."

Bill Brown fell silent on hearing the news. He had missed something in his investigation.

CHAPTER ELEVEN

While all these activities carried on in Tower Hamlets, Brown busily proceeded with his investigation, which seemed to be taking on a different lead. Vivien and the Ali family became more and more involved in actively helping with the aims of the Free Tower Hamlets Racism Forum. David and Susan found themselves questioning all that they had believed and held dear. Both found that the days following their mother's attack were filled with soul searching and reflection.

Each day David and Susan made their pilgrimage to their mother's bedside, having arranged to meet Vivien there. Graham did not phone them to arrange a time to meet and neither did they phone him. They were both hurt and angry at Graham's calculating and heartless attitude towards their mother's attack. It was Graham's reaction to Mrs Peters' attack that had finally brought home to them how deeply, deeply prejudiced Graham was. They realised too, that their brother's involvement with a racist and fascist party was evidence of what his intentions were for his future.

The day the meeting against racism was held, David had gone to Susan's house to pick her up to go and see their mother. Jamie was with him and Susan's daughter Martha also joined them. David was waiting in the sitting room talking to Martha about how unwell he felt and how he could not enjoy his food. Martha had noticed how much weight her big burly uncle had shed and she had asked him about this.

"Martha, since Mum got attacked, I don't feel meself anymore. Your Aunt Betty's been cooking all kinds of meals for me, but I can't eat like I usually do. I feel real down about Mum and I feel even worse about the way Graham is behaving."

"I know, Uncle David. Uncle Graham is being such a pig blaming the Ali family and then joining some bloody cause."

"He thinks he's doing something for King and Country," joined in Jamie. Jamie had heard about everything from his Aunt Vivien. His dad had not been keen to reveal much information about what Graham had done on the day of his Gran's attack and what he was currently involved in.

Susan had come in with some tea and had caught the gist of the conversation. She had not looked pleased with Martha and Jamie.

"Whatever Graham's up to or whatever he does, you two have no right to talk about him like that. He's your uncle and my brother and so I expect some respect to be given to him."

Martha and Jamie looked very angry at Susan's comments. Didn't she understand the extent of the kind of trouble her dear brother had brewed up? Did she not understand that many people were suffering because they were being almost persecuted for the colour of their skin? They had been blamed for things the government had cocked up, for the shit that politicians made and did not clean up. It was Susan's daughter who spoke darkly.

"No, Mum, you're wrong, we have every right to talk about what Uncle Graham is doing. This is a country where we're allowed to say what we want just like Uncle Graham is doing. You know he only went to see Gran a couple of times because he's been too busy taking advantage of the attack to improve his new political career. Uncle Graham and his party are responsible for the harassment the Ali family are facing everyday. For God sakes, Mum, little Ayesha and her mum were threatened in the streets on the way to school. Ayesha doesn't go to school anymore. She's being taught at her home because everything has got to her too much."

"Oh stop, being so ridiculous. You're going over the top. It's not gone that bad," said Susan, refusing to believe what her daughter was telling her. She had been listening too much to Vivien's extravagant exploits.

"No, Aunt Susan, Martha's telling you the truth. You can't handle the truth and you always try to stop others from accepting the obvious. For a change, Aunt Su, don't throw your weight around when Dad wants to have an opinion," Jamie said quietly but very seriously. He did not want Susan to interfere with the choices his dad wanted to make now. Jamie wanted his dad to see what Graham was really doing, to see the truth behind the web of lies that Graham fabricated.

Susan was completely lost for words by Jamie and Martha's response. She had not expected them to voice such strong opinions against her. Susan slowly sat down. She had seen some of the marches, gatherings and the leaflets Graham's racist party were carrying out on her way to see her mum at the London Hospital. Susan remembered the aggressive way the members of Graham's party had walked, the way some of them had sneered and jeered at the local coloured people who had looked frightened, and cowered from their aggressors. She remembered the fear now, because it reminded her of a time when she had also felt that same fear.

Susan had been in Spain at the time and one afternoon she had walked into a part of the town where she and her family had been staying which was not familiar to her. Susan had not realised how much further she had walked away from her familiar surroundings. She recalled enjoying the sun, the clear blue sky and sweet air. It was only when an old woman had spat on her and swore in Spanish that she became aware that she had entered a part of the town that did not welcome her. Behind the old woman, there had been a group of young people encouraging the old woman on with her aggression towards Susan. They were poor people but Susan knew from her basic instincts that they blamed her for their poverty and hardships. She had felt a sense of fear and nausea come over her and somehow she had managed to move her legs, willing them to run to safety. They had not followed her, but their aggression had instilled a great fear in Susan.

Susan had never told any member of her family of the incident. She had buried it deep in her memory, but today it had risen to the surface, forcing her to question her own moral conduct. A commodity which was so valuable but could easily be bought with money, fear, emotional blackmail, bribery and so many other ways, simply because it was a human commodity.

"Mum," Martha said, "are you all right?"

Susan looked at her daughter and felt suddenly drained. Susan was not one who liked to own up if she felt she had been wrong about something. But that did not mean she could not find ways of rectifying any wrongs.

"All right, so what's Viv being telling you two about?" she asked with a faint smile.

"Come on, Sis, I think we should pay a visit to the Ali family. My Jamie, found Shazia and her mum visiting our Mum a couple of times. Bet you didn't know that?" David said to his sister. "It's more than I can say about our Graham."

"Is that true then Jamie?" said Susan, knowing her brother was speaking the truth but still trying to find holes in what was the obvious.

"Oh, bloody hell, Susan, open your eyes and accept things. I'm learning to," bellowed David. He was angry at his sister's attitude, her constant denial of reality. It was unlike David to lose his temper with any of his family members but he was so frustrated with Susan and the overall situation that he just did not care anymore.

"I'm sorry," Susan suddenly began crying. "But I feel everything's falling apart. That club I go to, those middle class women know about everything that's happened and they've heard through the grapevine about Graham. They've been whispering about me behind my back, saying it's typical of common people to act like hooligans. My family ain't hooligans, it's Graham, he's lost it in the head and now I feel like some misfit in that club…" Susan broke down completely with her face in her hands crying bitterly.

David, Jamie and Martha looked at Susan and it dawned on them that perhaps part of Susan was very scared and insecure about the recent turn of events. They had assumed that she would be able to cope with most things and that she had been selfish in not broadening her understanding of what had happened. Martha went over to her mum, put an arm around her shoulders comfortingly and spoke to her gently.

"Sorry, mum, for being such a bitch, but I didn't know how bad you were feeling. You don't talk about it much and I just thought you were sort of supporting Uncle Graham. Anyway, those snobs at that club, they all look like Maggie Thatcher on a bad day and you stand out amongst them." Susan smiled through her tears.

"I'm really sorry Sis for biting your head off," said David softly.

"Me, too." James said apologetically.

Susan looked at them through her red-rimmed eyes.

"It's all right, you've got a right to snap at me. Me on my high horse, thinking nothing can touch me. Not wanting to get my hands dirty on anything messy. I just feel scared about everything. Most of all I'm scared of Graham. I didn't know he could go that far with all that race talk. I mean, you know, we all have our bitching sessions about coloured people now and then. Bit like having a bitch about the council tax, the price of fags going up. I'm not trying to justify what I've said in the past. I just thought Graham couldn't take such talk to such a violent point. He hasn't even gone to see Mum and she loved him the most. 'Cause he's too busy pissing around," Susan cried, scrunching her face with feelings of betrayal and frustration.

She turned to Jamie. "Jamie, luv, I believe you about Shazia and her mum visiting your Gran. You know why, 'cause that coloured family have done more for Mum in the past nine months than what Graham's done in his bloody lifetime. And you know something else, if Shazia or one of her family had ended up in hospital instead of Mum, she would have done the same for them and more but you see I didn't want to know about it all because I kept hoping Graham would suddenly turn up and change over a new leaf. So if Mum woke up, she wouldn't need to know what Graham had really been up to. It would hurt her so much to know that her son had been too busy with his own twisted activities to pay attention to her." Susan put her head onto her daughter's shoulder and gradually her crying subsided.

It was then David spoke, very cautiously, as if feeling the ground he was about to tread on. Making sure he didn't slip.

"But Sis, we don't have to be like Graham. We can be better than him. We can show the Ali family that we're like our Mum." He looked at Susan's face to see her reaction and found a weary smile and he knew she would be all right about visiting the Ali family."

Susan, David, Jamie and Martha were outside the Ali family's home. They had walked past their mum's flat. It was still sealed off; Detective Brown had made sure of that because he was continuing his investigations about certain aspects of the flat. Susan, David and Vivien had not understood what Brown could possibly be looking for. He would not say anything until he was crystal clear about things. And Brown was a person who would not reveal anything until he was sure he had hard evidence. They had all noticed the red paint on the flat wall and front door, the broken glass and eggshell that was littered in front of the flat. David knocked on the Ali family's front door and waited for someone to open it. Mr Ali opened the door and was completely taken aback by the group he saw in front of him.

"All right, mate," David said, and he meant it.

"Hello David," Mr Ali said and then he acknowledged, "Susan, Jamie."

Mr Ali smiled at Martha but he was unsure who she was.

"Um, all right, Mr Ali," Jamie said. He was wondering where Shazia was.

"Hello, Jamie, how are you?" Mr Ali greeted.

"Could we come in Unus?" David asked before his son could answer.

"Of course you can," said Mr Ali. He was rather uncertain of what David and Susan were doing here but he led them into the sitting room. Hamza was reading a book and Ayesha was lying on the settee. Mrs Ali was in the kitchen cooking and Shazia was in the bedroom. Yusuf was at the hospital doing his training.

When Susan and David walked into the sitting room and saw Ayesha lying on the settee, they were shocked at her appearance. The child they remembered had been a child of health, a vibrant little girl with a glowing complexion. Susan covered her mouth and without thinking she took quick strides towards Ayesha. As if knowing what Susan was going to do, Ayesha held her arms out and Susan had Ayesha in her arms.

"Susan, I'm scared, all the time," whispered Ayesha. Susan held her tighter, cursing herself for being so blind and ignorant. She finally understood what Vivien had been screaming at her about.

"All right, luv?" asked David gently. He too was shocked, but he heard Susan say gently, "I'm sorry, Ayesha. I'm so sorry. You went to visit my Mum and I never came to see you."

"No, it's not your fault. You didn't understand," said Ayesha.

"I'm old enough and ugly enough to know better," Susan said looking at Ayesha's hair, for the hair was less curly and less bouncy.

Ayesha started giggling and Hamza and her father smiled to hear her laugh. She didn't often laugh these days and there seemed no sweetness in their home without her laughter.

"What's happened to your face, Hamza?" David asked, thinking he might have been beaten up by racists.

"I got a bit of Paki-bashing," Hamza said sarcastically.

Mr Ali looked at him with tensed lips.

"Hamza, please don't speak like that," he chided.

"It's all right, mate, he don't mean any harm," said David.

"Hamza got beaten up by the two coppers who arrested him," Shazia said from the back. Jamie was the first to turn around. She looked a little thin but she was still beautiful. He had often thought of her since the attack on his Gran. Jamie had wondered how she was coping and then when he had met her in the hospital, he knew from the weary look in her eyes, how tough things were. Jamie became aware he was staring when Shazia walked past and whispered just for him to hear.

"Stop staring, you fool."

Bloody hell, why does she always have to do that to me, Jamie thought, but all he could feel was the rush of heat as Shazia had walked past him.

"Hamza, we didn't know," said Susan. Hamza's face still looked swollen and bruised. He looked so thin and worn out and Susan shuddered to think what it would feel like if her son, Michael, had come home looking like Hamza.

There was an awkward silence in the room, no one knew what to say, what to do, how to react or behave. It was one of those moments when people wanted to say so many things to each other but did not know how. Afraid if they spoke and said the wrong things, it might cause offence, hurt, anger and other complex human reactions. Ayesha looked around the room, she wanted

166

everyone to sit down and relax, talk to each other and laugh because she herself wanted to talk, to laugh, to feel safe and secure. "Why are you all quiet, like little mice? Sit down and act normal."

They all looked at her and started to laugh, she was right; they should be themselves amongst each other, since they knew each other. They were not strangers to one another and all they had to do was continue from when they had started to get to know each other, really know each other.

****

It was Monday morning and Hamza was in a meeting with a panel of four senior police officers, one from the police station where he had been beaten up by Blakely and Woods, two from outside police stations and a senior officer from the Police Complaints Authority. He had with him Nick Chambers as a representative. Hamza had made clear everything that he had stated in his written complaint against Blakely and Woods. Two of the investigating officers had tried to find flaws in his allegations against them but Hamza had stood firm and maintained his version of the events that had taken place. For Hamza it was easier to tell the truth than to spin a web of lies and deceit. The words had come from his lips so easily and honestly. He did not become angry but retained a respect for the police officers as they were still part of the system that governed him. That was the strength in his allegations and the wall which the two police officers failed to break down.

Nick Chambers had been impressed with the way Hamza had sat and spoken in a quiet, assertive voice, of how he had been treated. He felt disgusted at the way the two police officers had treated the young man. He could not believe that this could really happen in a service that was supposed to protect and serve people from all sectors in the community. Nick Chambers felt ashamed and deeply angry at Blakely and Woods' actions. He had looked forward to accompanying Hamza to the particular meeting. Not just because Nick felt that he could offer support to the Ali family in their time of crisis, but because of his increasing attraction to Shazia Ali. Nick Chambers, with Angela, had visited the Ali family after the Free Tower Hamlets from Racism Forum meeting. They had all talked about the proposed march and the current activities by the anti racist forum. Nick and Angela had taken notes about the harassment of the Ali family.

In that meeting, Nick Chambers had found himself staring at Shazia whenever the chance arose for him, manoeuvring questions to her. He wanted to talk to her, to be near her, hear her voice and look at her loveliness. Nick had found himself becoming more and more attracted to Shazia Ali. He had tried to shake the feeling off. Nick was twenty-nine years old and had had more than his share of women in his time, but for some unknown reason Shazia Ali affected him in ways he could not comprehend. Nick was a man who had always been in control of his emotions when it came to women. However the child woman he met in Shazia Ali disturbed him dreadfully. As he sat with Hamza Ali in the room with the police officers, Nick Chambers found his thoughts were on Shazia again. He had hoped she would come with her brother to the private meeting but she had not and he found himself deeply disappointed. The police officers were asking Nick if he had anything to say and he realised that they had asked him twice and he had not responded. Nick cleared his throat and looked at the grave looking police officers.

"I think one can gather from Hamza's words that he gives the image of a responsible, mature young man who is more interested in gaining a degree than a police record. I think many people in the community, both white and black, will begin to see that very clearly and ask whether it is the fault of racist, bad tempered police officers that he received such a battering at a police station which is supposed to protect rather than harm him. Would you not agree with me? We could also ask the public and the media?"

Detective Bill Brown was waiting for his seniors to call him when they needed him. Currently they were in a meeting with Blakely and Woods, talking to them separately. He knew why he was going to be called and looked forward to it. However, Detective Brown had other impending matters to deal with. New aspects of Mrs Peters' attack were emerging. Firstly the wooden club found as the weapon to attack Mrs Peters did not have Graham Peters' fingerprints, but had Mrs Peters' blood and hair on it. Bill Brown had managed to interview Graham Peters in his home. It had been incredibly hard to locate Graham Peters as he seemed to be in and out with his new political party, faster than the current Prime Minister. However, Bill had found him and the questions Bill Brown was bursting to ask him were finally answered by a rather bewildered looking Graham.

Bill Brown's first question to Graham had been to confirm where he was on the evening of his mother's attack. Graham had replied, looking red and pissed off. "Well, I was down at my local and then me and a couple of my mates went down Commercial Street. We met a couple of girls and we went back to my flat with them…"

"Who were the girls?" Bill had interrupted.

"You know girls, we just met," Graham had said looking at the floor.

"Graham, the only girls you meet down Commercial Street late in the evening are the working girls," Bill had said in a matter of fact tone.

"Oh, bloody hell, all right they were tarts. Are you gonna charge me for curb crawling 'cause there's a couple of well known judges who crawl down Commercial Street late in the evening and you're better off charging them than me," Graham had said indignantly.

"No, I'm not going to charge you with anything. But I want some answers, truthful answers," Brown added.

"Go on, shoot 'em at me."

"Do you know how to pick a lock?" Bill had asked.

"No I don't. For fuck's sake what kind of question is that?"

"Why did you just suddenly turn up on the day your mum was attacked?

That's a bit unlike you."

"Why, whose been telling you that I'm not an early riser?"

"I'm just assuming you aren't an early riser since you spend such late nights out and about."

"Look I turned up on that day, 'cause some geezer rang me on my mobile and told me what had happened to Mum."

"What man?" Brown had asked, very interested in Graham's revelation.

"Yea, some bloke 'phoned me up and told me to get down to me Mum, 'cause some Paki bastard had whacked her."

Instantly Brown had realised the jigsaw on Mrs Peters' attack was not as clear-cut as it had seemed. It occurred to Detective Brown that there was something else going on but he could not put his finger on it - something much more sinister that the attack was almost camouflaging. Brown intended to find out and he promised himself that he would.

"Can you remember the tone of the bloke, did you recognise him?" Brown had asked Graham.

"No, I didn't. I didn't have much of a conversation with him. He just hit me with the news and said he had to rush off and then hung up."

"But how did he get your mobile number?" Brown asked.

"I don't know. It beats me, but he done me one big favour by informing me about my mum. He was like some good angel," Graham had reflected.

Brown had sarcastically said to Graham,

"Well, we'll find out what kind of angel he really was. What time did he phone you?"

"Around about 9am."

Brown's reflexes were sharply aware that Hamza had not made the phone call to the police until 9.15am and police and ambulance had arrived at 9.30am. The person who had phoned Graham had known already that Mrs Peters had been attacked.

"Have you got your mobile with you?" asked Brown, revealing none of the thoughts that raced through his head to Graham.

"Yea, 'course I have. You want to have a look, it's not nicked," Graham had offered.

"Yea, hand it over."

Graham had handed it over and Brown had put it in his pocket.

"What are you doing?"

"I'm going to keep it for a couple of days to look after it. I'm going to do you a favour. I'm going to find out who your Guardian Angel was. Call it evidence that I'm keeping," Brown had said to a rather annoyed looking Graham.

"Graham, I suggest you visit your mum because I think your entire family may end up disowning you."

"More, I should be disowning them," Graham had replied angrily.

"What? Even your mum, who got whacked and ended up in a coma. For all you know you might not ever get the chance to disown her. Has it ever occurred to you that even doctors have to decide when to switch off a life support machine?" Brown had replied slamming the door behind him.

Brown had given the mobile to a colleague who was an expert and would be able to trace the call made to the phone on that day. The phone caller was the key to the events surrounding the attack on Mrs Peters. Brown had also found that the lock on Mrs Peter's front door had been picked so professionally, only another professional person in that field would have been able to identify the problem. Initially the door had conveyed the impression that someone had opened it with a key and had not shut it properly when they left. The front door had not shut properly because the lock had sprung back as it had been tampered with. However, there had been nothing taken from the flat apart from the money. There was something strange and unusual with Mrs Peters' attack. It was not fitting the typical burglary or even a random attack. There was something cold and calculating about the attack on Mrs Peters, almost as though it had been planned way back before it had happened. Brown's gut feelings were tapping into his unconscious mind and soon his conclusions would rise from within. That was the way Brown worked, thinking carefully before coming to conclusions. So often people came to rapid conclusions without clear and coherent thinking.

Downstairs Blakely and Woods were being questioned by the panel. They had both claimed that Hamza had become violent and had attacked Blakely. Blakely had pulled a punch in self-defence; Woods had insisted that he had tried to pull Hamza off Blakely but to no avail. The panel had smiled at them and they both felt rather pleased with their cunning story. It was obvious that the panel believed them, especially as one of the officers had said, "It's much easier for you both to verify your stories because there were two of you at the time of incident. You can both account for each other, thank God. And you should be glad that there were two of you to handle Hamza Ali's violent streak in his character."

"Yes sir," Blakely said. "I think my life would have been in extreme danger if I had been alone."

"That's right," said Woods hoping to get some of the limelight as well. "Sergeant Blakely was in extreme danger and thank God I was there."

Blakely and Woods sat smugly knowing that they had gotten away with their assault on Hamza Ali. How easy it was for them to lay the law down to coloureds and show their white supremacy. They would get back on duty and repeat such performances against non-white prisoners and persons in their community. It would be as simple as that. They knew how to get away with such incidents. They had the backing of people higher up and Hamza Ali would pay for whining over the treatment he had received. He would pay in full as far as Blakely and Woods were concerned.

"If that's all, Sir, may we be excused as there's a lot of good work for us to do and we'd like to get out onto our beat," Blakely said. He felt as though he had thoroughly impressed his audience. Woods wanted to make sure he left with a good impression too, so he simply added,

"Yes, that's right. We should be out working instead of sitting around. We're committed police officers."

"That's right." Brown said as he opened the door. "You two are so committed to your job that it often gets to your head."

Blakely and Woods turned around and saw Brown's face. As usual it did not reveal his thoughts but Blakely was quick to respond.

"Is there something you wish to spell out?"

Brown did not reply. They smiled at him, a smug smile, plastered with hypocrisy. The chair of the panel cleared his throat and spoke in a dangerously quiet voice.

"Sergeant Blakely and PC Woods, you will not be returning to your beat. We will be suspending you both from duty until further notice. Detective Sergeant Brown took photos of Hamza Ali's face and frankly it did not resemble the face of someone attacked in self-defence but more of someone who was intentionally beaten up. Further more, we have investigated Hamza Ali's character and found no evidence of violence in his past either on an official or unofficial record from other officers who know the East End very well. He is a young man studying for a degree and we have received two letters from his university voicing concerns over Hamza Ali's treatment while in police custody. There is a letter from the Principle of the University he attends and another from the University's Student Union. Both letters have stated clearly that Hamza Ali is not the kind of young man who seeks to disturb public peace, nor does he come from a family who cause trouble for police officers." The chair paused and watched the look of shock unfold on Blakely and Woods' faces. They were suddenly very unsure of their policing careers.

"You should also be aware," continued the chair of the panel, "Detective Sergeant Brown overheard the conversation between you about how you would make up a story to cover your racially violent treatment of Hamza Ali. He is an officer well known for his impeccable character and integrity both in the police force and in the community he serves. I should add that there is mounting evidence to suggest that Hamza Ali's allegations of racism against you both at his initial arrest, and the violence used against him in his police cell has a strong foundation. There are also two other witnesses who are willing to come forward and state certain incriminating evidence against you both. Both these witnesses are deemed as honest and responsible persons."

****

Blakely and Woods sat immobile and knew that they would now be in the face of the media not as heroes but as corrupt cowards. In their hearts they knew they were facing a very uncertain and not so bright future. The chair of the panel looked at them with distaste for he was thinking what bad timing it was for these two police officers to commit such an offence, in the light of the racial tension and the forthcoming elections.

"It is my duty to advise you both to seek legal advice as this particular case will be thoroughly dealt with at a much more senior level in the Police Constabulary. I am deeply appalled at the way you two have behaved as it is not only a reflection on your racist views, but it will give grounds for many ethnic communities to believe that the Police Force is a racist institution. You have done a great disservice not only to yourselves, to Hamza Ali and his family, Mrs Peters and her family, but to the wider community in this borough as a whole."

Blakely and Woods listened and instinctively knew they would most certainly not be going back to their beat. They had been driven by their own racist beliefs from the careers they had both truly wanted since their school days.

****

Malcolm King sat at his meeting with his senior staff in his flat. It was now only four days before the election and Malcolm was going through certain aspects of the NWBP's campaign for the seats in the local wards. He had been feeling extremely happy and very hopeful about what lay ahead, until recently. Malcolm's meticulous planning skills had helped the party to move to levels that would have been unachievable had he not been their leader. The party looked up to him and he enjoyed the authority he held with a perverse delight.

However, Malcolm had one slight hang up and that was the new organisation called Free Tower Hamlets from Racism Forum. It had sprung up from nowhere and seemed to be lashing out at all angles against the great work his party had painstakingly been doing for the past few weeks. Malcolm had countered a backlash from various groups in the community representing different people and backgrounds but he had not expected communities, groups, organisations - ordinary people from different races and backgrounds - to talk to each other and come together as one powerful force. For they had discovered what Malcolm had secretly thought they could not possibly find, unity in the midst of such aggressive tension.

Unity between people was a powerful force to be reckoned with by its enemies. Against odds, Malcolm had become sharply conscious of the power and influence they were having on many white, cockney East Enders, for the forum was in fact undoing the racist propaganda he and his party had been feeding to the ignorant, helpless masses. That was why Malcolm King was in a meeting with senior members of his party, looking sour faced and racking his brains to come up with an alternative plan, to hit out against the Free Tower Hamlets from Racism Forum. Margaret, Graham and a few others from the party were trying to find different tactics to gain more support for the seats they were trying to grab.

"Well, have any of you come up with anything else apart from the usual show we've been putting on?" Malcolm asked.

"We could get the SWAT team to do another rampage through Cannon Street on a quiet day. Scare the shit out of the Pakis. It would give off another message to the whites of white power and prestige," said a man called Jack Webster. He was an elite member in the SWAT team and the scars on his face were living proof of what he was capable of in the name of patriotism and nationalism.

"Don't you think we might scare them off with too much running around with dogs?" asked Graham.

"Why, you gone soft or something?" Jack darkly asked as he snaked out his tongue to dab saliva on a lip sore.

"No, I ain't, so bollocks to you," said Graham, defensively. The truth was he was feeling down in himself.

"Well what other ideas have you got then?" Malcolm said to Graham, for his reaction had not gone unnoticed on Malcolm.

"I heard them people at the Forum are gonna do a march the day before the election," said Graham.

"Where did you hear that from?" asked Malcolm, as an idea started to form in his head. He knew a vision would soon appear.

"Me sister told me," Graham replied.

"What that tart, Vivien?" Derek said.

"No, me older sister, Susan," Graham corrected almost agitatedly. He had been feeling like that since his meeting with Detective Brown. There was something eating inside him and he could not shake the feeling of uncertainty about what he was now involved in. He had been thinking of his father lately and wondering what he would have thought of his actions. He was burdened with the guilt of not visiting his mother and not keeping close with his other siblings but Malcolm had told him not to visit so often for the present time. The party needed his time and energy and that was very important. In reality Malcolm wanted Graham to have less and less contact with his family, in case they affected his emotions and views and he changed his mind about the party.

However Graham had been wondering who the man had been, informing him of his mother's attack. He had thought of that and it had been strange that the man had managed to get his mobile number, but then he had put it down to good kindred East End spirit. He just wanted to know who the man had been.

"Graham, we'd like you to join in the meeting and share your thoughts with us," interrupted Malcolm.

"Yeah, I want to but I keep thinking of me mum," said Graham clearly.

This was not the response Malcolm had wanted to hear and he knew Graham was feeling guilty about not seeing his mum. Through all his racist bravado, Graham loved his mum and had realized nothing could change his natural bond to her. Malcolm knew if he did not compromise, he could lose his blind support. It was easy to make him hate, but harder to break his love for his mother. Malcolm took a deep breath and said with the false gentleness so often used by politicians.

"Go and see her. You need to see her and give her my love."

Instantly Graham smiled and Malcolm felt relief to know he could pocket his ace back. The others smiled at him, proud of their leader's words.

"Alright, Malcolm, I'll see you lot later," Graham said and prepared to leave.

"Oh, by the way Graham, make sure you take a friend, you know to keep you safe," added Malcolm.

"Yeah, alright, mate." And with that Graham left.

"Should you have done that?" Margaret asked with a stone face.

"Well, what would you suggest, Maggie? If he doesn't see his mum, he'll end up resenting us and we could lose his total commitment. If he sees her now, he'll hate the Pakis more and we can make him move on to the next step," Malcolm replied, already planning on how to manipulate Graham's feelings further for the benefit of the party.

****

Graham was staring at his mother while his friend stood a little behind. She looked frail and bruised but the doctor had told him she was getting better. She had apparently been in and out of consciousness and mumbling words to herself. He remembered how his parents had tried to give him the best of everything with the little they could afford. His dad, with all his hard work and laying the law down to Graham, had been a kind and honest man, someone who believed in God and goodness. His mum, who had spent all her life caring for her family, loving them all, had not deserved such a tragic assault on her. His anger, hurt and vented frustration brought the tears he thought he was too manly to shed. Graham reached for his mother's hand and whispered, just as he used to as a child and even as man.

"Mum, come back and let me make it all up to you. I need you, I feel lost without you."

He held his mother's hand as if willing her to come round and say all the things he should have said to her when she was well. He wanted her comfort and her love and now perhaps her guidance. He stood there thinking of the past and his childhood, and he could only remember the warmth of the love he had been brought up in. Graham felt empty for he longed for that closeness again, something that only his family could give and not a racist political party.

Suddenly, Graham thought he saw his mother's eyes flutter and she seemed to be whimpering something. Overjoyed, he spoke quietly and tentatively.

"It's me, Mum, Graham, wake up. Go on, wake up and come home."

It was at that moment Mrs Peters' eyes opened and instead of her eyes lighting up at the sight of her son, her gnarled old hand pointed to his friend.

"It was him, him, him......."

Her eyes closed again as though she had worn herself out with that little sentence, but it did seem that the doctor had been right to say his patient was in and out of consciousness. However, Graham had clearly heard what his mother had said, and dumbfounded and bewildered, he looked at his friend, as though looking for answers. His friend looked back at him in shock, shaking his head in denial of Mrs Peters' accusation. For Graham, many thoughts ran through his head for he could not comprehend what his mother had meant in her hazy whimper.

Was there a much darker and sinister motive to Mrs Peters' attack than some frenzied and manic robbery? Her attack seemed to be linked into many issues and hostilities that had suddenly arisen out of her painful experience as everything was shrouded in mystery and uncertainties.

****

As Graham Peters stood near his mother, amazed at her revelation, the Ali family felt hope as Hamza came home and told them about the outcome of the Blakely and Woods hearing. It was a relief for them to realise that there was some kind of justice for victims of racial abuse. They knew this was a small step to getting back to some kind of normality in their lives but they could only tell how much of a step it was when the elections were over, if Mrs Peters came home and if her attacker was found and was not a Bangladeshi person. That was the greatest test for them as a family, for the Peters family and for the community in which they lived. These were trying times and if the future held a bleak and miserable awakening, the lives of many families whether black, white or Asian would be affected and the community itself would need to ask, where did we go wrong and why?

Look out for 'Shades of Tomorrow' the conclusion to Rainbow Hands and what happens during the elections and the effects it has on the Peters family and the Ali family and most of all the rest of the community.

Printed in the United Kingdom
by Lightning Source UK Ltd.
9818900001B/12-14